THOSE WHO SURVIVE

A POST-APOCALYPTIC DISASTER THRILLER

RING OF FIRE BOOK ONE

JACK HUNT

DIRECT RESPONSE PUBLISHING

ISBN: 9798862889925

For my Family

ALSO BY JACK HUNT

If you haven't joined *Jack Hunt's Private Facebook Group* just do a search on facebook to find it. This gives readers a way to chat with Jack, see cover reveals, enter contests and receive giveaways, and stay updated on upcoming releases. There is also his main facebook page below if you want to browse. facebook.com/jackhuntauthor

Go to the link below to receive special offers, bonus content, and news about new Jack Hunt's books. Sign up for the newsletter. http://www.jackhuntbooks.com/signup

A High Peaks Mystery series

In Cold Blood

Vanish From Sight

Her Final Hours

The Smart Killer

After it Turns Dark series

When the World Turns Dark

When Humanity Ends

When Hope is Lost

When Blood Lies

When Survivors Rise

Ring of Fire series

Those Who Survive

Book 2 coming soon in 2023

The Great Dying series

Extinct

Primal

Species

A Powerless World series

Escape the Breakdown

Survive the Lawless

Defend the Homestead

Outlive the Darkness

Evade the Ruthless

Outlaws of the Midwest series

Chaos Erupts

Panic Ensues

Havoc Endures

The Cyber Apocalypse series

As Our World Ends

As Our World Falls

As Our World Burns

The Agora Virus series

Phobia

Anxiety

Strain

The War Buds series

War Buds 1

War Buds 2

War Buds 3

Rules of Survival

Rules of Conflict

Rules of Darkness

Rules of Engagement

Lone Survivor series

All That Remains

All That Survives

All That Escapes

All That Rises

Single Novels

The Haze

The Delay

15 Floors

Blackout

Defiant

Darkest Hour

Final Impact

The Year Without Summer

The Last Storm

The Last Magician

The Lookout

Class of 1989

Out of the Wild

The Aging

Mavericks: Hunters Moon

Killing Time

PROLOGUE

U.S. territorial waters
Southeast of the Aleutian Islands
Two months before event

Commercial fishing was in his blood.

He thought he'd seen it all over 40 years of hauling golden king and snow crab out of the deepest, toughest, and most dangerous waters, yet nothing could have prepared him for the hell that day.

The *Alaskan Pearl,* a 116-foot fishing vessel, charged full speed ahead through the ferocious waters despite heavy resistance. A veteran of the ocean, the *Pearl* had earned its battle scars and gained the right to exist in territory that few vessels could withstand.

The rough seas, freezing conditions, and round-the-clock lashings by Mother Nature were brutal.

As one of only five boats with the hydraulic equipment to

harvest golden king crab from depths of 300 to 2,000 feet, it held a special place in the team's hearts.

There wasn't one of the seven guys on deck pulling gear that didn't regard it with some peculiar reverence. One of the seasoned men would kiss the steely deck each time he stepped onboard, and another would speak to it firmly but lovingly as a rancher might with his steed; the rest just held onto the steel beast for dear life, thanking it for bringing them back alive only once they planted their wet boots on dry land.

Strangeness aside, despite its age, the *Pearl* was solid, reliable, and always up for a challenge every year. For that and many other reasons, Captain Zac Erickson felt safe bringing out his wife and two young children. To him, it was just another day at sea. Except this time, it was meant to connect and instill into them the same love of the trade. He was pulling back the curtain and letting them see what their father did for a living. Coming from a long line of fisher-men, it was only natural that he wanted to pass on the legacy.

Enveloped by a gray sky, the boat pitched wildly from hard wind and waves as rain drenched the fishermen.

Inside the cabin, shielded from the relentless weather, he answered questions from his children as they observed deck-hands hauling in pots, emptying them into the hold, re-bait-ing, and returning them to the ocean floor.

"They work fast," Hannah said, her small hand clasped tightly around his, her eyes bulging out of her eleven-year-old head.

"No other choice," he replied. "Time is money."

Deckhands clothed in bright orange wet gear heaved and pushed 800-pound caged anchor pots by hand. Each had to be quick, decisive, and coordinated with the rest of the team to keep up with the high demands.

With pots coming up every 90 seconds, fifty pots per string, there were often no breaks for hours. Few could handle the grueling schedule. In his career, he'd seen a high turnover of crew. Many came and went, and those that stayed were a rare breed. Over the years, he'd gotten a good feel for those who could hack it. In a matter of minutes, he could tell if they would last as there were only two types he'd ever seen, the ones who groaned as they looked out at the crappy weather and complained, and the others who hooted and hollered like they were on their favorite roller-coaster ride at a fairground.

"Have you lost any crew members?" Liam, his thirteen-year-old, asked.

"Liam," his wife admonished.

"What? I'm just asking."

"It's all right, Kaitlyn. They deserve to know the truth." He looked at his son. "Yes. I won't cherry-coat it, son. What we do out here is dangerous. On average, around 30 die each year."

"How?"

"Drowning, hypothermia, capsizing, and other accidents," he replied without hesitation. As unfortunate as it was, risk came with the territory. Mother Nature was always ready to throw curveballs.

"What about your team?"

Zac exchanged a glance with Kaitlyn. Everyone from the fishery knew. He'd lived under the dark cloud that came with the loss. Two years earlier, a young guy he'd been training up had lost his life, crushed by one of the huge pots. It was a tragedy, an accident, a mistake made in the thick of huge waves crashing over them. They'd never told their kids, though word had gotten around, and his son would have eventually heard.

"One," he replied.

Silence stretched between them.

"We won't die, will we?" Hannah asked nervously.

Zac was quick to reassure her. "Oh, sweetheart. No. You're safe inside here."

Almost on key, as if Mother Nature was reminding him of who was in charge, the boat pitched hard again, and Kaitlyn moved in to take over. She'd been out more times than he could count. She was used to the rocky movement, and like any good mother, she knew when to distract. "Come on, Hannah, let me make you some hot cocoa. And you, Liam."

"I want to stay with Dad," Liam said.

"All right."

Zac got on the radio for a moment while his son gazed out with the same glint in his eye he had at that age when his father had taken him. There were vast amounts of money to be made quickly, but it relied upon bringing in a good catch.

And their success depended on so much.

The truth was the odds were stacked against them.

The relentless fury of the Bering Sea had become a ruthless adversary, battering the ship as it ventured into the heart of its domain. Zac increased the throttle, pushing the vessel forward and navigating the dangerous dance between their work and the raw power of nature.

"You think I can drive the boat?" Liam asked.

"In time. Observe for now." So many things could go wrong, and the deckhands relied upon his fast reactions. This wasn't a place to play around. Only a week earlier, he'd handed over the reins to someone while he used the washroom. While he was away, a deckhand had tossed a trailer bag over the rail, and the line had snagged in the picking hook. The newbie never took the boat out of gear. Tension was built, the line snapped, and the three-foot steel hook was catapulted at the crew, almost killing one.

Outside, daylight battled through the thick cloud cover, casting a pallid gloom over the turbulent seas. Rain continued to pelt the deck, driven sideways by gusts that promised no respite. The relentless pitching of the boat kept even the most seasoned deckhands on edge, but all of them were unyielding.

"But I wanted to..."

"Son. Listen to me. Navigating these waters is only a fraction of what this job entails. The greatest lessons are learned from the sea itself. Watch it. Observe the way it moves. In time, I will let you take the reins, but until then, you don't hand over a wild horse to a child."

"I'm not a child."

He grinned and ruffled his son's tousled brown hair. "Of course not."

Zac squinted as deckhands, silhouetted by the pale light, wrestled with anchor pots, their faces obscured by the spray and rain. The deck was a chaotic battleground, where men battled against the relentless forces to secure a prized bounty.

Zac looked out toward the horizon as the vessel moved back and forth in its usual rhythm. There was nothing out there. There were no boats for miles.

Then, an unexpected jolt rocked the vessel in an instant, a tremor so strong it jarred through Zac's spine. Radio chatter crackled to life, panicked voices reporting lines caught on something colossal and unyielding.

Zac's heart raced as he gripped the wheel and throttled

up, his every instinct honed to regain control. Waves, towering walls of frothy fury, swept over the deck, threatening to sweep everything and everyone away.

Desperation gripped him as he wrestled with the helm, but the vessel remained unresponsive. It was dragged like the hydraulic machinery pulling on the cages. He watched with dread and panic as the *Alaskan Pearl* was pulled faster. His heart clenched at the sound of his children's cries and the feel of his wife's frantic presence at his side.

"Zac! What's happening?" Kaitlyn's voice was a tremor in the storm as she fought to understand the chaos.

"I don't know," he shouted, his voice strained. "Take the kids down. Stay with them."

Deckhands braved the unforgiving onslaught, wielding knives to sever the tangled lines. Zac's jaw clenched as he fought to bring the ship under control, his gaze locked on the horizon that seemed a world away.

Just as despair began to cast its ominous shadow, and his radio call pierced the din — an urgent mayday, a plea for help — the lines snapped, the vessel righted itself, and a fleeting moment of relief hung in the air.

"What the hell was that?" he hollered over the radio to one of his few remaining deckhands. The others had gone over and disappeared into the rough sea.

"I think it was a submarine."

"Out here? That's impossible."

"I'm telling you what I saw. It was—"

Before he could finish, the calm was snatched away as abruptly as a lightning strike. An unfathomable force from below shifted the ship, and a monstrous hand of the deep asserted its power.

And then, chaos erupted anew.

The vessel groaned a tortured chorus that echoed Zac's anguish. The world was tilted, and reality flipped on its head. A surge of seawater engulfed the deck, throwing crew members into the abyss. Zac was torn from the helm, the world around him becoming an inky void where up and down lost all meaning.

Gasping for air, disoriented, and thrashing in the frothy abyss, Zac emerged from the depths. Waves hammered at his battered form as he fought for his life. He scanned the tumultuous waters, praying to see Kaitlyn and their children, but they were nowhere to be seen. A desperate sob escaped him as he felt the crushing weight of his failure.

And then, like a nightmare given form, it rose from the depths.

A behemoth — a Russian submarine — towered above, a monstrous specter of steel and menace. Its sheer size defied comprehension, an ominous sentinel of the deep. Zac's heart hammered his thoughts, a chaotic jumble of disbelief and dread.

As freezing waves crashed over him, engulfing him for the final time, Zac's last coherent thought was the promise to his daughter, an oath that she wouldn't die. But it was a vow shattered by the merciless sea, swallowed in the cold embrace of the depths, leaving behind only memories of a crew killed and a family lost.

FRIDAY, May 19, 1:10 p.m.
Hiroshima, Japan

NUCLEAR DETERRENCE WAS *on everyone's minds.*

Amidst the hushed corridors of the Grand Prince Hotel Hiroshima, where the G7 leaders had gathered for the annual summit, President Sam Devro of the United States engaged in an intense conversation with UK Prime Minister Emily Williams. The grandeur of the surroundings seemed at odds with the gravity of the discussions within its walls.

As the leaders finished their discussion on strengthening disarmament and non-proliferation efforts, President Devro's attention was abruptly diverted. His chief of staff, Lucas Reynolds, approached him with a sense of urgency that demanded immediate attention.

"Lucas?" Sam enquired, noting the gravity etched onto his face.

"Apologies for the interruption, sir," he began, "but there's an urgent matter that requires your attention."

Lucas gestured for them to step aside from the bustling crowd, his curiosity and anxiety piqued.

They walked a short distance, the tension palpable in the air. Lucas cleared his throat and proceeded. "We've received concerning intelligence. Yesterday, in the Bering Sea off the coast of the Aleutian Islands in Alaska, a mayday was received along with an EPIRB signal after 1700 hours. Debris from a crab vessel, fuel slick, and a life ring were found. There was no life raft, no survival suits, nothing. Whatever happened, it was sudden. The signal was lost. It's believed there was a collision with a sub."

"One of ours?"

"Russian."

Sam's brows furrowed, his mind racing to grasp the implications. "The Bering Sea, Russia's backyard," he mused aloud, his concern deepening. "How can you be sure?"

Lucas's eyes flicked to his right briefly before returning to the president. "There was a second sighting; a satellite captured it, this time in U.S. waters not far from the West Coast. We believe it's the BS-329 *Belgorod*."

Sam's expression darkened as he absorbed the information. The BS-329 *Belgorod,* the infamous Russian submarine known for its sheer size and terrifying capabilities, had been the topic of many closed-door meetings since a video had surfaced on the back of another threat from Russia. The US intelligence community had been keeping close tabs on it, considering it was the world's largest submarine and one of many in the Russian fleet. That all changed after the nuclear-powered sub went missing from its harbor in the Arctic.

Sam took a step back. "I don't understand. The USS *Ohio* and *Los Angeles* never picked up on it?"

"It seems it managed to evade sonar. Based on the photos that came back, we're positive it's the missing sub, sir, and we have to believe it's armed with the Poseidon nuclear torpedoes."

The weight of those words settled heavily upon the president. The sub could accommodate six 65-foot-long Poseidon nuclear torpedoes, each armed with a warhead of up to 100 megatons. If they were used, the destruction would be unimaginable. "Poseidon torpedoes," Sam repeated, his voice tinged with disbelief and dread. NATO had warned them that Russia might be planning to test the weapons system — a drone equipped with a nuclear bomb capable of creating radioactive tsunami waves 1,600 feet tall that could smash into the coast.

That was just the tip of the iceberg.

Lucas nodded solemnly. "If used in combination with the other subs carrying ballistic nukes that have been seen in the Atlantic, the potential devastation is beyond comprehension.

The seismic activity in the Ring of Fire would be off the charts, and it could trigger volcanoes, earthquakes, and..." He trailed off for a moment. "Well, it would kill millions, take the nation's grid down, and..."

Sam's thoughts swirled in a vortex of fear and strategic consideration. "No, the use of nuclear torpedoes would be madness," he murmured, his gaze distant as he imagined the horrors that could unfold. "They would suffer losses."

They resumed their walk, Sam's steps heavy with the weight of responsibility. "I agree, Mr. President," Lucas responded, his tone resolute. "Given Russia's recent actions and escalating threats, we can't underestimate the possibility of World War III. We need to take preemptive action and fast."

As they continued to stride through the corridors, Sam's mind flashed back to recent events, the tension after kicking Russia out of the G8, the provocations on the Nord Stream Pipeline, and the looming specter of conflict from NATO being drawn into the war in Europe. It was a powder keg that was just waiting to explode. He recalled the comment made by Russia's state chairman about them being more than capable of causing a global tragedy that could destroy multiple countries.

"Tell me we are on top of this," he said.

Lucas glanced at him. "We are doing everything in our power, Mr. President, but..."

"What is it?"

"Permission to speak freely, sir?"

"Lucas. Just spit it out."

"I can't say that this comes as a surprise. The director of the U.S. Northern Command and NORAD alerted us last year to the increased activity of the nuclear-powered Yasenclass submarines near our shores. With all the posturing activity in the Atlantic and the Pacific, and their fleet carrying many land-attack cruise missiles, the threat of an attack of this magnitude hasn't been this imminent since the Cold War."

A lump formed in Sam's throat as he grappled with the enormity of the situation. Lives, nations, and the delicate balance of the world — all rested on his decisions. He nodded slowly, his expression a blend of apprehension and steely resolve. "We can't afford to be complacent, but we must be careful. It could just be a ploy to bait us into war," he replied. Still, in the back of his mind, he recalled hearing about the Russian president's desire to abandon the "no first use" nuclear doctrine.

Who would be first to use nuclear weapons in a conflict was to be seen.

As the echoes of their conversation lingered in the air, the corridors of the Grand Prince Hotel seemed to hold their breath, bearing witness to the pivotal moment in history unfolding within its walls. The world's fate teetered on a knife's edge, and Sam knew that decisions made in the coming hours and days could shape humanity's future.

There were many he needed to consult first.

He only hoped it wasn't too late.

1

Sunday, July 2, 8:14 a.m.
Two days before the event

California's Camp Pendleton Base Brig was a different kind of hell from civilian prison, but it was still hell.

Bryce Mitchell sat on the edge of his bed in the one-person cell, waiting for a CO to escort him to freedom. His release date had been pushed up with good behavior. It had been a long time coming, and for many days, he thought he wouldn't see the end of the tunnel, but it had finally arrived.

He'd survived.

For five years, he'd been confined to the cramped quarters in the Level-2 facility at the Marine Corps base in San Diego. The brig served as a place of confinement for male prisoners serving sentences of up to ten years; those convicted of higher crimes ended up at the penitentiary in Leavenworth, Kansas.

He'd been fortunate to get a reduced charge in exchange for his testimony against the other six for their role in an overseas kill team targeting unarmed civilians.

Although the plea deal meant he'd be released sooner, he knew it also meant looking over his shoulder for the rest of his days.

Fortunately, he'd been kept separate from the others, who weren't looking to add more time to their sentence. Of course, the sixth, Mason Erikson, their platoon commander who had led the killings of unarmed civilians, had landed a tidy eleven years in Leavenworth.

Bryce glanced at the clock. The CO should have been here by now. What was holding things up?

Turning around in an 8-by-9-foot cell with a 10-foot ceiling, he felt relieved, knowing he wouldn't see this place again. The cell only had the bare essentials: a bed, mattress, toilet, sink, desk, and storage locker. The door was four feet wide and made of a steel mesh that allowed him to see the internal corridor.

Finally, a CO appeared behind the mesh, the door unlocked, and he stepped out of view just as Bryce stood up.

"For a second there, I thought you'd forgotten about me," he said.

"Forgotten? Who could forget you?" a familiar voice said before a broad-shouldered inmate in orange garb filled the doorway.

Bryce's brow furrowed, and a spike of fear went through him.

"Mason?"

"No salute?"

"But you were sentenced to Leavenworth."

"Was. I stole a page out of your book. I got myself transferred. You know, good behavior, making a deal, and whatnot. It worked well for you, didn't it?"

He sniffed hard as he took a step inside, looking around.

Behind him, the other five emerged. Bryce took a step back and swallowed. He'd expected an attack in the first few days of serving his sentence, not now, not on his release day. Bryce let out a lungful of air, resigned to his fate. In some ways, he'd been expecting to be jumped in the middle of the night, shanked in the showers, or beaten to death in the library.

The irony was almost humorous, but it made sense. Killing him within days of throwing them under the bus would have been an easy way out. What could be worse than letting him stew in the unknown? It meant he could never really relax. Five years of looking over his shoulder, never knowing when his number was up, only to show up on the last day when he could practically taste freedom and then end him — that was justice.

Bryce chuckled.

"Something funny?" Mason asked.

"Well, this just seems so cliched. You know — you all showing up here now. Let me guess, you've come to give me a parting gift, is that it?" He stepped back, clenched his jaw, and balled his hands. "C'mon on then. Which one of you is going to be first?"

Mason smirked before glancing over his shoulder at the others and then looking back at him. "We're not going touch you. What would that achieve? Nothing more than a longer sentence. More time to think about you. I've already had long enough. If I wanted you dead, these boys would have ended you by now. No. Like I said, I've taken a page out of your book, Bryce. I've been told I could be out of here in another two years with good behavior. That's right. Four years slashed from my sentence." He took a few steps closer, close enough that Bryce could smell his breath — the stale tobacco lingered. "But you're right about one thing. We do have a parting gift for you. I wish I had it here to see your reaction, but I've used up my favors." He gave a menacing smile at Bryce. "You look good, Bryce. We'll be seeing you," he said, turning to leave.

Mason reached the doorway, then stopped and glanced over his shoulder. "I hear your brother Chad is coming to collect you." He gave a wry smile. "Let's hope he didn't forget." The smile faded, and Bryce felt a cold chill run down his back.

With that said, Mason and the others wandered off, and the CO stepped back into view and gestured. "Let's go, Mitchell."

He hesitated momentarily, thinking it was just a ploy, another part of Mason's game. To draw him out, to make him feel he would walk out alive. However, there was no trick. Bryce exited his cell for the last time and glanced to his right. The six were gone.

Puzzled, he followed the CO out to collect his personal belongings. He would leave that day with a dishonorable discharge and no VA benefits. All that time serving his country, and yet after what he'd gotten involved in, he figured they wouldn't cut him any slack.

"Here you go. Don't spend it all at once," the CO said.

Bryce took the cash.

When being released from jail, those who didn't have money were given a small sum called "gate money." It was meant to assist with the basics like transportation, housing, or other essentials.

It was helpful, especially since he'd burned through whatever savings he had.

Bryce glanced at the pitiful handout of two hundred bucks before being taken to Camp Pendleton's Main Gate. It won't last the day, he thought.

Still, at least transportation wasn't an issue.

He'd already arranged two weeks ago for Chad, his younger brother, based out of Oregon City, to meet him in the parking lot. He only hoped he'd remembered.

"Where are you?" Bryce muttered.

He had the date and time. Bryce had confirmed with him three times to make sure.

Chad had promised to be there.

He was the only family he had left. Both of their parents had passed.

He breathed in the air for a few minutes and lifted his eyes to the sun, still trying to wrap his head around his release. There was so much he wanted to do, so much that he wished he hadn't done.

A smile formed as he wandered over to the parking lot to wait.

It soon faded as minutes turned into hours.

Standing with a small bag in hand, holding his only belongings, he felt sick in his stomach as he watched cars come and go. Almost two hours, and there was still no sign of him. The words of Mason slinked back in like a bad nightmare. "Let's hope he hasn't forgotten you."

Turning back to the gate, Bryce approached one of the

Marines on duty who'd been watching him like a hawk since he was let out. "Look, um, my ride hasn't shown up, and I don't have a cell phone. You think I could use the landline?"

The guard looked him up and down for a few seconds before jerking his head toward the phone.

"Make it quick."

Although he knew Bryce had been released from the brig, a Marine was a Marine.

Bryce dialed the number and waited, expecting to hear a remorseful apology. Instead, it rang until it went to his voicemail.

Bryce squeezed the bridge of his nose. "Chad. It's me. Pick up!" In the past, he'd called, and Chad had picked up late. He paused for a second, the phone in the crook of his neck as he glanced at the soldier eavesdropping. "I hope you're just stuck in traffic. I've been standing outside the gate for the last few hours. Where are you?" He paused again before he hung up. "Thanks," he said to the soldier as he walked by him out into the morning sunshine. He squatted on the edge of a curb and tried not to get worried. Chad told him he would fly into San Diego International Airport and rent a car. He'd planned to take him into the city for a night on the town before they would fly back to Oregon the following day.

Another hour passed before he decided he was done with waiting.

He returned to the guard station. "Do you think you can do me one more favor?" The soldier raised a tired eyebrow. "My brother was supposed to pick me up. He's a no-show. You don't think someone from the base could give me a ride into Oceanside, could they?"

The soldier offered back a deadpan expression.

Bryce nodded. "Right. Well then, can I use the phone again? I promise it's the last time."

The soldier grumbled but relented.

The call to his brother yielded more of the same—just his voicemail. Bryce set the phone down and gazed out into the lot. "Look, just in case my brother doesn't get the message, and he turns up asking for me. Tell him I'll be at the transportation station in Oceanside. His name is Chad Mitchell."

He stopped for a second, lifting a hand to his forehead as he looked back at the marine. "The station does still exist, right?"

He was familiar with the area but imagined many places had closed down since his incarceration.

"Yeah, about two miles south of here. Turn left onto San Luis Rey Drive, then get on the Coast Highway. You can't miss it; it's across from an auto service place and a huge lot with the Blink Charging Station."

Bryce stabbed the air with a finger. "That way."

"You got it."

With that, he set out for the Oceanside Transportation Center. It would have been a short drive by car, but he was looking at forty minutes on foot. If it wasn't for the fact that he was free, he might have found himself in a foul mood.

Not that day.

Nothing was going to ruin it.

Gone were the CO's, the unruly men, and all the orders.

As much as he'd hoped his brother would be there, he'd seen life throw enough curveballs. One more wasn't going to topple him.

As he trudged away into the California heat, blissfully unaware of the coming chaos, a newspaper blew across the street behind him; its front-page headline revealed growing tension between the USA and Russia.

Is World War III on the horizon?

The war in Europe has created global ripples.

2

Gatlinburg, Tennessee

His rage was nuclear.

Natalie Reid had worked as a supervisor at GEMS, a foster-care facility for at-risk kids, for as long as she could remember. She'd come across a wide gamut of troubled youth. Kids aged 13 to 17 were there for all kinds of behaviors such as violence, self-harm, abuse, suicidal thoughts, trauma, and disciplinary problems.

The list seemed endless.

Friends of hers were divided on her choice of career. Some felt it was admirable that she held out a hand of hope; most just thought it was insanely dangerous.

It was both.

The fact was as terrifying as it was — the rewards outweighed the daily risk.

As Natalie's legs pumped like pistons, hurrying down the corridor to respond to the call for backup, she could already hear the familiar cacophony and knew who it was.

The cries were ungodly. She knew some folks would have called the kid possessed by a demon with all the thrashing around, but she knew better — it was emotional pain.

As she rounded the corner toward his dorm, she was met by the usual sight of staff lingering outside. The cries from the teenage boy's room were so unnerving that they were hesitant to go in out of fear of being hit, or they were biding their time for the right moment to strike.

Inside, the small room was in total disarray. Bed sheets ripped, a mattress torn apart, a study table tipped over, several holes in the walls, and a section of the door frame missing.

The teen's room was one of ten. Only four were occupied. The group home was housing the lowest number they'd had in years. Still, the danger to them or the teens was never reduced.

"Come any closer, and I will do it," he shouted, holding the sharpened end of the wood frame up to his wrist. It pressed into his skin, causing a trickle of blood. He continued his tirade, kicking over a waste paper basket and driving his fist into the drywall, creating a perfect indentation of his knuckles.

Natalie squeezed through the knot, eyeing the newest hire — Dante Anderson, a black guy with a tight head of hair, forty-nine, a few years older than her. Age, however, meant little here; experience trumped it. He'd only been working there a few days. It was always the same — that familiar deer in the headlights stare. That was because the work was unpredictable. They had to think on their feet.

The job was simple. It didn't involve parenting or giving therapy, simply ensuring the teens were safe until the state determined where they would go. Easier said than done. No amount of training classes could prepare anyone for this. The situation was dynamic, and every individual was different. They learned fast or quit. It was that simple. The turnover in a facility like this was high. Few could handle it, especially when new rules had been brought in preventing them from legally stopping a kid from leaving the facility. And they had — many times. Run off, that is. So, instead, they would follow and try to talk them into coming back, or the cops would return them.

"Jordan. Come on now," Natalie said, inching her way in. "Put that down."

"I'll do it," he said in a threatening manner.

"No one is here to fight you. We want to make sure you're safe. Talk to me. What's going on?"

Susan, one of the other workers, leaned forward and whispered into her ear. "It's his father. He got a call from him."

Natalie frowned. "He spoke to him?"

Susan nodded and glanced at the new hire, who lowered his chin. It was a rookie mistake. A file overlooked. A regulation forgotten. Often, the first few days were information overload. Natalie groaned.

The pieces fell into place. Jordan came from a rough family. A single parent. His father drank and would take it out on him. Dishing out beatings daily. After he was taken away and placed in the system, his father tried to track him down. He was supposed to have no contact.

"I can hear you!" Jordan said. The conversation between them only enraged him more. Like a Tasmanian devil moving faster and faster around the room, a whirlwind of chaos, yelling curse words better than any sailor, he unleashed his fury, kicking the walls and even elbowing the window and causing it to smash.

"Okay, put it down, Jordan," she said multiple times, hoping to coax him, but it was doing little to help.

"All right. You know what to do," she said to those beside her. Although they had a couple of guys on staff, and it would have made sense to let them handle it, she was used to getting her hands dirty. Often, backup arrived too late, and if she hadn't learned to defend herself, the teens would have chewed her up and spat her out at the first sign of weakness. There was no easy way. The risk of harm to him or them was too high.

Timing was everything.

Natalie saw an opening and went for it, exploding forward off the balls of her feet. She saw his hand come down. But pure adrenaline took over, blocking out the rest. Jordan landed hard on the carpeted floor. The other staff members were seconds behind her, grappling and holding him until he calmed down.

He cursed loudly, thrashing around like a wildcat.

"Just breathe, Jordan. Breathe!"

Seconds turned to minutes.

"It's going to be okay, Jordan."

She felt his muscles relax, his breathing slow as he muttered, "I hate him. I hate him."

Nearby, there were numerous droplets of blood.

"Is he bleeding?" Natalie asked.

"No. You are," Dante said. She reached up and felt a gash at the back of her neck.

∾

Minutes later, Natalie leaned over a sink in a bathroom while Dante cleaned the back of her head. "Listen, about earlier. I'm sorry. Had I known, I wouldn't have."

"It happens," she said, glancing up at him through a curtain of brown hair. He dabbed at her neck, dried it, then applied a small bandage.

"There, that should do it."

"So, you were an EMT before this?" she asked.

"Trainee. Never made it through the course."

"Why not?"

"Seems I don't like the sight of blood as much as I thought," he said.

She chuckled. "Well, you seem to be doing just fine."

"Working here?"

"Patching things up," she said, straightening up and then placing a hand over the bandage. With the adrenaline dumped out of her system, the shock kicked in, and she felt a little unsteady.

"Whoa. It would be best if you took a seat. I'll get you a drink."

"Appreciate that," she said, perched on the edge of a bathtub. As Dante went out, the phone in her pocket buzzed to life. She reached in and pulled it out, answering it automatically. She could hear the hissing of a truck and chatter in the background; the usual sounds common to life on the road.

"Hey, how goes the battle?" Jackson Reid asked.

She winced. "Just awesome. Where are you?"

"Not far from San Francisco. I have a few drops to make, and then I'll swing by and pick up Zoe."

"Did you get the text?"

"Text?"

"Jax. The counselor."

"Ah, yeah. Sorry, it's been a little busy." He muffled the phone for a second, and she heard him shout to someone to keep it down. He came back on again. "Are you sure you want to go with that one?"

"Jax, we're not doing that again. You promised."

"I know. I know. I'm just remembering how it went last time," he replied. He was referring to couples counseling and the disaster it had been. They'd already been through three; one of the counselors even told them not to return. Jax found that funny. Her, not so much.

Having been married for twenty-one years, they had experienced the roller-coaster that came with having that many miles behind them. They'd made it through the first five years with flying colors and leaped over the seven-year itch. However, it was all the years after that.

Statistically, anyone who made it past fifteen years had a good chance. Jax had always said he was baffled by why anyone needed to keep a record. Like no one earned a medal by seeing how long they could endure one another.

In his mind, just because two people were still together x number of years later, that didn't mean they were happy. And happiness was the key point in it all. An elusive marker that appeared to keep moving. That no one ever really achieved. It was only experienced as a side effect of a series of ongoing life experiences. Their last counselor had told them that the secret was to stop trying. The more they tried, the less it happened.

"Are you on board or not?" she asked.

There was a pause. She knew he didn't think much could be gained from it. The way he saw counselors was different from hers. She felt that outside help could guide them and give them sound advice. Jax felt like all of the advice would be colored by that counselor's own experiences and world views. If they felt jaded by men, that would come out; if they felt let down by women, that could steer the conversation. And what made them an expert? A piece of paper? Half of them hadn't been married. The rest divorced. He wanted to interrogate them, get a background check, the regular over-the-top nonsense, anything to avoid going to one.

"Of course," he replied.

"Good, because I was beginning to think you didn't care."

She heard him groan. "I do. Look, can we talk about something else for once?"

"So, I'm taking the teens downtown tomorrow for the July Fourth parade."

"You think that's a good idea?" Jax asked.

"Yeah, about as much as I think driving for four days across the country when you could have flown out to San Francisco is, but I couldn't dissuade you."

"I told you I want to spend some time with Zoe. It won't be long before she's flying out to Europe, and we'll be lucky to see her once a year."

"You won't if you keep driving that truck."

It had been a sore point in their marriage for years. There had been times he was away from home for two to three weeks at a time. They'd talked about him giving it up, but much like her career choice, it was all he'd ever done.

"Natalie. Cut me some slack."

"I was just hoping to spend July Fourth with her."

"You'll get the rest of the summer to be with her. I have to work."

"Don't I know."

"I gotta go. See you in four days."

"Yeah."

"Nat."

"What?"

There was a short pause.

"Ah, it doesn't matter," he said before hanging up.

Dante appeared in the doorway.

"How long have you been standing there?" she asked as he handed her a bottle of water.

"I didn't hear anything, if that's what you're asking. I should get back to work," he said. She nodded. She took a swig of the water and was about to get up when her phone rang. She thought it was Jax calling back again; instead, when she glanced at it, an unknown number was on the caller ID. Usually, she would ignore a call like that, notch it up to a tele-marketer, but after the morning she had, she was about ready to give them a piece of her mind.

"No, I don't want my ducts cleaned," she hollered.

"What? Is this Natalie Alvarez?"

"I haven't been called that in a long time. Who is this?"

"Bryce Mitchell."

"Bryce?" A flood of good and painful memories from the past came rushing back in.

3

Monday, July 3
San Francisco
Day of event

Traffic was brutal getting into San Francisco before July 4th.

As it was one of the most anticipated holidays, celebrating heritage, history, and independence, everyone expected the roads to be gridlocked. Nothing could have been truer that morning. He'd made it to the city the previous evening, dropped a few loads off, and hunkered down for the night, expecting to collect his daughter Zoe and hit the road before it was bumper to bumper.

The problem was everyone must have had the same idea.

As the early morning sun cast its golden hue over the Stanford University campus, the black Peterbilt 579 truck rolled over a rise. Its powerful engine hummed as it moved through the streets. Jackson Reid had been a seasoned commercial trucker since he left high school. His father before him had passed on the baton to him. Thirty years later, he still carried the flame even though it burned a little dimmer.

Trucking was different from what it once was. With pitiful pay increases, a paycheck of less than fifty grand, and bonuses being a complete joke because of the strings attached, companies needed help to attract anyone.

The lifestyle had always been rough, with barely seeing family, rarely showering, gaining weight from unhealthy food, and getting little to no respect from those who shared the road. It wasn't any wonder that America faced a trucker shortage.

It was a thankless job but essential.

Three days. That's all it would have taken to see the nation come to a grinding halt if truckers weren't delivering goods, gas, and the essentials.

Still, it remained one of the easiest ways to make money that didn't require a college degree. He hadn't been the brightest spark in the classroom, but out here, he knew how to navigate a country full of pitfalls and trouble. And he'd seen a lot in his thirty years riding the country's veins.

But despite it all, the most significant trouble wasn't found tailing a slew of cars; it was at home. He hadn't met one driver that hadn't been divorced at least once, him included. His first wife had called it quits after taking off with another man; his second threw in the towel the first time he was away from home. That's what made Natalie an anomaly. They'd been together for just over twenty-one years.

His marriage mattered to him. She mattered to him. He'd done his time. Thirty years driving was more than enough. The trouble was he'd considered giving his notice every day, but had yet to do it. Whether it was fear or habit, it was the one thing that kept him sane, and if Natalie was honest, her as well. For one reason or another, time away from each other allowed them to breathe. It made the times together sweeter. And yet she was still vying for him to toss in the towel or risk losing her. That's why he'd agreed to see a counselor.

The truck's brakes hissed as he put his foot down.

After completing his last delivery that morning, he'd arrived at Stanford.

The trailer-less truck maneuvered the roads with precision. Its commanding presence amidst the ordinary cars and pedestrians made it stand out.

Easing off the gas, he stopped at the security gate; the guard glanced up.

"The loading area is around back, and you need to—"

Jackson cut him off, leaning out of the window. "I'm here to pick up my daughter, Zoe Reid."

The young security guard momentarily seemed caught off guard. "Alright, sir. Drive up the road, take a right, and you'll find the quad."

He acknowledged him with a nod and pulled ahead. Towering trees flanked the avenue before him, the leaves casting dappled shadows across the road. He marveled at the serene beauty of the campus, the calmness of a July morning hanging in the air. As he drove forward, the grandeur of the Main Quad unfolded before him.

It was a sight to behold, a picturesque scene of vibrant green grass surrounded by historic buildings with intricate architectural designs. Sunlight glinted off the windows, and the tranquil setting was alive with a few early risers strolling or preparing to leave for home. Jackson slowed his truck, the deep rumble of its engine falling into a peaceful pause.

His arrival was not inconspicuous. Curious glances came from students who were drawn to the massive truck. Jackson, aware of the attention, couldn't help but smile. After all, he was used to being a lone figure on the road, and the truck's size made it hard to ignore.

Zoe emerged from the university with two friends. At twenty-one, her long black hair framed her face, her features reminiscent of Natalie. Zoe's gaze met his as Jackson brought the truck to a stop. A faint hint of embarrassment colored her expression but quickly dissolved when she saw him step out.

"That's your dad?" he heard one of her friends say.

She nodded and smiled. "Hey!" Zoe greeted him with an affectionate hug. He took her bag and greeted her friends before effortlessly tossing the bag into the cabin.

"We're not flying?" Zoe quipped as he went to get in his side.

Jackson chuckled, climbing in and starting the engine. The truck grumbled to life. "I told you we're driving back."

Zoe raised an eyebrow as she pulled out some earbuds for her phone. "I thought you were joking."

"It will be fine," Jackson reassured her. "Besides, you always said you wanted to camp. We have four days together; we'll pass through multiple states and see some sights."

Her hesitation didn't escape his notice.

"What is it?" he probed gently.

Zoe hesitated before speaking. "It's just..." she trailed off, glancing at her phone.

"What?" Jackson prompted.

"Ah, it's okay. Forget it," she murmured, sticking the earbud in one ear and fixating on the screen.

The moment felt awkward, but he masked it with a smile. "Trust me. We'll have a good time. It'll be like old times."

Zoe met his gaze, her eyes holding a mix of emotions as the truck began to move. "I was twelve."

Jackson laughed heartily. "Yeah, and look at how well you've grown up. My daughter is attending Stanford; who would have thought?" Sending her to the prestigious and private university had been challenging between his job and Natalie's, but they'd been fortunate enough to start early, setting aside a small amount from their monthly income. Had they not done so, she wouldn't have gone or would have been buried under a mountain of debt before she even got started on life. Too many were in that boat. It was no life for anyone.

A driver honked, before swerving aggressively around him, bringing Jackson's attention back to the road. He gave a wave and called out. "My bad!"

Zoe's cheeks flushed as she shrank down in her seat. Jackson noticed but said nothing.

They had yet to make it a mile outside the campus when his phone rang. Natalie's name came up on the caller ID.

He tapped to accept. "I've got our gal," he informed her. "We're heading out now if that's why you're calling."

Natalie's voice hesitated for a moment. "That's good. Actually, I was calling to..."

Curiosity crept into his mind. "Yes?"

"You know I don't often ask favors from you," Natalie began. "But I was hoping you might do one for me."

Jackson's grip tightened on the steering wheel as he eyed the road. "Sure. Shoot."

"I have a friend who needs a ride to Oregon City."

His eyebrows shot up. "Okay...?" he said slowly. "But I'm spending time with Zoe, and we are heading east, not ten hours north."

"I understand. But you could work it in. She always said she wanted to see Oregon."

"Nat—"

"And you'd still be coming east after."

"Nat."

"Will you give *him* a ride?"

Jackson's thoughts raced as the silence stretched before him. "Him?" he asked. "I thought it was a female. Do I know him?"

"No."

"Is there something I need to know here?"

"No. He's just an old friend. We go way back."

Jackson nodded. "Okay," he said slowly. "But why doesn't he just catch a flight, or take a bus?"

Another empty beat followed.

"Because he's out of cash."

"Is this guy homeless?"

"No."

"Then everyone has cash, and if they don't, they get a loan. We've had to scramble at times."

"Jax. Please. Can you just do this one thing?"

He shook his head. "Who is he?"

"I just told you. A friend."

Zoe was looking at Jackson. Even she was a little perplexed.

"Nat, you're asking me to bring a stranger along with us for ten hours, take us out of our way, and all you can tell me is he's a friend?"

Nat was quick to reply. "His name is Bryce Mitchell. Will you do it or not?"

He grumbled, his grip tightening even more, but not because of the increased traffic. "And if I say no, is that something you'll bring up in couples therapy?"

She didn't respond to that, but the non-response was an answer.

"Nat?"

"Yes or no, Jackson?"

"Then it's no. It's the wrong timing. I'm with Zoe. It's inconvenient, let alone odd. We don't know him. He doesn't know us. And I get the sense you aren't telling me everything."

She sighed. "Fine. I'll pay for his flight."

Jackson veered over to the side of the road, causing Zoe to glance at him again. "Are you serious?" he said.

Natalie's voice came over the phone again, this time pleading. "All I'm asking for is a small favor."

"No, you're asking for a lot more than that," Jackson retorted, irritation seeping into his tone. "Did this guy ask you?"

Natalie hesitated. "No. He didn't even know you were out there. It was my suggestion, and he turned it down. He didn't want to put anyone out."

"Good. He won't be," Jackson replied curtly.

Natalie's tone turned earnest. "So, you'll do it?"

"I didn't say I would." Jackson sighed, briefly leaning his elbows against the steering wheel as traffic rushed by. "I don't get it. Doesn't this guy have family, or other friends who can help?"

"Yeah, a brother, but..." Natalie's voice trailed off.

"So let his family pick him up."

In an instant she shot back, "His brother was meant to; he didn't show up. And he used what funds he had to get to San Francisco."

The silence that followed was heavy. "I'm sorry to hear that, Nat, but I've got Zoe, and this is meant to be our time together. Any other truck run and I would have gladly done it, but..."

Natalie interrupted softly. "I owe him."

There was silence.

"Money?" Jackson's tone took a sharp edge.

"No. Not like that," she said quietly.

"But he wants payback?"

"No. Not at all. Look, will you do this for me or not?"

Jackson gritted his teeth as he leaned back in his seat, torn between his protective instincts and his desire to support his wife. She wore her heart on her sleeve. That's why she worked at a group home. Everyone was a rescue to her. "Where is he now?"

"Waiting at the Greyhound station in San Francisco," she answered.

He released a heavy sigh. "Is there anything you need to tell me, Nat?"

Silence hung in the air, and then she replied, "No. Like I said, he's just an old friend."

Trust had been a fragile element in their relationship. He didn't think she would ever cheat on him. However, Natalie had doubts about him during his long weeks on the road, and he had his during her late nights at the group home. Jackson's uncertainty was palpable. "All right," he finally conceded. "But I won't be back in four days now."

"That's fine. When can you get there?"

"I'm on my way. If he's not there, I'm leaving. I'm not waiting around."

As the conversation ended, Jackson glanced at Zoe, who had been watching him closely. "You always give in to her," she said.

He managed a half-hearted smile. "I know. Look, it's just a detour."

"But you said we were going to camp and..."

"And we are. Listen, for all we know, he might not even be there."

It was a hope. The last thing he wanted to do was head north, but with his marriage already on thin ice, he wanted to avoid creating more conflict.

They resumed the journey, leaving the tranquil Stanford campus in his side mirrors. Natalie's request tugged at his thoughts; a lingering unease settled in his mind. He couldn't shake the feeling that there was more to this story than she had revealed, and the uncertainty was casting a generous-sized shadow over the adventure he had planned for his daughter.

With the sun continuing to climb, Jackson's truck rolled northward up to the peninsula, traversing the familiar roads that linked Stanford to the city. The traffic was pretty good for the morning commute, although there were a few sluggish moments as they merged onto Highway 101.

The expanse of the Bay Area sprawled before them, the waters of the bay glistening under the early summer sun.

As they journeyed, the cityscape gradually unfolded. Skyscrapers punctuated the horizon, and the urban rhythm of life surrounded them. The air was tinged with the scent of exhaust fumes and the faint aroma of coffee shops wafting through open windows. The drone of the city traffic hummed in their ears, the soundtrack of a bustling metropolis

Finally, after about forty minutes on the road, they arrived at the Greyhound station. The station was located on Mission Street. It was a mix of urban hustle and transient travelers. The moment Jackson pulled in, the scene hit them in layers — a mosaic of sounds, sights, and scents.

The scuffling of shoes on the pavement mingled with the cacophony of honking horns from the busy streets that criss-crossed over one another. The smell of food wafted through his window, making his stomach growl. People bustled about, some with determination, others lost in their world. Home-less individuals and panhandlers were a sad but familiar sight in most cities, lingering at the periphery, their eyes seeking some form of charity.

"What if he's a bum and stinks up the cab?"

Jackson laughed. "I hardly think mom knows any street people."

"She said he didn't have any cash."

"He's probably making the most of the opportunity, and you know how mom is; she has a big heart and wants to help everyone."

As he brought the truck to a halt, Zoe leaned over and peered out her window, her expression one of mixed fascina-tion and wariness. "This is weird. What if he's some serial killer?"

"A bum who kills other bums? You have a wild imagina-tion, my girl," he said, raising an eyebrow and shooting her a half-amused look.

Jackson hopped out of the truck and glanced around. Just as he was about to close the door, his gaze settled on a figure rising from a bench near the main building. The man who stood was a paradox of ruggedness and charm. He had the rough edges of someone who had seen the whole gamut of life's challenges, yet his features were handsome in a way that was hard to ignore — hard for any woman to ignore, even his wife.

The stranger began making his way over.

Dressed in a casual T-shirt with lots of muscle and jeans that seemed to fit him just right, the guy exuded an air of confidence. He wasn't fazed by those around him, as if none seemed a threat. A jean jacket hung loosely over his shoulder, and a pair of military boots added an authoritative touch to his appearance.

"Bryce?" Jackson called out.

The man's attention turned toward him, and a warm smile curved his lips. "Jackson, right?"

Jackson nodded, a small smile forming. He approached, and Bryce extended a hand, which Jackson shook firmly. "Nice rig," Bryce commented, glancing toward the truck.

Jackson nodded appreciatively. "Yeah, thanks. So, you and uh... Natalie, go way back?"

A relaxed smile accompanied Bryce's nod. "Yeah. We knew each other growing up. I didn't realize she was married. Though I expected she would be."

Jackson studied him for a moment, suspicion flickering in his eyes. "Huh, you did?"

Bryce's attention wavered briefly, drawn to Zoe as she climbed out of the truck. "I just meant that she's that type. A caring individual and whatnot. I figured she'd eventually settle down, except..." He trailed off, his words leaving a lingering curiosity.

Jackson tried to read between the lines. "You didn't expect her to end up with a trucker?"

Bryce's eyes met Jackson's, and momentarily, they seemed to share an unspoken understanding. "No. In fact, that makes sense."

Jackson's eyebrows shot up in surprise. "It does?"

Before Bryce could respond, he extended a hand towards Zoe, who stood there with interest. "You must be Zoe. You look a lot like your mother did at that age."

Zoe's smile tugged at the corner of her face, her fingers absentmindedly playing with the earbud. "Nice to meet you," she said shyly.

"And what is it you do, Bryce?" Jackson asked.

"Nothing right now. I was in the Marine Corps."

"Huh."

While the introductions unfolded, many questions raced through Jackson's mind. He couldn't help but feel a little intimidated by Bryce's presence, both for his rugged charm and the fact that he was an ex-Marine.

"Listen, I appreciate you giving me a ride. Nat said you were going to swing by Oregon, so..."

"Did she," he said, eyeing him and thinking about what he would have said to Natalie had he known this.

"Yeah, I didn't want to put anyone out," Bryce replied, addressing Jackson. "I haven't had the best luck lately since getting out, and well..." He glanced over his shoulder, a touch of vulnerability in his eyes. "What little I had only got me so far."

Jackson nodded, understanding the unspoken plea. He wanted to drill him with questions to get a better sense of who this person was that Natalie had asked him to help. But time was ticking, and as much as he wished to probe deeper, they needed to hit the road. "Climb in."

Bryce and Zoe conversed as they got in. Jackson glanced

up at the sound of multiple jet fighters roaring overhead. He eyed them speeding into the distance and found himself caught in a mix of curiosity and uncertainty. "All right then," he muttered. The journey ahead was becoming more complex than he anticipated, and the stranger's presence was more than a little unnerving.

4

Bryce was an expert at it.

He'd had to feign sleeping many a time inside the pen. Threats were a constant, the fear of retribution even more likely when he shared the same block with those he'd thrown under the bus to get that plea deal. There was no telling who might slit his throat in the night.

This time, however, that wasn't the case.

He'd feigned sleep for the better part of an eleven-hour drive from San Francisco to Oregon, keeping his eyes closed in the rear cab. It was easier that way. It gave Jackson and his daughter time to converse without him being in the middle; it allowed him to eavesdrop and hold up his end of the agreement with Natalie.

She didn't want them to know about his stint in the can or his history with her.

Although he didn't see it as a problem, she did.

"I know Jax better than you," she'd said.

Had he sat up front, Jackson would have grilled him, and even if he couldn't draw the truth out of him, it would at least create enough doubt in his mind about Natalie that it would only cause issues at home. That was the last thing he wanted for her.

So instead, he'd told Jackson within minutes of getting into the cab that he was exhausted from a lack of sleep the night before. It wasn't a lie. He'd waited in Oceanside for his brother to show for most of the day before he opted to use what little gate cash he'd been given for food and a ride as far as it would take him.

That had gotten him to San Francisco.

He'd considered panhandling to raise funds to get him the rest of the way or thumbing a ride but couldn't bring himself to do it. As he sat in a café with less than five bucks to his name and a cup of coffee before him, his past came rushing back; promises made, relationships formed. That's when Natalie came to mind.

Finding her was easier than he thought. He figured he would have to phone friends from his hometown; instead, he quickly searched the internet on the café owner's phone and found her. Her name was listed as a supervisor of a group home in Gatlinburg on LinkedIn. There was even a photo of her. He'd smiled. The last time he'd seen her was over twenty years ago. She was younger then, but not even the years had stolen her good looks. Dark hair, shorter than it was in her twenties. Her piercing blue eyes reminded him of an Arctic wolf. Her gaze had strength and resilience from being forged in the fires of life. She and he had experienced more in those early years than few would in their lifetime.

Phoning her was a shot in the dark, but it paid off.

There was no hidden agenda. Bryce never asked her for money or a ride. That came after he spewed to her the last five years of his life and his situation. Natalie did what she always did — offered to help. Even then, he declined the offer. But just like her, she was persistent. *It' not a big deal.* She played it down. Made out that Jackson would be happy to do so, that it wasn't infringing on anything as he had drops to make.

He knew that that wasn't the case from eavesdropping on their whispered conversations. That only bolstered his reasons to feign sleep. Jackson was pissed, and rightly so. He would have been, too.

"Hey, uh, Bryce. We're in Oregon. You want to give me some directions to your brother's place?"

Although he'd been awake most of the time, there had been moments he'd drifted off. He yawned, stretching his arms as he opened his eyes.

"We're here?"

"Yeah, we're just a few minutes outside of Portland."

"What time is it?"

"Almost midnight."

"What road are we on?"

"Interstate 5 just south of Wilsonville."

"If you take the 205 east, that will take you right into Oregon City," he said as he climbed from the back into the front, sitting beside Zoe.

"You slept a long time."

"Sure did," he said. As the truck continued its trek into Oregon, Bryce peered out the windshield, his gaze eagerly scanning the landscape. Oregon didn't wait until the Fourth to begin celebrations. Fireworks, parades, it was just one giant time for people to get wasted or spend time with family. The world around them painted the scene with vibrant red, white, and blue hues. The streets bustled with activity as people prepared for the upcoming parade. Families draped in patriotic attire waved American flags, and laughter and excitement filled the air.

"So, how did you celebrate July 4th last year?" Jackson asked casually, his attention on the road ahead.

Bryce hesitated momentarily, his mind conjuring an answer that would conceal the truth of his imprisonment. "Oh, you know, just kept it low-key. Nothing too extravagant."

Jackson nodded in understanding, seemingly satisfied with his response. He turned his attention back to the road.

"Besides your brother, do you have any other family?" Jackson asked.

And there it was, the beginning of the questions. These were the questions Bryce had hoped to avoid on the way up. He only hoped the traffic ahead picked up, as he wanted to avoid answering, especially when they were so close.

"None."

"Sorry to hear that."

Bryce used that moment to steer the conversation in another direction. "I hear Gatlinburg knows how to throw a party."

"I got a sense you were from around there."

"Bryson City," Bryce replied.

"Bryce from Bryson City. What are the odds of that?"

"Tell me about it. That was what everyone said growing up."

A smile played at the corner of Jackson's lips as memories

resurfaced. "Yeah. Gatlinburg holds a celebration parade at midnight just as the clock ticks over to July 4th every year. Everyone comes out and lines the streets to watch. It's nuts."

"Sounds like you don't like it."

"He doesn't," Zoe said, grinning. "Dad's only been once."

"And that was more than enough," Jackson replied.

Bryce smiled. "Not a fan?"

"To me, it's all smoke and mirrors. It has less to do with Independence Day and more with advertising. All those floats, all those ads for different companies in the town. Makes me want to gag."

"Oh, Dad," Zoe said, shaking her head. "Here we go again."

"What?" Jackson replied with a chuckle. "Anyway. Natalie will be there again this year. She's taking the teens from the group home."

"Must be hard."

"Huh?" Jackson replied.

"You know, you being on the road. Her back there supervising a group home."

"Ah, it is what it is. At least she just has to watch over a few kids."

Bryce chuckled. "Is that all you think she does?"

Jackson glanced at him. "You sound like you know what it entails."

"I should. I was one of those teens in a group home at one time."

Jackson shot him another glance, but a police officer flagged them down before he could follow up with another question. The truck hissed to a halt, and Jackson brought his window down. Music seeped in, the sound of a marching band.

"Sorry, sir, you'll have to take a left up here. The road is closed."

"Right," Jackson replied with a thumbs-up. He veered down a different road.

"After the left up here, take another left, and then a right, and that will bring us back on track," Bryce said.

"You were saying?" Jackson asked, trying to probe him for more information.

"About?"

Jackson slammed on the brakes as a group of kids rushed into the road. He honked the horn. "Seriously!?" he hollered at them before moving on, frustration rising. Fortunately, Jackson dropped the topic.

"Your brother. What's he do for a living?"

"Farmer."

His brother's home was located on the north side of Oregon City, a farm close to the winding Clackamas River.

Bryce cleared his throat, his voice more confident. "All right. Take the next turn from here. You can drop me up here on the road's edge."

Jackson followed his directions; his brow furrowed in confusion. "I don't mind dropping you outside his house."

Bryce met his gaze, a mixture of determination and hidden unease in his eyes. "Nah, it's fine. I want to surprise my brother."

Jackson eased off the gas, and the truck stopped along a long, winding forest road. Bryce climbed out of the truck. "I appreciate the ride," he said as he turned back to Jackson and Zoe, who exchanged puzzled glances.

"No worries. Take care, Bryce," Jackson said, his tone tinged with relief.

With a wave, Bryce watched as the truck rumbled back to

life, the sound of its engine fading into the distance as it went around a bend in the road. As silence settled around him, he took a deep breath and turned to face the forest.

As Bryce left the road, entering the forest, he couldn't help but wonder what lay ahead. The truth, his past, and the intricate web of emotions that bound him to his brother were all about to converge in a quiet corner of Oregon.

JACKSON EYED his side mirror as the truck rumbled away, about to leave the forest road. He saw Bryce duck into the woodland. He shook his head, muttering to himself. "Man, your mother sure knows how to pick friends. That whole encounter was just odd."

"You're telling me. He slept all the way here."

They hadn't driven more than one hundred yards when Zoe's voice broke the silence, her tone urgent. "Dad, he left his bag behind."

Jackson glanced over, groaned, and his grip on the steering wheel tightened as he slowed the truck. "Stay here, Zoe. I'll be right back." He parked the truck on the side of the road, grabbed the bag, and jogged back in the direction they had just come from.

"Bryce!" he hollered.

There was no reply.

As he ventured into the dense forest at the location he'd seen Bryce enter, sweat dotted Jackson's brow. The trees, towering giants of fir and pine, made it seem darker than it was. The air was thick with the early scent of moss and damp leaves as he waded through, expecting to meet him on the way in.

"Bryce! Hey, you forgot your bag!" Jackson's voice echoed among the trees as he navigated through the underbrush. Ahead, he noticed a clearing and the outline of a house nestled between the trees. Its wooden exterior blended seamlessly with the natural surroundings as if nature had woven it into existence.

Glowing lanterns illuminated the outside.

Moving out of the tree line and approaching the home, Jackson made his way up onto the porch step and knocked on the door. From inside, he could hear voices. He heard footsteps, and the door opened partially, revealing a stranger on the other side.

"Sorry to bother you. Is this Chad Mitchell's home?"

The stranger's voice was cautious. "I think you have the wrong address."

"Oh. Sorry. I was looking for Bryce Mitchell. He left his bag behind," he said, holding it up for a second. "He's not a neighbor of yours, is he?"

The man gave him a blank expression.

"Right. Thanks," Jackson said as he turned to leave, but another man appeared at the foot of the steps, catching him off guard.

"You said that bag is Bryce Mitchell's?" the stranger asked.

"I already told him," the man behind him said.

Jackson nodded. "Yeah. Look, is Bryce here or..." He looked over his shoulder and caught sight of an overturned chair just beyond the door. A spike of fear shot through him. "Forget it, I'll just be going."

Before he could step away, the stranger who had appeared at the foot of the porch steps pulled out a revolver. "How about you give me that, and you go into the house."

Jackson froze.

Fear gnawed at his insides, but thoughts of Zoe pushed him forward. "Listen, whatever I've walked in on, I haven't seen anything. I'm gone."

The stranger motioned for Jackson to head inside.

He hesitated for a second but complied when the guy cocked the gun. "All right. All right."

He backed up, and as he turned to go in, the bag was taken from him. Almost immediately, once he was inside, he was pushed into a dimly lit area of the house. There, he found two more men, and his eyes widened at a lifeless man lying on the floor in a pool of blood. Someone shoved him from behind, and he landed hard next to the dead man.

"Who the hell is he?" one of the other men asked.

"Don't know, but he had this on him," another said as Jackson heard him throw the bag to one of the other men. "Says he knows Bryce."

"Is that so? Who are you?"

"Nobody. Just a trucker," Jackson replied, unable to peel his eyes away from the lifeless man's face staring right back at him with a tidy hole in the side of his temple.

"Then how did you come to get Bryce's bag? Where is he?" The grizzled man's voice was harsh and demanding.

Jackson's shock momentarily silenced him until a kick to his stomach spurred a response. "Answer!" the grizzled man barked.

"I... I just gave him a ride here. I don't know the guy," Jackson stammered, his mind racing to comprehend the unfolding chaos.

A creak from outside drew the men's attention, and one of them hurried to the door while another peered out the window. Fear tightened Jackson's chest as he struggled for words.

"Where is your ride?" The man's voice was relentless. Jackson's thoughts turned to Zoe. Before he could answer, another noise from the rear of the house stole his attention. The guy at the door peering through the peephole disappeared out the back. The thug grilling him asked again, "Where is your truck?"

Jackson went to get up but was forced back down; this time, the guy held his foot hard between his shoulder blades.

"It's on the road, beyond the driveway."

The man motioned to a fifth man who appeared at the bottom of the stairs.

"Check it out."

Jackson saw him head out the front door, withdrawing a Glock from the back of his jeans. Terror gripped him.

What happened next occurred so fast.

Suddenly, a gunshot pierced the air from outside, and chaos erupted. One of the other men raced to the rear of the house.

That was his moment to seize the opportunity to escape.

Jackson scrambled, sprang up, and bolted for the door.

He burst out, making it to the edge of the porch before a searing pain shot through his leg. His legs buckled, and he collapsed, missing the steps and rolling across the dirt.

Groaning and squirming in agony, he turned to see the grizzled man exit the house.

Jackson lifted a hand. "No!"

A gun erupted multiple times, and for a brief second, in all his pain, he thought he'd been shot a second time. He unclenched his eyes to see Bryce emerging from the house, his gun trained on the grizzled man.

"What the fuck is going on, Bryce!?" Jackson shouted in a mixture of confusion and anger.

"You shouldn't have come back. You weren't supposed to come back!" Bryce replied, bitter, as he crouched down to help Jackson.

"You left your bag behind," Jackson grunted as Bryce helped him, wrapping his arm around him for support.

Inside the house, carnage awaited them. Blood pooled around lifeless bodies, and the atmosphere was thick with tension. "Shit. Zoe. He sent one of the men to the truck." Jackson's voice trembled with urgency as Bryce laid him down on the couch. He unbuckled his belt, pulled it out, and wrapped it around his thigh above the gunshot wound.

Bryce tightened it, his eyes darkening with concern. He turned, scooped a rifle from one of the downed men, and headed for the door. "I'll get her. Just hold tight."

As Bryce rushed out, Jackson's cries of agony mingled with the turmoil of the forest.

ZOE'S FINGERS danced across her phone's screen as she sat in the truck, the music from her earbuds creating a cocoon of sound around her. Her feet rested on the dashboard, swaying slightly to the rhythm of the music. Oblivious to the unfolding chaos, she was focused on a conversation with her friend, the messages scrolling on the screen.

As the beats of music enveloped her, distant gunshots punctuated the air. Zoe furrowed her brows momentarily, wondering if she had imagined the sounds. She pulled out one earbud and tilted her head, listening intently. Another shot reverberated through the air, undeniable this time. Her heart skipped a beat, and she looked around, uncertainty and fear clouding her features.

Movement off to her right caused her to glance at the side mirror.

Then she noticed the stranger emerging from the trees and heading toward the truck. Her pulse quickened as her eyes fell on the glint of metal — a gun — in his hand. Panic surged through her veins, replacing the music's soothing cadence with a harsh adrenaline-fueled rush.

Swiftly, with instincts honed by the unexpected, Zoe grabbed her phone and removed the remaining earbud, her fingers fumbling slightly. She locked eyes with the approaching stranger, her breath caught in her throat as she assessed the situation.

Quickly, Zoe stabbed the control panel on the door. With a decisive click, the locks engaged, her actions motivated by self-preservation.

The man hopped up and tried the handle. When it didn't open, he tapped on the window with the side of his gun, his demand cutting through the air like a blade.

"Open the door."

Zoe backed up, shaking her head. The thought of getting out the other side shot through her mind but was quickly replaced as the man stepped down and moved around to the front of the truck, lifting the gun toward the windshield. "Open the door!"

With her heart pounding in her chest, she sank, making herself as small as possible. The man jumped back onto the door, tugging it furiously and looking at her through the glass.

The stranger's persistence escalated, and fear tightened its grip around Zoe's heart as he shattered the window with a violent crash. Shards of glass sprayed inside, glistening like malevolent stars as they scattered across the truck's interior.

He reached in and unlocked the door.

Before Zoe could react, the man reached for her, his movements quick and purposeful. He tucked the gun into the small of his back, then lunged for her leg.

"No. No. Get off!" she screamed.

Panic surged through her as his fingers closed around her ankle. She fought back, her kicks fierce and desperate, her survival instincts guiding her every move. Her attempts to free herself intensified as the man's grip remained tenacious, dragging her towards the open door.

In the struggle, her body twisted, and she found herself facing away from her assailant, clinging to anything that would hold her.

As terror threatened to consume her, Zoe heard a sound that cut through the chaos of her screams — a sharp gunshot. The man's grip faltered, and for a brief moment, Zoe felt herself freed from his grasp. Her heart raced as she turned, her eyes wide with disbelief.

The door was empty.

The forest looked peaceful, a stark contrast to the intense struggle that had just taken place. A surge of relief and confusion swept over her as she moved cautiously toward the open door.

A new figure emerged from the shadows, a familiar face that seemed both surreal and surrealistically comforting at that moment. It was Bryce.

"It's all right. It's over," he assured her, his voice a lifeline in the turmoil. "You're safe. Could you do me a favor? Close your eyes and give me your hand."

Zoe hesitated; her gaze locked on him as a rush of emotion surfaced. She was torn between her instinct to trust him and the lingering shock. "Where is my dad?" she cried, her voice laced with fear.

Bryce's expression softened with understanding. "He's at the house. Listen, I'll explain everything, but we need to get back to him now." He motioned for her to give him her hand.

Reluctantly, Zoe's trembling hand reached out, meeting Bryce's steady grasp. With careful gentleness, he helped her out of the truck. Her eyes were closed as her feet touched the ground, but she couldn't resist looking back.

Beside the truck was the same man that had smashed the window.

Blood oozed from the back of his head.

As Bryce and Zoe hurried back toward the house, a sudden screeching of tires erupted from the driveway down the road. In the fading light, Bryce's instincts kicked in, and he reached for his gun. He raised it, his finger on the trigger, but the car was already too far away for him to take an effective shot. Instead, he lowered his weapon, concern and frustration mingling on his face.

"We need to go inside," Bryce told Zoe, his voice full of urgency.

Bryce's attention shifted to her as they reached the house's threshold. He placed a hand on her shoulder, his voice measured. "Listen, I'd suggest you keep your eyes closed, but if you don't, just know it will be difficult to see."

Zoe's gaze held a stubborn determination.

As they approached the house, a gasp caught in her throat at the sight of another lifeless figure on the ground, bathed in an eerie pool of blood. Without hesitation, she rushed into the house, catching sight of her father on the couch. Her emotions swirled like a storm in her chest. "Dad!"

"You're okay," he said, relieved.

As she looked at him, it was clear he wasn't. The color had run from his face. Her gaze drifted to the stain of blood that marred his clothing. The realization struck her like a physical blow. Her heart clenched with a suffocating fear.

As the tension in the room remained palpable, Bryce's focus shifted from the grim scene around them to the task at hand. With a determined expression, he said, "Help me get him on the dining table." Bryce entered the dining area and swiped everything off, tossing it to one side. Plates and cutlery clattered on the tiled floor.

"What?" Zoe asked, rising.

"We need to treat that wound."

"No, we need to get him to a hospital."

"No hospital," Bryce said, moving past her.

Zoe looked at him in total confusion. "Are you a doctor?"

"No."

"Then have you lost your mind? We need to..."

"Get him to a hospital. Yeah, you said that. But then what? What do you think is the first thing they will ask when he arrives? How did it happen?" He put an arm under Jackson to get ready to lift him. "And then you know what's going to happen? Police will show up, and..."

"You just tell them what happened."

Bryce replied. "Oh yeah. It's that simple. I just killed five men because they killed my brother, and they were seconds away from doing the same to your father. Now, do you want to give me a hand or not?" he asked.

"Zoe," Jackson said, fading in and out of consciousness. "Listen to him."

Anger held her even as she moved in and helped him move her father out of the living room into the dining area.

Jackson winced as his injured leg was maneuvered onto the table, his teeth gritted against the pain.

Bryce laid him down and then turned and disappeared farther into the house. She heard a water faucet turn on and him rooting around inside a cupboard. Pots and pans were being tossed. He was cursing up a storm.

All the while, she gripped her father's bloody hand. "Don't leave me."

"I'm not going anywhere," Jackson replied.

Bryce returned with a pot of water to clean the wound. He had a small red medical bag; he dumped it down, took out a pair of scissors, and started to cut into Jackson's pant leg to get access to the wound to treat it.

His hands moved with a practiced efficiency as he worked on Jackson's leg, his face a mask of concentration. Sterile medical supplies lay scattered beside him, ready to use.

"Who the hell are you?" her father asked. "And don't give me any bullshit about a long-lost friend of Natalie."

As Bryce went to work on his leg, her father demanded an answer.

"If you won't tell me. Then tell me who they were."

Bryce stopped momentarily, glancing over at his dead brother, whom he hadn't even had a chance to mourn. "Just rest. I'll explain later. Right now, it doesn't matter."

"Like hell it does. If I'm going to die, I —"

"Dad."

"If I'm going to die," her father said even stronger, "I want to know why."

Bryce looked at him momentarily, then began to explain as he worked on him. "You know I said I got out recently."

"Yeah. Out of the military."

"No. Out of prison. Military prison," he said.

Zoe and her father exchanged a glance.

"Natalie didn't say anything about that."

"She thought it was best you didn't know. Look, you were meant to drop me off. That's it. Those men are related to some of the people I was involved with before I went away. My brother's death. All of this. This was payback. The first of it."

"Payback? For what? Why were you put inside?"

As Bryce was about to respond, a low rumble began to resonate through the room, vibrations coursing through the floor. It grew steadily, and the objects on the walls started to sway precariously. The room seemed to come alive with movement as if the house's very foundation were quaking.

Books tumbled from shelves, their pages fluttering like frightened birds, and picture frames clattered to the floor, their glass surfaces shattering into a myriad of crystalline fragments.

The light fixtures swayed ominously overhead.

The quake intensified, and the room seemed to shudder in protest against the unseen forces. Dust billowed from the ceiling, filling the air with a haze that caught the light in an ethereal dance of particles. The once-steady light now flickered as the trembling threatened to extinguish it.

Zoe fell to the floor as the tumultuous surroundings shook.

As the quake climaxed, a powerful jolt shook the room with renewed vigor. The impact sent a shockwave through the room, and a loud crash reverberated as a bookshelf finally surrendered to gravity, plummeting to the floor in a shower of splintered wood and books.

Bryce's gaze flicked toward the window, waiting for it to smash, his heart pounding in time with the earth's upheaval.

Jackson's grip tightened on the table's edge, his eyes wide with pain and apprehension.

As the quake finally began to subside, the room gradually stilled, leaving a scene of disarray and destruction.

Bryce exhaled a tense breath, his hands still as he surveyed the room. Then his attention shifted to Zoe; concern etched his features.

"Everyone okay?"

Almost immediately, both her father's and his cell phones emitted the ominous ring of an emergency alert. Zoe pulled hers out and glanced at it.

EMERGENCY ALERT

Ballistic missiles inbound to the nation. Seek immediate shelter.
THIS IS NOT A TEST: NWS: TSUNAMI danger to all West Coast residents. Move to high ground or inland now. This is not a drill.

Bryce glanced over at the television that was playing in the background. He told Zoe to apply pressure to her father's leg while he crossed the room, picked up a remote, and turned up the volume. He switched channels several times and landed on a news broadcast displaying devastation beyond anything he'd ever seen. Much of San Francisco was gone, replaced by an ocean of water.

5

The explosion startled everyone.

It was a new and unexpected treat for those in attendance.

The sky above downtown Gatlinburg exploded in a kaleidoscope of colors as fireworks burst in a mesmerizing display. Brilliant streaks of crimson, sapphire, and emerald painted the night canvas, creating a breathtaking tapestry against the darkened heavens. Golden sparkles rained down like stardust, their glow reflected in the stunned faces of the crowd below. The air crackled with anticipation, each burst of light accompanied by an echo of oohs and aahs from the gathered spectators.

In all the years she'd attended, fireworks were reserved

for the evening of the fourth. It was out of the norm for such celebrations; the rest was tradition.

Every year at the stroke of midnight, Gatlinburg rang in the Fourth of July with its Midnight Independence Day Parade. Hundreds of people were lined up along the Parkway, eagerly awaiting the parade to pass them.

Amid the radiant spectacle, Natalie Reid stood in awe, her heart racing with excitement and responsibility. As supervisor of the group home facility, she'd opted this year to bring four of her charges to downtown Gatlinburg to witness the enchantment of the Midnight Independence Day Parade.

The teenagers gazed out, pressed up against a railing, their eyes wide and jaws slack as the fireworks painted the night sky with vibrant hues.

"Whoa, that is incredible!" Selena exclaimed, her voice barely audible over the explosive crackling of fireworks. She turned to Natalie with a wide grin, her eyes reflecting the colorful bursts above. There was an immense amount of satisfaction in seeing her smile.

Selena Redfox had a terrible family background of abuse and alcoholism. Originally from the reservation, she'd learned at a young age how to survive. Her entire early years, up until her arrival in the home at fourteen, had consisted of living hand to mouth, dodging sexual advances, and sniffing gasoline. It pained her to see a fantastic girl with such low self-esteem almost commit suicide. In a matter of two years, she'd come a long way.

"I'm glad you're enjoying it. Just wait until the parade," she said, glancing at the other three and then stepping in and snatching a cigarette out of the hand of one of them. "I'll take that."

"Oh, come on, Ms. Reid," Liam Bennet said.

"Where did you get this from?" she asked, holding it up before his nose.

He shrugged. "I bummed it off some bum over there."

"Not impressed. You're better than that." She dropped it and twisted it below her foot but grinned. Liam smirked and returned to looking back out.

Liam had long hair buried beneath a baseball cap, and his arms were already covered in tattoos. At seventeen, he was in his last year before he would venture out on his own. He was a good kid. Bright. Amazing at art. No one had ever told him until he arrived at the home. He'd been with the group home the longest. The only child of a single mother, he'd grown up sleeping in cars and being told he would never amount to anything. That was one of the first walls they had to dismantle: the belief that he was nothing.

Her eyes flicked to Daniel Calloway, an overweight sixteen-year-old with glasses and a limp from an injury sustained while in the foster system. Only a few months in, he'd already run away twice. Each time, the cops brought him back, and each time, he vowed to leave.

Then, of course, there was Jordan Parker. Pressed against the fence, he didn't even crack a smile. His mind was in another place. Tall, broad-shouldered, he could have easily made one heck of a football player. His trouble with his father was the talk of the group home. All he'd ever known was pain. He had been used like a human punching bag. It was odd that his father wanted to have him back. It made no sense.

So many traumas were unseen.

It would take years to rebuild their self-esteem, but it all began by offering a safe place and surrounding them with people that gave a damn.

Natalie gathered the group together as the final crescendo of fireworks faded into the darkness. "All right, everyone," she called, her voice carrying through the lingering echoes of the explosions. "Close in tight. I don't want to lose you in the crowd. Safety first."

Dante Anderson, the recent addition to the team, stood by her side, offering a reassuring sense of security. He exuded a calm confidence that helped put the teenagers and her at ease.

"Does it ever get easy?" Dante asked.

"Not really."

"What does your husband do for a living?"

"What?"

"Noticed you were married," he said, motioning to her ring.

"Oh. Yeah. He's a trucker."

"Out on the road right now?"

"Visiting San Francisco to pick up our daughter. She's been studying at Stanford for the past few years. He's spending time with her over the next few days."

He nodded, eyeing the turn in the road.

"What about you? Have any family? Married?"

"Family is out east around Rhode Island. I never had a good relationship with them, to be honest. Strained, you could say," he replied.

"So, what brought you this way?"

"A relationship. Didn't last though. It went balls up after eighteen months here. She wanted something else — adventure. The reality was she was in love with the uniform, not the man inside it. So, when I bailed out of the course, she didn't want to know. I figure her idea of showing off an EMT husband wasn't in the cards."

"Her loss, I guess."

He smiled. "Yeah. Right."

As the parade's first float rounded the corner, Natalie couldn't help but feel a sense of wonder. It didn't matter how many years she'd been coming to the event; it was always a joy. The float was a vision of opulent grandeur, adorned with intricate decorations that glimmered and shone under the glow of the streetlights. The marching band played infectiously, the melody interweaving with the scene's energy.

Her gaze swept from the ornate float to the bustling crowd around them. A feeling of unity and exhilaration hung in the air, transcending individual backgrounds and differences. Families walked hand in hand, couples shared intimate moments beneath the neon-lit signs, and children laughed and pointed as they caught glimpses of the passing floats.

Although she was eyeing the teens, her gaze kept being distracted by the parade.

"Get off me," Jordan said.

"You're coming with me," a stern voice said.

Natalie glanced to her right to see Jordan's father and two others. Clyde Parker was a rotten piece of work. After reviewing Jordan's intake file, she'd dug into his background. Much of her research was to understand Jordan better, as teens often wouldn't open up for months. It was like trying to pry a barnacle from a stone. Every attempt to uncover his past only meant more pain for the teen as he relived it.

"Hey! Hey!" Natalie said, charging forward, getting between Jordan and Clyde, and pushing him back. The look he gave her could have stopped anyone in their tracks. She saw his fist clench as if he was about to swing. "Go on. Try it. I'll be the last person you hit."

"Get the fuck out of the way. He's my son. I'm taking him home."

Dante sidled up beside her, offering support. Clyde's two pals, cousins, brothers, whoever the hell they were, eyed him with venom. All of them stank of alcohol. Celebrations brought out the best in most, but not all.

She jabbed a finger at him. "You are breaking a no-contact order."

"Screw the orders. He's coming home with me." He lunged forward to grab Jordan's wrist, but Natalie batted his hand away, shoving him back because he'd drank so much.

"I'm warning you. Walk away!"

Clyde sneered. "And if we don't?"

"Selena, alert the cops," she said, motioning to a couple patrolling the street to keep order. She'd never seen the parade produce a fight in all her years. There were a few yelling matches from those who drank too much, but nothing like what was about to take place. Selena hopped over the railing, dodging the floats to the other side.

Clyde spoke to his son like a dog, calling for him to come to his side. "Jordan. Here!"

Natalie placed her arm back, keeping Jordan from moving. "He's not going with you."

"You don't get to make that choice."

"No, the state did it for him."

"You are making a big mistake."

"You've already made one. Get the hell out of here."

Clyde scowled at her. Fortunately, the other two must have had some sense as they glanced off toward the cops on the other side of the street and then tugged at Clyde's arm.

"Another time, Clyde," one of them muttered. "Let's go."

Clyde spat a wad of tobacco at Natalie. It sprayed her face, dripping down her cheek. He flashed a black toothy grin and strode away, disappearing into the crowd. Dante handed her a tissue.

"Thank you."

She wiped the disgusting mess from her face.

Jordan turned and kicked the railing, holding it tight with both hands. Every interaction only brought out the worst, and she knew the evening was over before it started. Cops jogged over.

"Everything good here?"

"They already left," Dante said. "Went that way."

"You okay, ma'am?" an officer asked, watching Natalie wipe the spit from her face.

"Been better. Look, it was just a misunderstanding."

"You want to give me a name and description?"

"You didn't see them?" Dante asked.

"A lot of people here, sir."

"Don't worry about it. I think he got the message."

"You want to tell me what it was about?"

While they were explaining about Jordan's father, the vibrant celebration turned into a surreal nightmare.

Darkness enveloped everything; a suffocating shroud swallowed the streetlights and neon signs and quieted the crowd's laughter. The floats ground to a halt, their dazzling allure extinguishing instantly.

The police officer turned; his exclamation echoed in the shocked silence. "What the...?"

Natalie's heart sped up.

The air crackled with unease as everyone on the street strained their senses, trying to fathom the inexplicable darkness that had descended upon them.

Strangers became silhouettes against the night, their faces masks of uncertainty and fear.

Then, piercing the stillness, a scream sliced through the air.

Heads turned skyward, and horror gripped everyone as a plane hurtled toward them. It all happened so fast. The dark and deadly projectile cut through buildings, destroyed cars, and obliterated a crowd.

Multiple explosions erupted as another plane struck the ground further afield, then another several streets over. Buildings shattered, vehicles burst into flames, and chaos cascaded through the once-celebratory streets.

"Run! Move!" someone shouted, their words almost drowned in the din of disaster.

Natalie's survival instincts kicked in as the nightmare unfolded before her. "Guys, let's go!" she cried, her voice firm as she ushered her charges away from the impending danger.

Above them, the sky became a tapestry of hellish reds, oranges, and yellows as flames erupted from broken structures. The wind howled, an evil force that seemed to feed the fire's ravenous appetite, consuming everything in its path.

Pushing forward through the torrent of terrified people, Natalie gripped Selena's hand and glanced at Dante, her determination mirroring his.

The scene was one of instant pandemonium: families were torn apart as they desperately fought to escape, and children cried out for their parents as the street transformed into a chaotic frenzy to survive.

Many were trampled beneath the tide of feet.

"Ms. Reid, what's happening?" Daniel's voice wavered with fear as he followed behind her.

"I don't know. Keep moving," Natalie admitted, her heart

pounding as they navigated back to where they had parked. "Once we are safe, I'll figure it out..." Her voice trailed off as they reached the open lot. She watched as people clamored toward their vehicles in parking lots only to discover they were lifeless and unresponsive.

Panic and desperation fueled the scene as those trapped in the town held up inoperative phones. All communication devices had been rendered useless.

Tears streamed down faces illuminated by the ghastly glow of the inferno as the injured walked through smoke, dazed and muttering to themselves. One woman was unconscious, being helped by two others. Blood was on the ground from where a driver had lost control and barreled into a lamppost. His driver's door was open. He was on his knees, gripping his stomach where a chunk of metal was stuck in him.

"Guys, this way! Stay together!" she bellowed over the tumultuous chorus of screams. As they pushed through the human tidal wave, Natalie could feel the ground tremble beneath her feet; it wasn't the impact of the plane's devastation reverberating through the town, but something worse.

Desperation etched their features as they glanced toward the heavens, a gasp escaping her lips as fiery plumes illuminated the night with savage brilliance.

"What do we do?" Selena asked, her voice quivering.

Amid the chaos, vehicles became useless hulks, only adding to the sheer number of people rushing down the sidewalk. The very fabric of their reality seemed to have unraveled.

A young girl's shrieks cut through Natalie as she glanced across the road to see a motionless woman. A child no older than four was patting her mother. "Wake up. Mommy, wake up!" An adult came by, scooping up the child. The kid reached out, her cries blending in with the rest.

Tears mingled with the ash and soot that fell from the sky like a dreadful rain.

"Find cover!" Dante's voice rang out above the din. "We need to find shelter!"

Natalie's heart hammered as Dante led the group toward a building, its entrance offering only an uncertain promise of safety. It was a sports bar. The air was thick with the smell of smoke as the ground quaked with the force of another impact or an earthquake.

Inside, other people huddled together, seeking a moment of reprieve. Everyone coughed watching the madness unfold through the windows. Outside, flames danced in wild abandon, whipping into a frenzy and consuming everything their glowing fingers could reach.

"Anyone know what's happening?" someone asked from far back in the bar.

"Hell. That's what's happening," someone covered in soot muttered as Gatlinburg's sirens began to play out. The city's new emergency warning system had been created after the wildfires and floods years earlier. It was meant to signal people to move to higher ground. Its ominous echo was too late this time.

Natalie's gaze flickered from face to face, a silent promise of survival and solidarity. Standing there, arms around the teens who had no home to return to, she thought of the safety of her husband and only child.

6

Tuesday, July 4, 12:05 a.m.
Portland, Oregon

T alis O'Brien carved his initials into the man's forehead so he wouldn't forget him. Muffled cries escaped from behind a gag as blood trailed into his eyes, blurring his vision. Satisfied and holding the scruff of his collar, Talis leaned close to his ear, speaking in almost a controlled whisper.

"If we see you or your scum-loving antifa buddies again, it will be the last time."

With that, Talis gestured with a nod to one of his pals. The rear doors opened on the moving van, and with a quick shove, the man fell out the back, hitting the ground hard and rolling to a stop.

He was alive. Barely.

They'd spent the past hour snatching up strays lost in the

fog of smoke bombs.

"That's another who will have one hell of a story to tell the others."

"Yeah, and an excuse to explain why he can't attend the next rally."

Laughter erupted inside.

Portland was alive with a buzz that only the summer months brought.

It was dubbed fighting season, and he fucking loved every second of it.

Like European soccer hooligans who lived for the thrill of drinking, filling out coaches, and showing up at matches intending to launch vicious assaults on opposing team fans, this was their high.

A long-time member of the Proud Boys, a group that had gained notoriety as extremists involved in the Capitol riots, he begged to disagree.

Were they misunderstood? Yeah. Feared? No doubt. Were they reviled by man? Hell, yeah.

But terrorists? That's where he drew the line.

He chuckled at the very mention of it.

A spokesman for their group had tried to clarify, but it didn't matter. As long as they spoke up, folks would associate them with white nationalists, misogynists, and anti-immigrants. There was some truth to that. And? It wasn't like the world wasn't full of their own biases.

Everyone loved to throw them into a box, but the truth was beliefs and hatred had evolved. In many, they were a consequence of an oppressed, pussy-ass society that had succumbed to the complaints of a fringe minority. In his eyes, they were no different than a government hell-bent on war against another country, their fight was justified.

Chris Harrison glanced over his shoulder into the back of the van.

"They've moved the rally from the Waterfront Park to a commercial parking lot in the northeast to avoid the police." He paused. "Shall we?"

"Hell, yeah," Talis replied.

Hundreds of people, many from the anti-fascist group, had assembled downtown earlier that day. What started as peaceful soon culminated in a gunfight with both them and others firing rounds at each other. One of those rounds had struck a member of theirs, and so to find out who was responsible, they'd been pulling anti-fascists into the van all day, grilling and torturing them.

The problem was that unlike the Proud Boys, the antifa movement didn't have a centralized leadership. So, rooting out those responsible was a tough job, especially when they all wore masks and black attire, a tactic known as "black bloc," a way to unify their efforts but hide their identities.

They were cowards and hypocrites.

They said their goal was peace and inclusivity, yet their actions said otherwise.

No better than them, their methods were as violent as the Proud Boys, even if it was done under the umbrella of stopping racism and hatred. What was overlooked until recent months were the windows smashed and cars set on fire during protests at a university in California.

Both groups blamed each other for being the first to be aggressive.

There was all this talk about hard left and hard right, but Talis didn't give two shits about any of that. That kind of talk was for pussies. For him, this wasn't political. He left that to others. He was in it purely for the brotherhood and thrills, and as long as that continued, he was game.

Sitting in the back of the van, jostling around, they glanced over each other, all clothed in black. Like a SWAT team, they were ready. They'd shed the familiar yellow and black attire to blend in with antifa. It was easier that way. If they were spotted grabbing one or two and tossing them into the back of a van, other antifa protesters would assume they were injured and doing the noble thing and getting their guys out there.

It couldn't be further from the truth.

It was a new tactic they were employing. Talis liked to think he thought outside the box; his elder brother Ryland, on the other hand, hadn't been so open-minded.

He was more about diplomacy, taking ground through being a voice for the next generation. And to be fair, he'd achieved it. Chapters across America had grown exponentially under his leadership.

Still, where Ryland was the bark, Talis was the teeth, ready to tear into the fabric of society if necessary.

Drawn into it by his family, Talis had risen through the ranks, utilizing any method possible to gain new members and keep those who tried to stop them at bay. Going incognito had done wonders for their group. The kind of intel they'd been able to extract through blending in was priceless.

That was the whole point: to look, move, and even smell like them. The only different thing was how they thought.

"This is going to be epic," Sawyer said.

Talis glanced down at his phone.

"You heard back from your brother yet?" Jagger asked.

He turned it off and pocketed it. "Nothing."

"Did he tell you what it was about?"

Talis shook his head. "He said he was doing a favor for a guy inside — an old war buddy of his. I don't ask. Ryland handles his own business; we handle ours."

In the urban sprawl of Portland, the night sky hung heavy with the absence of stars. The moon cast only a faint glow, revealing silhouettes of buildings and streets as they drove toward the commercial car lot. In the heart of the darkness, an electric tension surged through the air, signaling the collision of opposing forces.

In the thick summer heat, the van's headlights sliced through the obscurity, its tires rolling to a soft stop. Talis prepared for another round of snatch-and-grab under the cover of smoke. His face was etched with seriousness as he stepped out of the van, his silhouette illuminated by the faint glow of the lot.

Jeering, shouts, and the batting of shields strangled the air.

Beside him, his friends emerged, clad in their black attire, their faces concealed by masks that added an enigma to their presence.

There was the risk of being caught up in the fights, so they had to make it quick.

Nearby, a large gathering of individuals all in black wore hoodies, bandanas, and masks as they formed a united front. Their intent was palpable, their voices a symphony of genuine conviction. This was the rallying point for those who stood against perceived injustices and social inequalities, the symbol of resistance against his brothers.

As the two groups faced off, a volatile equilibrium held. Tempers simmered beneath the surface like molten lava on the brink of eruption. Dialogue served as kindling, igniting flames of confrontation that threatened to engulf them all.

The cacophony of voices on both sides grew louder, each word a spark in the storm.

Talis grinned. This was his backyard, his playground, where he thrived.

"You know what to do," he said as they reached for smoke grenades and unleashed them into the crowd.

Suddenly, a gust of wind carried the scent of something acrid — a hiss of smoke bombs being released. Wisps of gray fog began to curl through the air, creating an ethereal and menacing atmosphere. The world became hazy and distorted as if reality had shifted into an alternate dimension.

Amidst the smoke, individuals on both sides surged forward, the clash of bodies a chaotic ballet. Fists met flesh, shouts rose in a crescendo, and a tapestry of flags — each representing a different stance — flapped like banners in the wind. The scene was a storm of movement and emotion, a dance of opposing forces, as Independence Day carried a different meaning for each side.

Talis led his group forward into the midst of the tumult, seeking out anyone carrying a handgun. Most avoided it out of fear of being arrested. But the police weren't there. They wouldn't be for a while. The move from one place to another was done on purpose, to give each side a fair chance on a battlefield where voices faded into the background and blood could be shed.

Before he could move forward with the next grab, Jagger pulled his arm. "Talis. Foster is back."

"Is my brother here?"

He turned and elbowed through the ruckus until they stood beside the van. An out-of-breath man, heavily bearded, a part of the older generation, was already inside the van. It was too dangerous to linger outside.

Talis ducked into the van, and Jagger pulled the doors closed.

"Is that blood?" Talis asked.

Chris handed Foster a bottle of water. He was sweating badly.

"It's Ryland," Foster muttered.

"What about him?"

Their gaze locked amidst the chaos outside.

"He's dead," Foster said.

Talis' jaw went slack. "What are you talking about?"

"We were ambushed. Bryce, the brother — he shot Ryland in the head. I saw it."

Talis leaned back, shock and despair mixing into a volatile cocktail. His hand balled, ready to unleash even though it had no target.

"Start from the beginning. Where did you go tonight?"

"Ryland never told you?"

"No," Talis replied.

Foster lowered the bottle of water. "East of here. North of Oregon City. Ryland was meant to kidnap, torture, and kill a man then wait for Bryce to show. Except when he did, there was someone else there. It all got complex. I don't know. I was upstairs at the time. All I heard was the gunshots, the commotion. I saw Ryland get shot in the back of the head. There was nothing I could do. All of them are dead."

"Except you?"

"What do you expect? He killed the other five. I managed to climb out the top window and go down to the car."

"Who killed Ryland?"

"I assume it was the brother. I don't know. I never saw the shooter. I did see the man that Ryland was about to shoot before he was ambushed from behind. I could point him out." He paused to catch his breath. "I'm sorry, Talis. If there were anything I could have done — anything — I would have. You got to believe me."

If it wasn't for the fact that he needed him, Talis might have been inclined to turn the gun on Foster. Still, there were times he'd seen rallies go sideways. Nothing was ever guaranteed. The irony was that Ryland was always telling him if continued on a path of violence things would end badly. "How many were there?"

"Two. Could have been more."

"And this house. You can take me to it?"

Foster nodded.

Talis' breathing became labored as the weight of the loss bore down on him. He removed the mask he'd been wearing; sweat trickled down his brow.

He reached for a machete lying on the van floor, and in an act of pure anger, he opened the doors and went to get out and inflict damage on antifa members. Jagger grabbed him.

"Talis."

"Get off me."

Jagger held him for a beat longer.

In an instant he pulled his arm away, rushed into the smoke cloud, and began hacking, unleashing his rage on those around him. They never saw it coming. Cries were smothered by the noise of fighting and guns erupting. By the time he was done, multiple people lay seriously wounded, a few dead.

Emerging from the chaos, as blue, red, and white strobe lights from police vehicles burst into view, he dropped the machete, his face and hands covered in blood.

His anger was no closer to releasing its grip on him.

Jagger took hold of him and bundled him into the back of the van.

"Chris. Let's go!" Jagger shouted.

In shock, Talis stared at Foster while the others got in, and the van swerved out of the lot. It didn't get far.

In an instant the engine died.

Lights went out, and the van slowed to a crawl and stopped.

Jagger, still aware of cops rushing into the midst of the rioting, yelled, "Get it started. Let's go."

"I can't. It won't start," Chris replied.

Jagger clawed his way to the front of the van and looked out the windshield, and that's when he noticed. Every vehicle was at a standstill, all the lights had gone out.

"Talis. TALIS!" Jagger cried. He glanced back at his friend, blood dripping from his hands. "We should..."

Before anyone could move, an explosive force seemed to surge from nowhere. The van shuddered violently as if seized by an unseen hand. A blast of air slammed against the side of the vehicle, the world tilting at a disorienting angle.

The van groaned and creaked, the force of the impact causing jarring chaos within its confines. Metal screeched against concrete, a haunting symphony of destruction that painted the air with tension. The effect seemed to stretch time, each second an eternity of disarray.

Amid the nightmare, Talis' breath caught in his throat. Through the shattered windshield, he glimpsed a scene of surreal devastation — a section of a plane engine engulfed in flames sprawled before them. Black smoke billowed, thick and suffocating, engulfing the night in a sinister embrace. The stench of burning filled the air, making each breath a struggle.

Coughing and choking, they exchanged frantic glances, their eyes reflecting a shared fear transcending the conflict they had arrived to participate in. Fueled by adrenaline, Sawyer kicked open the back doors. One by one, they clambered out into a world that had transformed into a nightmare.

The sight that greeted them was a scene of unfathomable destruction.

Flames licked at the night sky, painting it with a hellish glow. The commercial building they had parked near had suffered a direct hit from the plummeting plane. The wreckage was an ominous reminder; its twisted metal and shattered windows bore witness to the explosive force of the impact.

Adrenaline coursed through Talis' veins, shifting from confrontation to survival. The plane's wreckage was an eerie and sad tableau of chaos before them. The flames danced, casting monstrous shadows that flickered and contorted.

The night vibrated — the crackling of flames, the groaning of metal, the faint cries that seemed to linger just beyond the periphery all underscored the fragility of existence.

Talis' gaze shifted from the wreckage to his friends. Their faces illuminated, expressions locked in disbelief and shock. As they stood on the precipice of confusing chaos, Talis realized that the world had shifted its narrative, revealing a truth that transcended the conflicts that had brought them here.

The flames roared, and shadows danced, but a shared humanity emerged among it all as he watched some from antifa assist those from the opposing group.

Speechless, Jagger approached him.

"What now?"

7

Oregon City, Oregon

The light from the TV winked out, as did all the bulbs in the house.

What little Bryce had gleaned from the broadcast before the power went out made it clear the situation was dire. As he stood before the TV, remote in hand, still thinking the power might switch back on, the weight of the unknown bore down, hard and heavy.

"What's happened?" Zoe said in a panicked state.

Bryce's mind was a turmoil of thoughts as he tossed the clicker and headed for the front door, swinging it wide and stepping out into the night to see if he could make out the lights of other homes on the street. Nothing. Absolute inky black. Not even one street light was illuminated.

"Shit," he muttered, turning back inside.

Zoe followed him as he rifled through drawers in the house, searching for a flashlight. "Bryce. Bryce!"

"Besides what you heard on the TV, I don't know, Zoe. The country is under attack."

"Why are the phones not working?" she asked.

He found a wind-up flashlight and gave it a tap against his hand before winding and illuminating the room.

"Off the top of my head, I think it could be an EMP."

"A what?"

He charged across the room, answering as he went. "An electro-magnetic pulse caused by a high-altitude nuclear missile. It takes out the grid, vehicles, smartphones, power stations, you name it; unless it's in a Faraday cage, it could be affected. Of course, what might be affected is all speculation as many factors can come into play — type, distance, size, intensity, and so on, but it's not good." Bryce shone the light on Jackson.

Jackson squinted.

"Speak to me, Jackson. How are we doing?"

Jax muttered something but was going in and out of consciousness. Bryce continued working on him, doing the best he could. It was clear to see that he needed real medical attention.

"Well, when will it come back on again?"

"It may not," Bryce replied, still concentrating on her father's leg.

"How do you even know about this?"

"You learn a thing or two in the military," he said.

Zoe sidled up beside him. "But it can be fixed, right? I mean, the government will handle this."

He shook his head. "How can they when the infrastructure

is affected? Delivery trucks bringing groceries, medication, fuel, and assistance won't run. Factories that produce items will stop. Everything you know will grind to a halt. And that's just the beginning." He held the flashlight between his teeth, focusing it on the wound. His hands were gloved in blood as he stepped back and sighed. "Well, that's it. That's all I can do."

Zoe's gaze bounced between them. "That's it?"

Bryce walked out of the house and stuck his hands in a pail of water, washing them clean before scooping up a handful and running it over his face. Zoe followed him, standing in the doorway.

"What now?"

"Now I get the hell out of here, and you should too before more trouble shows up," he muttered, going over to one of the dead men and dropping to a knee to root through his pockets.

"But what about my father? We can't just leave him in there. And if you're right about this EMP thing, the truck won't be working anymore. How am I supposed to help him?"

"I'm sorry. I never wanted either of you to get caught up in this, but there's nothing more I can do."

"Nothing more you can do?" Zoe yelled, making her way down the porch steps.

Bryce turned in a flash and grabbed her by the arms; keeping his voice low, "He's not going to make it. Okay? I'm sorry. But he's lost too much blood."

"So, help me get him a doctor."

"Okay. Sure. How?" he said sarcastically. "We are miles from the nearest hospital. We have no transportation. And even if we did, he could die en route. No, right now, the safest thing to do is to get away from here before—"

"Your friends come back?"

He released his grip. "They're not my friends."

"No, but we are. At least, I thought we were. I mean, you know my mother. That's got to count for something." She shifted from one foot to the next, studying him.

Bryce looked at her under the moon's glow, the light danced off her features. He could see Natalie in her. He swallowed hard, pushing the memories of the past away. He couldn't let it sway him. Not now. Not under these conditions.

"Zoe. I knew your mother a long time ago. Besides, I haven't even had time to grieve the loss of my brother."

"Yeah, well, if we don't do something, my father will join him."

"Join who?" her father said. Zoe turned to see him staggering out of the doorway. He collapsed on the porch, and Zoe ran to him. She dropped down, holding his head, tears streaming down her cheeks.

"Please," she said, looking back at Bryce.

Bryce gritted his teeth. "Fuck!"

He hurried over and helped her take him back into the house. They set him back on the table coated in a thin layer of blood. Bryce turned and went back into the depths of the house.

"Bryce!" Zoe yelled.

"Hold on a second. I'm trying to find a map."

"There's several in the truck."

He re-emerged and bolted out of the door.

As he jogged past the dead, he couldn't push from his mind the last conversation he had with his ex-platoon commander, Mason Erikson. This was exactly what he wanted. It was the he gift he'd mentioned.

Bryce felt a wave of stress hit him.

If it wasn't that, now he had other things to contend with, the nation in darkness, and... before he could finish that thought and reach the truck, another rumble echoed, and fissures split the road in two, upheaving the ground and shaking everything.

Bryce's legs buckled, and he scrambled to his feet to reach the truck before it got sucked into an opening.

He hoisted himself up onto the truck that had pitched to one side.

"C'mon!" he yelled, pulling on the door before using the butt end of his handgun to smash the window, then unlock the driver's side.

Once in, he fished around on the floor; even as the truck tilted to one side, smoke and fire rose around vehicle as if a dragon's mouth was consuming the steel beast. He snagged two maps and scrambled back out.

He had to escape vertically as the driver's door was now skyward.

Hoisting himself through the opening, he launched off the edge, landing hard in a ditch and rolling into the under-brush. He turned in time to see the ground swallow the 18-wheeler like it was nothing.

Plumes of dust and smoke exploded upward, raining dirt down on him.

Bryce scrambled to his feet and raced back to the house without wasting another second. When he entered, Zoe was still grasping her father's hand but was on the floor, taking shelter under the table. "You, okay?" he asked.

"No. No, I'm not."

Bryce opened the map and located Oregon; he shone the light over the grid and pinpointed his brother's farm and the nearest hospital. "We're looking at roughly four, maybe five miles to the nearest hospital. It's south of here."

"So, we carry him."

"You know how long that will take?" he asked.

She shrugged.

"About an hour and a half, walking at a good clip. Add your father into the mix and..." He shook his head and stepped away from the map, exiting the house again. Zoe wasn't far behind him.

"So, we find a way to carry him," she said. "There must be—"

"Zoe. Listen! There's a chance he's not going to make it. He's lost a lot of blood. He's already going in and out of consciousness."

"So?"

"You saw the news before it went off the air. You've felt the earth shake. There's no telling if the hospital is even running. They might have some backup generators or something that was protected and working, but they're likely fried. He needs medical help, but there is a chance..."

"Don't say it. I don't want to hear it."

"Zoe."

"NO! I'm taking him with or without you. Now, which way is the hospital?"

"It's pitch dark. You won't find it."

She made a beeline for the door and entered again. Bryce lifted both hands to the back of his head, interlocking his fingers and releasing a heavy sigh. Zoe was as stubborn as Natalie.

Back inside the house, Bryce found her holding her father's hand, sobbing hard, asking him to help her, but he was out cold. The longer they waited, the higher the chances he would die.

"All right. I'll help you, but it would be quicker if I went by myself and got a doctor to visit him, and you stay behind."

"How do I know you'll come back?"

"You don't. I guess you'll have to trust me."

He eyed her and could see the skepticism.

"Anyway, even if I agree to stay behind? How would that work? You just said more trouble could be coming this way."

"I did. You wouldn't stay here. Down the road is a good friend of my brother who will be able to help."

"How would you know that if you've been inside?"

"Because I was offered a job by him. Chad arranged it. Look. It's not ideal, but at least you'd be safe."

"Safe?" She stared at him.

"All right. Reasonably safe. Look, what do you want me to say, Zoe? I'm trying my best here. I never wanted this. No one did. I can't guarantee your father will make it, but it's the best option under the circumstances."

"Circumstances. I am still determining what we're facing."

"I just told you. Listen, we are wasting time here. The longer we take, the quicker things are going to spiral down. Looting, riots, it won't take long for cities to descend into chaos. Now, do you want help or not?"

"Listen to him, Zoe," Jackson muttered, his eyes fluttering to life. He squeezed his daughter's hand, and she began to cry.

Bryce went off to search for a bag. He glanced at his brother. Everything inside of him wanted to unravel, but death wasn't foreign to him. He just wished his brother hadn't suffered. He collected a few bottles of water from the fridge, a couple of cans of food, and several granola bars. He scooped up a rifle from one of the dead men, set it on his back, gathered some ammo and the map, and then went outside to see what he could find in his brother's barn. He'd need something he could use as a stretcher. Worst-case scenario, he would gather two tree limbs and some sheets.

Ten minutes later, Bryce worked with Zoe to move Jackson from the table. He'd rigged up the makeshift stretcher with a cord that he could wrap over his backpack. It wouldn't dig into his chest and shoulders as he dragged him.

"How far down the road?"

"Less than a mile. You remember the junkyard we passed on the way?"

She nodded.

Chad had asked around. Bryce knew that his chances of landing a job after getting out would be meager. No one would want someone with a record. Fortunately, an army vet knew all too well what it was like to get out and be kicked to the curb. He'd had to rebuild his life from scratch, so he was willing to give Bryce a shot. It wouldn't have been glamorous or high-paid. Days would have involved a lot of sweat and long hours, and he'd spend hours scrubbing oil off his hands, but it would have been honest work.

"How are you doing back there, Jackson?" Bryce asked.

Jackson managed to summon a grunt.

"It's going to be bumpy from here on out. Hang in there." Bryce dragged the stretcher behind him. It was now that he was glad that he'd caught a few hours' sleep on the way up. Zoe, on the other hand, was running on steam.

What should have been a silent lug less than half a mile down the road turned into a disaster scene. The reality of the new world hit them fast and hard. Thick plumes of smoke drifted up over the sky like outstretched fingers. The road had several cars that had been abandoned. In the distance, Bryce could see buildings smoldering as if a vast missile had torn a gash through town. Many of the signposts had been snapped like toothpicks. Fissures ran across the ground, with some of the asphalt heaved up, leaving debris scattered.

The acrid smell was overpowering.

The forest nearby was on fire where a jetliner had burned through it. Tongues of fire danced in the night sky. He could see the impact had cut a huge gash in the ground and had left behind a massive engine.

Chunks of shrapnel scattered.

"Cover your mouth," Bryce said as Zoe began coughing hard.

He could feel a burn in the back of his throat from the toxic fumes.

"Maybe I can go with you," Zoe said.

"What?"

"To the hospital."

He groaned. "Your father needs you."

"But..."

"Zoe. I know you don't trust me, but your mother does, and right now, I'm all you've got. I might have made a few mistakes, but my word is golden."

There was silence between them for a few minutes before Zoe piped up again. "Were you screwing my mother?"

"You don't beat around the bush."

"Well, it's not every day she asks my father to give a guy a ride. You said you knew her. How?"

Bryce glanced back over his shoulder at Jackson, hoping he wasn't listening.

"How much do you know about your mother's past?"

Zoe shrugged. "Only that she grew up around Bryson."

"And grandparents?"

"I only knew those on my father's side."

Bryce nodded, his thoughts turning to the day he met Natalie. Her past. His. The upbringing he left behind. "I think it's best you hear it from your mother."

Zoe shook her head. "If I see her again."

Bryce glanced at her; he wanted to reassure her that she would, that somehow, he'd manage to make good and find a doctor for her father and maybe even help them find their way home to Tennessee, but one look at the landscape and it was clear they were on the precipice of an unknown disaster.

Even if another nation didn't invade, a country could quickly turn on itself.

"Then, at least tell me this. Why does she owe you?" Zoe asked.

"She doesn't."

"That's not what she said."

Bryce considered the question. There was a reason why Natalie could have felt indebted, but before he could respond, he noted the address on a mailbox outside a wreckers yard. "We're here."

8

Gatlinburg, Tennessee

Confusion gripped the group, heightening fear.

In the heart of Gatlinburg, amidst the chaos and turmoil that had engulfed the streets, the small sports bar stood as a fragile sanctuary. Its neon signs were darkened with no power, offering no light to the faces of the weary and scared huddled inside.

The situation was unlike anything they'd seen in eastern Tennessee. Sure, severe weather had knocked out the power before, sending thousands into darkness and damaging many buildings, but that was a storm.

This was something far more terrifying.

Natalie stared out the window at the main street that now resembled a road straight out of hell. Fire and smoke dominated, and the silhouettes of people moving through it all looked eerie.

"Planes just don't fall out of the sky. Cars don't just stop working," someone said from inside the sports bar. "And why is this damn phone not working?"

Natalie glanced back.

"It was a ballistic missile," another said.

"How do you know?"

"You didn't get the emergency message?"

"Unlike some of you, I don't walk around with my phone on me every hour of the day. I like to be present in the moment," an older woman said.

She wasn't far wrong. It had taken years of convincing for Natalie to buy a phone. Even then, she often left it behind, using a landline to call home. She'd seen how zombified society had become, staring at their screens all day.

"Ballistic missile?" Natalie asked, peering into the black.

Before an answer came, a small light illuminated an area behind the bar. "Here, take this," the bartender said, handing someone a candle.

"Can I get one of those?" a woman asked.

"Sure. Hold on," he replied.

Natalie inched her way back through the knot of people. "You said something about a ballistic missile?"

"Yeah, an emergency message was displayed on my phone just before the shit hit the fan. There was also some warning about a tsunami hitting the West Coast."

"Are you sure?"

"Lady, I might be hard of hearing, but I can see perfectly well."

Natalie felt her stomach drop at the thought of Jackson and Zoe. As she turned to head back to the group of teenagers, there was another rumble and a jolt. Glasses in the back of the bar rattled, and multiple bottles shattered on the floor. Many cried out, just voices of peril in the darkness.

"It's getting worse. We should leave," Dante said, gazing out. "These old buildings aren't secure."

"What did he say?" someone asked.

"He said these buildings…"

As the woman's words came out, the whole building shook hard, and the floor beneath them began to tremble with an unsettling ferocity. Glasses rattled on the bar shelves, and the walls emitted a low, ominous groan. Panic spread like wildfire among the group, and the room was filled with a chorus of frightened cries.

Then, the room shattered.

The ceiling cracked with a deafening roar, and plaster and debris rained down. Bottles smashed on the floor, and chairs toppled over, the chaos intensifying. A table near the entrance was torn apart as a jagged fissure snaked through the wooden floor.

In what felt like a heart-stopping moment, the floor beneath them yawned open, and the abyss instantly swallowed several people.

Natalie's eyes widened in horror; instinctively moving to avoid it, she stumbled back, losing her footing on the shifting floor. But before she could fall into the darkness, Dante clasped her hand, pulling her back to safety.

As the violent shaking subsided, the room fell into an eerie silence, except for the stifled sobs punctuating the air. Dust hung like a veil, casting an otherworldly haze over the scene. Those who had survived coughed hard. The familiar walls now bore gaping cracks, and the ceiling bulged, threatening to collapse at any moment.

"We need to leave," Dante's voice cut through the stillness, his words a grim reminder. Her gaze met his, a silent understanding.

As the group spilled out onto the street, their eyes widened at the scene of devastation. There were no flashes of red and blue illuminating the night from emergency strobe lights; all that could be seen was a landscape of destruction.

Natalie's heart clenched as she soaked in the sight of a police officer scrambling to help the injured. Cries for help echoed through the air, and she could see shadows of people buried under debris. Instinct and empathy drove her forward, pushing toward a trapped figure.

A young woman sat helpless in her car, her eyes wide with fear as a colossal tree trunk bore down on the vehicle, the weight of it crushing the metal shell. Nat caught her breath, pushed down her fear, and got on the hood of the wreckage.

Without hesitation, her hands reached out, gripping the remains of the roof. She forced open the dented metal, her muscles straining. "Here, let me help you," Dante said, pulling on the other side of the metal.

Inside the wreckage, the woman's face was streaked with tears, her voice trembling as she implored for help.

Natalie squeezed through the narrow opening. Her fingers brushed against the woman's form, offering reassurance. "It's all right. We'll get you out," she said, her voice a soothing balm.

The woman seemed to care less for herself and more for what was behind her. Her eyes darted toward the back seat, her voice cracking. "My child... my baby's back there. Please, help her."

Dread and determination mingled.

"I'll get the baby," Jordan said, offering additional support.

Jordan reacted as Natalie pulled the woman free, slipping through the shattered window. He slipped around twisted metal and broken branches, agile and determined. He was small enough to fit through the wreckage, and his courage lent him an unnatural strength.

"I got you. I got you," he said.

There was a moment when Natalie lost sight of him in the darkness and branches. Then, she heard the sound of the child being unbuckled from a car seat and then him emerging with an unconscious infant.

With the utmost care, Jordan hoisted the child through the shattered window and into the waiting arms of Natalie. Relief surged as she cradled the baby, her heart swelling at the teen's courage.

Dante took over performing CPR on the child — blowing into her airway.

A moment later, the child let out a cry.

He handed the kid back to the mother, and she broke down in tears, thanking them while rocking back and forth. "Come on, let's get you out of here," Natalie said, guiding her toward where emergency personnel could assess the baby and ensure she and the mother were safe.

WITHOUT ANY VEHICLES IN OPERATION, they were looking at a walk of at least forty minutes to reach the group home. It was sandwiched between Mountain Fox Lodge and Smokey's Lodge on the east side, nestled in the woodland but within driving distance of everything they needed.

Together, they carefully navigated the debris-laden street, the weight of the moment a potent reminder of the fragility of life. As they moved away from the sounds of cries, they saw no looting, only people helping others.

Natalie's thoughts circled from family to the teens.

"I just don't understand why the vehicles have stopped," Natalie remarked.

"I wish I knew," Dante replied, glancing down the road.

"That's simple," Liam said as he adjusted his ball cap. "America is under attack. It's been coming down the pipeline since the Cold War. All that prodding, puffing out your chest, and peacocking only gets you so far. Eventually, it was going to backfire."

"And you would know this because?" Selena asked.

"The internet."

"Right, because the internet is the source of all truth."

"No, he might be right," Dante said as they walked along the road, seeing destroyed buildings. "Who else can hit this hard? And the timing of it on the Fourth of July of all days? They know America has its guard down. It couldn't be any better."

"Well, if they think they are going to muscle in and take over, they are going to be in for a rude awakening when they find themselves staring down the barrel of guns," Liam muttered.

"I don't think they need to invade. It's estimated that almost 90 percent of the U.S. could die if the grid went out for longer than a year or two. A lack of food, clean water, medicine, it wouldn't take long for the young and old to drop off," Dante said.

"Well, that's not happening," Liam replied. "It will take more than a country in the dark to take me down."

"He means infants and old folks, dipshit. Isn't that right, Mr. Anderson?" Selena muttered.

"Selena," Natalie said in a reprimanding tone.

"What? I'm just clarifying for the lower-level thinkers."

"Low level? I'm pretty sure it's your kind sniffing gasoline."

"Your kind?" Selena barked, offended by his remark about stories he'd heard from the reservation. It wasn't that far off, but it wasn't their fault. There were so many more variables that came into play.

"That's enough!" Natalie snarled, stopping and looking at the two of them. She swallowed hard and took a deep breath. It wasn't like her to yell. She was usually the calm one, but the evening had unnerved her.

Daniel and Jordan stared for a second before continuing.

Natalie had them all walk ahead while she tried to have a moment to think. "If you have to head back home, I'd understand," Natalie said to Dante.

"And leave you to bear the weight. Forget it."

"I'm just saying... I'd get it."

They said nothing for a moment or two before he piped up. "They left early. They made it out, Natalie."

"Yeah."

She knew he was referring to her family. While she appreciated the confidence, she couldn't help but wonder if they were still alive and, even if they were, how they would ever make it back.

As they continued the journey east, they threaded their way through a multitude of people working their way back to their homes. The trouble was the downed planes had caused some of the forest to catch fire. It had been a dry summer, and that only brought even further complications. Gatlinburg had already suffered from wildfires in 2016, starting as a small fire and forcing thousands to flee. Now, it looked like it could happen again.

Natalie glanced at where several planes had crashed and saw a fire burning sideways. Without electricity, there would be no means of pumping water to fight the fires. It wasn't like lakes surrounded them. The nearest one, Douglas Lake, was over an hour away by car.

"We should help," she said.

"What?" Dante shot back.

She motioned with her head to the fire that had surged since they'd been in the heart of the downtown. It had chewed into the valley and cut a path through the forest.

"You don't help with that," Dante said. "You run from it."

They all stopped and looked back as the flames grew more prominent.

"How the hell can they fight that?" Selena asked.

"Like they did back in the 1900s. People used to keep buckets of water at the front of their homes, firemen used to use hand-pumped fire engines," Liam said. "Except we don't have that."

The orange glow continued arching over the town, a terrifying sight revealing only a fraction of what must have been happening nationwide. Liam continued, "I expect the country is on fire. It's said that there is anywhere from 8,000 to 13,000 planes over the U.S. at any given time," he said. "If all of them have crashed, this country may never come back from this."

Natalie thought about what Dante had said — a country might not need to be invaded by a foreign nation as the devastation would be so vast that the domino effect would wipe them out.

She patted him on the arm. "Come on, we should go and help."

"Wait a second," Dante said, taking her by the arm. "Help with what?"

"The fires. There are emergency personnel and residents down there trying to battle it alone. We'll take water from the rivers in buckets. Whatever it takes."

"You saw it down there. It was like walking through hell. If we get any more earthquakes, we might find ourselves swallowed. No. We stay clear. We leave the city if need be."

"And go where? These kids don't have family. This is home. This is all we have. I'm going to help. You want to be useful; take the teens back to the group home. I'll be back later." Natalie turned to the teens. "Go with him."

"No. I'm going with you, Ms. Reid," Daniel piped up.

"Me too," Jordan added.

It wasn't long before all of them except Dante had agreed. He sighed. "Lead the way," he said.

"Shit. They're turning back, Clyde," Bobby said, lowering high-power binoculars. Clyde worked a pinch of tobacco between his gums and then spat a thick wad on the floor of the group home. Only half an hour earlier, they'd broken into the home and turned the place upside down. They smashed windows, spray-painted the walls, and emptied the fridge before making their way up to the balcony to sit and wait for that bitch to return.

He wasn't going to have someone speak to him like that.

She'd stepped over the line, and he fully intended to make an example of her and her colleague.

After, he'd take Jordan back and get back to his life.

Life? What life?

That had all changed when those damn planes had dropped out of the sky, and the lights went out. Clyde tore the binoculars out of his cousin's hands and peered out. Under the greenish glow of the night vision, he watched as the group vanished around a bend. "What do you want to do?" Ricky asked.

"Burn this place down."

"What?"

"You heard me. Burn it down."

"But I think it will anyway if we just leave it. Those fires are..."

"Did you not hear me? I said burn it. I'm not taking any chances."

"All right. All right."

Clyde made his way down to the truck outside. Ricky and Bobby took out two ten-gallon gasoline cans and began shaking them out through the huge home.

Clyde watched with a grin. "You want to fuck with me? Take my kid, will you? Let's see how you like this."

He waited until the two of them trailed gasoline out of the house before he took out a small, thin cigar and lit the end with a Zippo. Keeping the lighter open, he tossed it into the doorway and backed away at the sound of the whoosh.

9

Oregon City, Oregon

The world seemed to hold its breath in the predawn hours of the Fourth of July.

Bryce trudged forward; determination etched into every step. His worn boots stirred up small eddies of dust as he led the way, his gaze fixed ahead on the looming silhouette of McAllister's Auto Salvage and Recycling. Beside him, Zoe remained stoic, her youthful gaze wide and wary, scanning the darkest areas around them.

Behind them, the makeshift stretcher groaned under its burden. Pallid and grimacing, Jackson lay prone, his leg bound in a hastily fashioned tourniquet. Each shuffle of their feet jostled him, and muffled groans escaped his lips, carried away by the breeze.

"Listen, best to let me do the talking."

"Why do I detect a hint of uncertainty?"

"Besides the obvious? It's the middle of the night, Zoe. And look, just—"

"Let you do all the talking. I heard you."

The encroaching darkness shrouded the landscape, and the distant stars offered little more than faint glimmers in the ink-blank canvas above. An intense amount of smoke seemed to have swallowed the world around them, blotting out the light that might have illuminated the rusted remains of forgotten vehicles.

The trio moved up the unpaved driveway. The looming junkyard seemed both menacing and strangely welcoming.

Corrugated steel fencing and chain-link barricades enclosed the space like the ramparts of a fortress, promising protection from the outside world.

As they neared the entrance, an American flag, tattered and proud, caught the rays of light from a feeble moon. It stood tall, a silent testament to a spirit that refused to waver even in the face of the unknown.

Bryce noted a trailer beyond the entrance. It stood weathered and worn, like a sentinel guarding the secrets of the past. Its peeling paint told tales of countless storms endured, just as its battered appearance masked the resilience within.

"Looks closed," Zoe said.

"Yeah, but..."

Before he could finish speaking, the stillness of the night was pierced by an unexpected crack, the sound of a shotgun echoing through the air. Jackson tensed on the stretcher, a mixture of fear and pain contorting his features. Zoe's grip on Bryce's hand tightened.

"We're closed!" The gruff voice carried a warning.

Jackson's groans intensified. Bryce raised a free hand, his

eyes narrowing as he tried to make out the figure emerging from the trailer.

Rusty McAllister was a living embodiment of stubborn resilience. His stance was wary, his eyes sharp like a sentinel guarding his domain. He wore faded jeans and a weathered American flag T-shirt.

A battered cowboy hat rested atop his head, casting a shadow that concealed the depths of his gaze. A flask peeked out from his chest pocket, a promise of liquid courage.

"I was hoping to…"

Bryce was cut off by a whistle. What little silence existed was disrupted by the sudden appearance of two pit bulls. They charged toward the gate. The chorus of their barks joined the tension, creating a symphony of fury.

As abruptly as a conductor's final note, there was a whirring sound followed by a bright light illuminating the scene. Floodlights. Bryce shielded his eyes against the harsh glare, the sudden brilliance painting an afterimage on his retinas.

"Who are you?" Rusty asked, full of suspicion.

Bryce squinted, struggling to see past the blinding light. "Bryce Mitchell."

"Don't know you!"

Bryce took a few steps forward, glancing back at Zoe for but a second. "My brother Chad. He arranged to have you give me a job once I got out of military jail."

There was a pause, and then Rusty said, "Chad Mitchell?"

Bryce replied. "Yeah. His farm is half a mile down the road."

"Where is he then?"

Bryce dropped his chin as he responded. "Dead."

"Duchess! Lady! Stand down!" Rusty's command sliced

the night, and the dogs, obedient but reluctant, retreated to the trailer, their energy absorbed into the shadows beneath it.

The door on the trailer closed.

The floodlights shut off.

There was no movement, no sound.

Zoe sidled up to Bryce. "I thought you knew him?"

"I said my brother did. I..."

Before he could finish, a glint of metal caught his eye — a gun barrel slid through an opening in the corrugated fence, gleaming menacingly. A spotlight clicked on, its harsh beam illuminating his face. "Come a little closer. Let me get a look at you," Rusty's voice commanded from the shadows.

With a hesitant step, Bryce moved forward, unsure if he would pull the trigger.

"You got an ID?"

"ID?" Bryce replied, his heart pounding.

Rusty's voice dripped with impatience. "Is there an echo?"

Suppressing his exasperation, Bryce reached into his pocket and retrieved an old, worn ID card. He held it out toward the fence. The light from the end of the gun glinted off its battered surface.

Rusty examined it in the harsh glow. "You sure look like a criminal. More than a Marine." The tension was palpable, and a coiled energy hung in the air. "And you say your brother's dead?"

Bryce's voice caught in his throat; the words heavy as stone. "Yeah. That's right."

"Hard to see anything in this light. You packing any heat?"

"Yes."

"Good." Rusty's tone held a hint of approval. He disappeared momentarily, and then the gate began to creak open, revealing a narrow path into the heart of the salvage yard.

As the gap widened, Bryce exchanged a glance with Jackson, who remained silent but pained, his body betraying the torment he'd endured.

"Well, come on then, before I change my mind," Rusty said, standing at the entrance, beckoning them into a world of forgotten relics and discarded memories.

Rusty's gaze lingered on the stretcher. His eyes narrowed, dissecting the scene before him. "Whoa, whoa, whoa. What the hell is this?"

Bryce's voice was firm yet respectful. "This is a friend of mine. Jackson Reid. That's his daughter Zoe. He got shot in the leg. Look, I can explain, but maybe we can do that inside?" he said as the sound of gunfire in the distance caught his attention.

"And then what?"

"I just need a safe place to tend to his wounds while..."

A dry chuckle escaped Rusty's lips. "And you think this is it? You think I'm running a hospital?"

Jackson's groans underscored the urgency of the situation. "We won't be a problem," Zoe added.

Rusty looked at her; a hint of empathy flashed across his face, replaced by a healthy dose of skepticism. "I'll be the judge of that."

With cautious progress, they navigated into the salvage yard and over to the trailer. The interior revealed itself in shades of dim lamplight with a space that mirrored the chaos of the outside junkyard. It was a mishmash of salvaged furniture, worn but functional. The air held the faint scent of oil and rust, a testament to the proximity of their surroundings. The seating area consisted of mismatched couches and chairs, all bearing the scars of use and time.

Rusty headed straight for the small kitchen area, illuminated by a flickering overhead light. The fridge, plastered with magnets and faded photos, loomed like a monolith of sustenance. He opened the door, retrieving water bottles and handing them out with a curt nod, a rare gesture of hospitality.

As the water changed hands, Rusty's attention turned to his needs. He retrieved a bottle of beer. The familiar hiss of carbonation punctuating the air followed. With a swift motion, he cracked the top, the sound a release of tension. He tossed the cap aside and downed the beer in a few hearty swigs.

He tossed the bottle after; the sound of it joining a heap of others echoed, a reminder of Rusty's preference for function over form. He wiped his mouth with the back of his hand, his gaze shifting from Bryce to Jackson before settling on Zoe.

"How do you have power?" Zoe asked, her innocent curiosity breaking the silence.

Rusty's lips quirked into a half-smile, a trace of pride touching his features. "Kept a generator in a Faraday cage. I got my own stash of fuel, too. Unlike all the idiots of this world, I knew this shit was coming. Maybe not exactly like this, but enough to know how to prepare a little. The sound of the trumpet has been echoing for years, but oh no, everyone has been too distracted by shiny technology, award shows, and the poison they sell for five bucks a cup. Damn idiots. You of all people know what I'm talking about..." He tapped the bottle toward Zoe as if she embodied everything terrible about the new generation.

"Hey. She just asked a question," Bryce said.

"And I answered it. Or are you those folks who get all bent out of shape and offended when an opinion doesn't agree with your own?"

"How about we change the subject?"

"Hey, you asked." Rusty took another swig. His answer revealed the extent of his preparedness amidst the chaos of the outside world. He grabbed another beer from the fridge, his manner unhurried, starkly contrasting the urgency that had brought Bryce to his door.

Rusty leaned against a battered countertop, the lamplight casting his features into shadow and light. "Now, how about you tell me why you're here and what mess you've dragged in with you? Because I sure as hell know you aren't here for that job. Which I might add, I never offered."

"My brother said..."

"Your brother is full of shit. The fact is he came around here saying I owed him money. Something about when he dropped off his old car, I never gave him enough cash. He thinks I scammed him. And like I told him, it's supply and demand. Take today's new cars, for instance. Every Tom, Dick, and Harry is wondering how to get their hands on a new one, at least those that can afford them. So, they browse online, build one out, and get a price for the new car. Then they go to a dealer and find they have been charged an extra four thousand. For what? Who the hell knows? Dealers do whatever they want when supply is low and demand is high. Now, your brother could have taken his car to any other place. He may have gotten more, but he came to me. So, there we go. Either way, I didn't offer a job despite his ramblings about me owing him and him coming to collect someday. I assume this is that day, am I right?"

Bryce felt an uncomfortable twist in his gut.

Zoe took hold of his arm and yanked him toward the door.

"A moment of your time," she said.

"Don't mind me; you two just confer outside." Rusty chuckled before taking another swig.

Outside the trailer, she turned on a dime. "What is this, Bryce? You said you knew him. You said he would help."

"I am as much in the dark as you are. My brother said…" He shook his head. "Fuck. It doesn't even matter what he said. Just leave it to me," he replied before charging back inside. He took a deep breath, his gaze steady as he recounted the events that led them to Rusty's doorstep. The story unfolded with a mix of honesty and caution, painting a picture of a life unraveling and lives upended.

Rusty's expression remained inscrutable as the tale unfolded, his eyes flickering between the trio as if assessing the truth in their words. When Bryce finally finished, the silence seemed to stretch, the weight of judgment hanging in the air.

"So? Will you help?"

Rusty's lip curled into a wry smile, his eyes holding a hint of begrudging respect. "Well, I'll be damned. You've certainly managed to get yourselves tangled in a fine mess."

Bryce's shoulders relaxed imperceptibly at Rusty's response. "We didn't have anywhere else to turn. Look, it won't be long. Two hours tops. If you have a bicycle, maybe I can get there faster."

"Oh, so dumping your baggage here isn't enough; you want a bicycle?"

Bryce ran a hand around the back of his neck. That's when Zoe stepped up.

"Forget it, Bryce. You're wasting your time. It seems he lost trust in people a long time ago. We'll drag my father to the hospital."

She turned to leave, and Rusty laughed. "A woman with

fire and spunk. I like that. It's a rare thing to see in the youth today. With so many acting so self-entitled, like the world owes them something. Hold up. I'll help. He can stay until you get this doctor if you can get a doctor. I highly doubt it now with the shit that's happened, but I love to see people prove me wrong."

The moment was interrupted by a blaring beeping cutting through the air, red lights casting an eerie glow within the trailer. "Son of a bitch! They're back!" Rusty's voice crackled with frustration as he snatched up his shotgun, his movements practiced and swift. "Duchess! Lady! Time for supper!"

The dogs bounded out from their hiding spots, whisking by them and out the door.

Bryce watched in confusion, heart pounding in his chest. "What the hell is going on?"

Rusty turned, his eyes flashing as he answered before disappearing out the door. "Oh, it's just the self-entitled."

Bryce exchanged a bewildered glance with Zoe, the gravity of the situation sinking in. He ushered her to a corner, telling her to wait while he followed Rusty's lead.

Outside, the night air was charged with tension. Rusty held his shotgun high, a figure of authority. Two rounds tore through the stillness, the sharp retort echoing like a warning bell. "I know you're in here. This is your final warning. If you little bastards don't leave here now, you never will. I'll ensure that by tossing your dead body in the compactor."

His whistle sliced through the night, and Duchess and Lady sprang into action, their forms disappearing into the darkness on separate paths. "Go find 'em, girls!"

Bryce approached cautiously; his handgun held at the ready. "You want to clue me in on what's happening here?"

Rusty turned abruptly, his expression tight with resolve. "Off to catch me some rodents. I'd advise you to go back inside and stay down. Things could get ugly."

A dog's aggressive barking erupted in the distance, followed by Rusty's response, loud and commanding. "I'm coming!"

Bryce's heart raced as he stood at the precipice of the unknown. He glanced back at Zoe through a window, her eyes wide with fear and curiosity, before he moved to follow Rusty.

The night embraced them as Rusty and Bryce pressed through the labyrinth of steel bones. The air was thick with the scent of rust and oil, a tangible reminder of the mechanical corpses surrounding them. As they moved deeper into the heart of the junkyard, the landscape transformed into a mesmerizing and eerie maze.

"If you want my help, you should leave now," Rusty said.

"And leave Zoe here while this shit is happening?"

"I can handle it; it's not the first time."

"Who is it, Rusty?"

"A disgruntled buyer who bought a part here and thought that it should come with a warranty, a thief looking to get their hands on some extra steel that they can sell at a time when they think I wouldn't be here. How the fuck do I know? Like you, I have a history, and it's laden with plenty of assholes who would love to see me in the ground."

Mountains of vehicles towered around them, forming intricate alleys of steel and decay. Each car, once a prized possession, now lay stripped and broken, a mere shadow of its former self. Stacked atop each other with calculated chaos, the haphazard arrangement of vehicles created a haunting mosaic of forgotten memories.

The barking led them to a tangled heap of discarded metal, a hiding place for those who sought to disturb the fragile peace Rusty had carved out. As they approached, a figure could be seen high above, off the ground, trying to avoid Duchess.

"What we got here, my girl?" he said, looking up. "Come on out, you little rodent. Last chance to get out of here alive."

The intruder's voice was laced with bravado, a false sense of superiority. "Fuck you, old man."

"You little bastard," Rusty said, lifting his shotgun.

Bryce intervened, placing a hand on the barrel and pushing it down. "He's just a kid."

"A kid that should know better!" he bellowed.

"Let me get him," Bryce whispered, moving away and disappearing into the dark. He made his way around and began to climb. All the while, he could hear Rusty arguing with the boy. Bryce climbed up the steel, trying to be as quiet as possible. Just as he reached the vehicle that the kid was in, a boot struck him in the face, sending him down.

He landed hard, knocking the wind out of him.

Several rounds were fired on the other side. Bryce looked up just in time to see a large kid leap toward him. Bryce rolled out of the way, sweeping the boy's leg and bringing him down. The kid was agile and fast, bouncing up, ready to run, but Rusty beat him to the punch. As the kid ran, looking over his shoulder and laughing at Bryce, he didn't see Rusty step out of the darkness. The butt of his shotgun hit him square in the side of the face, knocking him out cold. The night seemed to hold its breath as the kid crumpled to the ground, the echo of the impact resonating through the air.

The intruder lay motionless, a still form amid the junkyard's chaotic expanse.

Rusty looked at Bryce as he got up and brushed dirt off him.

"I'll get him. I can handle this," he said before chuckling. "The only way you handle these punks is at the end of a barrel. Get up!" he said, kicking the boy in the stomach. The boy never groaned or moved. Bryce heard movement behind him and saw two other kids emerge and run.

"That's it. You get the hell out of here," Rusty said before unloading two rounds. Meanwhile, the boy wasn't moving. "Kid. Get up."

Still, he wasn't moving.

Bryce dashed over, dropping to a crouch.

The adrenaline rush masked the steady beat of his heart as he observed him. Bryce leaned in, his instincts shifting from caution to concern. Rusty's strike had rendered the intruder unconscious, his chest unmoving in the stillness of the night. Time hung suspended as they both stared at the kid.

Rusty's stern façade softened momentarily, replaced by a flicker of uncertainty. "Is he...? No, he's playing around. Slap him," Rusty said.

"Hey kid, c'mon," Bryce said, placing his hand on him and shaking him. But he didn't move. He placed two fingers to the side of the Adam's apple, in the soft, hollow area. Bryce pressed gently to locate a pulse and then he looked up at Rusty. His heart sank.

"He's playing with you."

"He's not breathing," Bryce shot back.

"No. I only struck him with the end of the gun barrel."

Almost immediately, Bryce began doing CPR on the kid. His response was swift, his training kicking in as he knelt beside the intruder. His hands found their place, his palms pressing against the kid's sternum as he initiated a rhythm of compressions. Each push was a desperate plea, a demand for life to return to the motionless body. "Come on." He breathed in through his mouth and pumped his chest. "Come on back. Come on, kid."

Time seemed to blur as Bryce's movements became a steady cadence. His world narrowed to the rise and fall of the chest beneath his hands; the pressure and rhythm a lifeline.

All the while, Rusty paced, distraught. "I warned them. I told them not to come back." He looked on with a mixture of trepidation and hope. The passage of time was marked by the sound of the symphony of breath and movement.

Then, a gasp — a sudden inhalation of air — shattered the quiet like a crack of thunder. The young intruder's body jerked, reacting to the influx of oxygen as life surged back into his lungs.

Relief flooded Bryce's features as he leaned back, his breath shaky as he watched the kid's chest rise and fall in its own rhythm.

Rusty's voice, full of gratitude, cut through the air. "He's breathing."

The intruder's eyes fluttered, his consciousness returning in fits and starts. Confusion and disorientation clouded his features as he blinked at the faces above him.

Rusty extended his hand, a gesture of assistance and understanding. "Easy now, son. You're okay."

Bryce and Rusty shared a glance, a silent exchange of emotions encompassing relief and the understanding of a second chance. Together, they helped the young man to his feet, his steps shaky but determined.

"Let's get him inside," Bryce's voice was steady, his gaze focused on the young man who had once been a threat.

With careful coordination, they guided him back toward the trailer; their movements synchronized like a dance born of necessity. The moonlight cast elongated shadows across the path.

As they reached the trailer, Zoe held the door open, her features full of confusion. Bringing the young man inside, they set him down, and Rusty got a bottle of water.

"Who's he?" Zoe asked.

"That's the question, isn't it," Rusty said, handing the kid some water. "Tell them."

The kid's gaze bounced between them.

From a distance, Bryce had figured he was in his late teens, but now it was clear he was at least in his early twenties. The young man's breathing steadied as he settled, his gaze flitting between the faces around him, his eyes focused more on Zoe than anyone else.

"Well?" Rusty asked.

"Rusty. Give the kid a moment."

"Yeah, before I send him packing. Which reminds me, you need to get going. I'm not here to help everyone. I've about used up my patience for the night."

"Then do you have a bicycle?"

"It's a wrecker's yard. What do you think? Of course," he pointed outside. "To your right, there's a stack of them. However..."

As much as Bryce didn't want to leave while things were still tense and unresolved, they'd already used up much of the night, and Jackson wasn't looking any better.

Bryce headed out before Rusty could finish.

"Wait up, Bryce. I'm coming with you," Zoe said.

"No, you need to stay with your father."

"You're going to need me."

"How so?"

"Why do you think he let us in here?" Bryce considered her words. For someone who was only twenty-one, she was a smart gal, much like her mother. "Besides, Rusty's right. The chances are we won't even be able to find a doctor, let alone convince one to come back here with us. Let's face it, he won't make it, and I..."

"If your father dies, you need to be there."

"I can't. I can't..."

"It's not about you, Zoe. It's about him — about having family around him when he passes. Now, I need to leave. It's going to take at least twenty minutes to get to the hospital, longer to find someone."

"Not if you take an old truck," Rusty said from the doorway.

"What?"

"That's what I was trying to tell you, but like I said, no one listens, too busy and distracted." He glanced over his shoulder at the young man to ensure he wasn't up to anything, but it was clear he was in no state.

"But no vehicles are working," Zoe said.

"No newer vehicles." He disappeared inside and then returned, holding a set of keys. "Duchess, Lady, keep an eye on our guest," he muttered. The dogs posted outside the doorway, growling at the young man while Rusty confidently strode into the maze of vehicles. "The reason vehicles aren't working is because they are shit. Plain and simple. No point in cherry-coating. That's the short version. Today's vehicles are using chips, computers, you name it, wireless crap, hooked up to the damn cloud, and what happens when one country wants to bring another to its knees? They press a button. Boom. Cyber hacking. Electromagnetic pulse weapons. It doesn't take much now to take out transportation and communication — the things that keep our country ticking over, and you and I alive. But here's the thing: most manufacturers didn't begin placing computer chips inside vehicles until the early '80s, even though, to be fair, there were some in the mid-'70s that were rocking integrated circuits. What I'm saying is these kinds of things are a bit hit-and-miss. However, a place like this is an absolute goldmine for finding old vehicles. Old vehicles that work, I might add. I don't care what Russia, China, or Mongolia is rocking regarding high-tech equipment; you can't beat a good old American-made truck — the old classic Chevy, Ford, Dodge, these beauties are perfect for times like these." He took a deep breath and shone a flashlight into the slew of automobiles. "There we go!"

He illuminated a red Chevy truck.

"1967 to 1972. Oh, those were great years. They don't make them like this anymore," he said, tossing the keys to Bryce. Bryce hopped in. The seats were torn up, and it stank to high hell of rust.

"Hold on a tick," Rusty said, taking a gas can and filling it up. "All right, fire it up."

He turned over the ignition. It coughed and spluttered.

"Give it some gas."

"I am."

"Well, it's been here a while."

He tried a few more times. Then, as if fate had laid out the road before them, it growled to life, spluttering a few more times. "Yes! Yes!" Bryce hollered. "Get in, Zoe."

"Now you can take her father to the hospital, and while you're at it, take that little punk too. Not that I care what happens to him, but I'd rather he was with you than me."

"All right."

Bryce put it in gear and hit the gas, but it struggled to move.

"What the—"

He glanced out as Rusty shone the flashlight down on the wheels. They were flat.

"I thought you said it would work," Bryce said.

"It does. But this is a wrecker's yard."

10

Oregon City, Oregon

The oppressive darkness smothered the farm. The tension seemed to seep into every crevice of the house. Talis O'Brien knelt beside the lifeless form of his brother Ryland, a mixture of grief and rage etched across his features. The moon spread a pale glow over the scene outside, illuminating the blood that stained his hands — a macabre testament to the violence that unfolded.

Rubbing blood between his thumb and two fingers, Talis stared down at his brother's face, the weight of their shared history hanging heavy between them. His hand hovered above Ryland's chest, a final connection in a world turned upside down. In a calm voice, he murmured words of farewell, a private ritual of closure for a bond severed too soon.

Pushing himself upright, Talis turned away from his

brother's body and approached the house. The sight that awaited him inside was a tableau of horror — the aftermath of a massacre that had claimed the lives of an older generation. They were his brother's close friends, but also his comrades.

His gaze swept over the carnage as disbelief and anger churned inside him. The familiar faces that had once shown the way for his generation now lay silent, their lives extinguished instantly, not by antifa but by a convict.

The walls bore the scars of violence with streaks of blood, and the air held the scent of smoke and tragedy, clinging to everything it touched.

The moonlight filtered through shattered windows, casting elongated shadows over the fallen bodies. Talis' fists clenched at his sides, his anger simmering beneath the surface. He was a man consumed by a singular purpose — vengeance.

The fire of rage fueled his every moment. "I want him found," his voice was a low growl, the words laced with promise of retribution.

"How?" Foster asked.

"What did you say?"

"Well, I hate to point out the obvious, but the grid is down, we are still experiencing quakes, the city has turned into a hellish glow, and there is talk over the radio of ocean water still heading this way from the tsunami."

"It won't get past the Oregon Coast Range," Jagger said. "The forested mountains and hills are dense and far too hilly. Tsunamis travel no more than ten miles inland, and the landscape determines much of that."

"How do you know this shit?"

He shrugged. "I pay attention to the news."

"What I'm saying is, how are we supposed to find him?" Foster asked.

"We don't. He finds us," Talis said, walking across the room to the only body he couldn't recognize. "This is his brother, right?"

Foster nodded.

"Then he'll return."

"How can you be sure?"

"Because I did," he said, referring to his brother. "Now, find me a shovel. I need to bury him."

"Here? But..." Foster stuttered.

It was taking everything inside Talis not to lash out and strangle him. Instead, he shot him a menacing glare and clenched his fist. That was enough. Foster ventured out the back to find one.

11

Oregon City, Oregon

T he city was pure pandemonium.

Providence Willamette Memorial Hospital was a beacon of hope, a lighthouse to those lost in a sea of despair, and yet thoughts of finding it closed or worse — destroyed — lingered in Bryce's mind.

The journey from the wrecker's yard into the heart of Oregon City had been less than straightforward. On a good day, it would have taken at most fifteen minutes with traffic lights, but with so many stalled vehicles, navigating the roads was beyond problematic; it was a nightmare.

Inside the truck, tension crackled in the air like static electricity. Bryce gripped the steering wheel, his knuckles white against the dim glow of the dashboard lights. The soft groans of the engine provided a haunting soundtrack to the journey, each clunk and rumble echoing their unease.

In the back, Jackson winced, his face a mask of pain as he held his injured leg. Zoe sat up front next to Bryce, her finger tapping nervously on her knees. Beside Jackson, the young guy sat with his head tilted slightly, his eyes glazed, lost in his world of confusion.

The only information they'd managed to get out of him was his name was Colton, and he was twenty years old. After being struck in the side of the head, he was grateful to Bryce for delivering CPR and apologetic for his attack. Bryce never pressed him for more until he left Rusty's yard, as he seemed hesitant to say anything with Rusty listening in.

The hospital loomed ahead, a faint oasis of light amid the darkness. As they pulled into the parking lot, the truck's engine roared defiantly, a stark contrast to the silence of the abandoned vehicles that lay dormant around them. The scene that greeted them was one of controlled chaos. People milled about, some huddled in groups, others paced back and forth, their faces etched with worry.

Outside, police officers had set up a barricade and were doing their best to stem the flow, only allowing in the most critical patients to ensure the hospital wasn't overwhelmed beyond what it already was.

"They've got power?" Zoe asked.

Bryce shrugged. "Generators, I guess."

"But wouldn't they have been affected?"

"Of course, but with all the talk of EMP attacks in the news over the past few years, I wouldn't be surprised if precautions have been taken to insulate critical infrastructure. Hospitals, police departments, and military establishments would be some of the first, if any. With lives hanging in the balance and having ridden out multiple power outages, it was only a matter of time before medical services would look at continuity. Now having enough fuel to power them long term is another thing entirely."

Injured individuals lay outside the entrance on makeshift stretchers; blankets were their only source of comfort. Several Red Cross tents had been erected to offer additional help, but they were pushed to the max. The emergency room doors swung open and shut in a never-ending rhythm, a revolving door of pain and despair.

Beyond the glass, nurses in scrubs rushed between patients; their expressions strained but determined, working with a sense of urgency that echoed the gravity of the situation.

Everyone was in survival mode.

As the Chevy rolled to a stop, the four of them exchanged glances, their eyes wide with trepidation. With so few vehicles operating, they stood out, attracting the attention of many outside the hospital. "I might need to stay with the vehicle," Bryce said.

"But I thought..."

"Zoe, how many working vehicles did you see on the way down here?"

"Including ours? Three."

"Right. We are in the minority. This situation isn't getting any better, only worse. Once folks know they are shit out of luck, they will turn to their own devices if they haven't already. Some already have. Crime existed before, and this is now a green light for the worst of society to do whatever they like, which means a working truck will look attractive."

Bryce parked on the far side of the lot. The glow of the hospital's emergency lights cast an eerie pallor on the scene, painting those outside in stark and unnatural hues.

Zoe's breath hitched as she turned to her father in the

back, speaking through the window. Her voice trembled. "Dad. You, okay?"

Jackson was as tough as they come. Bryce had seen many a man wounded in the Middle East. Everyone dealt with pain differently. Jackson mustered a weak smile, his voice strained but reassuring. "I'm still here, sweetheart. Don't you worry."

"What about you?" Bryce asked.

Colton shifted uneasily, his fingers gingerly touching the side of his head where a dark bruise had formed. His voice was distant as if he was only half there. "Breathing."

Bryce stepped out onto the asphalt, immediately feeling the weight of the situation pressing upon him as a disheveled man approached. "Hey, mister. How is your vehicle working and most aren't?"

"Age," he replied.

There was no point in lying. Eventually folks would figure it out.

The guy's shifty eyes bounced between them. He nodded and strode away. He might not have been a threat, but others would be. "I'll help carry him in, then I should take the truck back," Bryce said.

Zoe frowned. "Back? I thought you would stay and watch over the vehicle."

"Rusty loaned it to us."

"He had others there."

"Still."

"You're going to leave us, aren't you?" Zoe said.

"I need to go back. My brother..." he trailed off. "Look, c'mon," he said, returning his attention to Jackson. No matter what he said, it wouldn't sit well with them. He was also aware, from the sheer number of people outside the hospital, that the idea of being in and out in a matter of hours was a pipe dream. The medical system had all but failed long before the disaster, with wait times up to ten hours in some places, but now, after this, he wasn't going to linger.

As they helped Jackson out of the truck, he muttered, "Thank you. For your help."

"You're welcome."

The sense of urgency grew more palpable as they made their way toward the hospital entrance. A line of injured people stretched out before them, demanding attention. The injuries were vast, with many bleeding out; some looked like they might die there on the spot. Hushed conversation mixed with the occasional cry of pain only added to the sense of suffering.

Bryce's heart raced as he guided Jackson through the crowd.

"Excuse me. Make way."

Every step forward felt like a small victory.

The hospital's façade, once a symbol of healing and hope, now stood as a defiant bastion against the chaos that had engulfed the world.

As they approached the entrance, their steps heavy with exhaustion, a stern-faced police officer blocked their path. His uniform was rumpled, and his eyes held a weariness that mirrored theirs. He raised a hand, his gaze washing over the group.

"I'm sorry," the cop said with a sigh. "You have to get in line. We're full right now, and until they get an opening—"

Bryce's heart sank at the officer's words. The severity of the chaos outside had penetrated even the hospital's walls. He couldn't afford to wait, not with Jackson barely conscious. He took a step forward. "Look, my friend was shot. He's lost a lot of blood. Please."

His expression remained unyielding; his resolve hardened by those complaining behind them. "He's not the only one. I can't make any exceptions."

Frustration welled up within Bryce, fear and anger taking hold. He opened his mouth to protest and fight for Jackson's chance at survival, but Zoe's voice rang out before he could find the words. "This man is a Marine. He's served our country to keep us safe. I think you can make an exception."

The cop's gaze shifted to Zoe, and his stony façade seemed to waver for a moment. He hesitated, caught between duty and empathy. Zoe laid it on thick, seizing the opportunity. "Please, officer. My father could die."

The cop shook his head, torn by the weight of the decision and the overflow of people in similar conditions for one reason or another. "I understand. I do, but I don't get to make that decision. I'm sorry."

Defeat settled over them, resignation weighing down Bryce's shoulders. He nodded, his eyes cast downward, and he turned to leave, leading the group away from the entrance.

But just as they were about to give up and navigate the sea of suffering, another cop approached — a fresh face, his uniform bespeaking a different energy. "Hey, uh, what division did you serve in?" he asked, his voice full of curiosity.

Bryce met his gaze, a glint of hope rekindling within him. He noticed his tag had the surname Saunders. "Fifth," Bryce replied.

A smile tugged at the corner of the cop's lips as he pushed up his sleeve, revealing a Semper Fi tattoo. "I was part of the First Division." He gazed around and then met Bryce's gaze. "Look, I shouldn't be doing this, but... well, follow me."

The officer led them to a side door, away from the bustling emergency room and its throngs of patients. He

opened it and gestured for them to go in. The overhead fluorescent lights cast a clinical pallor on everything, starkly
contrasting the outside. As they walked in, the officer handed
Bryce a red tag, a lifeline to expedited care on a night when
exceptions were rare.

"Zone three, show them that. I hope your friend makes
it," he said, opening a door to reveal a new scene. Bryce
thanked him, and their hurried footsteps echoed down the
corridor.

"Smart thinking," he said to Zoe.

She shrugged, just glad to bypass the crowds.

Inside, it was pandemonium. Cries. Blood on the floor.
Walls smeared with bloody handprints. Patients on gurneys,
groaning and waiting for help.

Nurses moved with purpose, attending to patients with
methodical precision; although there were few of them.
Medical equipment beeped and hummed in the background.

As he approached a nurse stationed at a desk, Bryce's
heart pounded with apprehension. He cleared his throat.
"Excuse me, ma'am. We were directed here."

The nurse looked up from her paperwork, her eyes
annoyed.

"Your tag?" She extended a hand.

He handed it over. "Could you please get someone to look
at my friend? He's lost a lot of blood." She observed his skin
and the blood-soaked fabric around his leg, revealing the
extent of his injuries.

"I see. We're busy right now, but we'll do our best."

She collected a wheelchair and placed Jackson in it.

"And I have someone here with a head injury."

The nurse sighed and motioned for another nurse to

bring a gurney over but was told they didn't have any more. "Sorry, but you'll have to sit over there and wait."

"Ma'am, he stopped breathing earlier. I think it's a little more serious than that."

"If you haven't looked around. Everyone here is because of something serious. People are dying, and we are doing our best to keep them alive. Take a seat. I will try to get someone to see him," she said, her tone harsh but warranted under the conditions.

"That's fine," Colton replied, rubbing his head and doing as she said.

"Are you leaving now?" Zoe asked.

"I haven't decided. I do need to go check on the vehicle."

Zoe nodded. "Thank you. For everything."

"Least I could do. I'm sorry any of this happened. I didn't want either of you to be dragged into this mess. I just..." He trailed off. "I should go." He placed a hand on her shoulder and then walked away. In the mirror in the corner of the room, he could see Zoe watching him walk off before she turned and hovered close to her father, her eyes never leaving his face as the wheelchair began to move, guided by capable hands towards a room where he would receive medical attention.

The din of the emergency room faded behind him, replaced by the muted hum of machinery and the rhythmic beeping of monitors.

Pushing out of the side door back into the tension and uncertainty, Bryce navigated the shadows, making his way up the side of the hospital. The darkness embraced him as he headed for the old Chevy truck parked at the far side of the lot. He hadn't even gotten to the front of the building when something slammed into him, and he was yanked violently off his feet.

Pain seared through his body as he crashed to the ground; the roughness of the earth and the weight of his attackers knocked the breath from his lungs. He fought back as he was dragged into a grove of trees, his fists striking out in the darkness. He landed a few solid blows that resonated with a satisfying thud. But it was short-lived.

The odds were against him, and he quickly realized he was outnumbered.

"Get the keys!" a voice hissed.

As Bryce lifted his gaze, a boot struck, knocking him down. Another glance under his arm, and he saw the familiar face of the man who had been eyeballing their vehicle earlier. Four others flanked him, their silhouettes menacing against the night.

Bryce struggled against their iron grip, his attempts to break free met by more brute force as someone rifled through his pockets. Pain blossomed across his abdomen as he was kicked repeatedly, the blows a relentless barrage that left him gasping for air.

"Where are the keys?" the man demanded, his voice a vicious snarl.

His mind raced, his thoughts jumbled as he clung to his last shred of control. Ahead of time, he had hidden the keys in the truck's wheel well, anticipating the possibility of this situation. He knew he couldn't afford to let anyone take the truck.

"I don't have them," he managed to gasp out, his voice strained. His ribs ached, and blood trickled down his face, mingling with the dirt on his skin.

"Don't lie to me," one of the men growled, his fist connecting with Bryce's jaw in a vicious blow.

"I'm telling the truth. They're in the hospital," he continued, pushing through the pain to form his words. "I was just driving. It isn't my truck. It's my friend's truck, and he's getting medical attention."

Frustration simmered among the attackers, their hostility palpable as they exchanged glances, realizing that the intended prize was beyond their reach. Bryce's words only seemed to fuel their aggression, and he was repeatedly struck, the blows raining down like a storm.

As abruptly as they appeared, the men decided their efforts were in vain. With one final kick to Bryce's side, they turned and fled, melting into the darkness and disappearing into the chaos of the night.

Bryce lay there for a moment, the world spinning around him. He ran a trembling hand over his face, his fingers coming away slick with blood. His lip was split, and his eye throbbed with a dull ache. Gingerly, he touched his ribs, wincing as pain flared through his side. He couldn't be sure, but it felt like a bone might be broken.

Summoning all his strength, Bryce staggered to his feet, his movement unsteady. He cast a wary glance around, scanning the crowd for any signs of the men who had attacked him. Was it over? Or were they still watching, biding their time to see if he would return to the truck?

"You, okay?" A voice cut through the haze of his thoughts, and Bryce turned to see the officer he had spoken to earlier rushing over, concern etched on his features. He hunched over slightly, his ribs protesting the movement.

"Yeah. Just a little disagreement," Bryce managed to

mutter, his voice strained. The officer's arm slipped around Bryce's shoulders, providing steady support.

"Yeah, never out of the fight, right," he said.

"You're right about that."

"Let me guess, a guy with a goatee?" the officer said, a note of recognition in his tone.

Bryce nodded and winced as pain coursed anew with the movement. "So, you know him."

The officer chuckled. "We've had some problems with him and others this evening. Come on, let's get you patched up."

He guided Bryce toward the Red Cross tent, and the officer spoke into his radio, updating his colleagues about the men and urging them to be on the lookout. As they reached the tent, a sense of relief washed over Bryce.

A lady stepped in to help.

"I'm Joe, by the way."

"Bryce."

"So, what happened to your friend, Bryce?" Joe asked.

"He was jumped." Bryce wasn't about to give him the whole story. Instead, he figured he'd take the opportunity to glean more about the unfolding situation.

"So not as lucky as you."

"Guess not."

The officer stood in the tent's opening, speaking into his radio and glancing at the crowd.

"Any update on what's happening?" Bryce asked.

"That depends. How much do you know?"

"Only that San Francisco was hit, and there was some incoming ballistic missile."

"Missiles. Multiple ones came in from the east and erupted high in the atmosphere."

"And the West Coast tsunami?"

"Mostly to the south. San Francisco took the brunt of that. That was courtesy of a torpedo fired from a Russian sub if the reports we've heard are accurate. Our department got a heads-up a few hours before the event occurred that something big could hit and to be prepared. We weren't given specifics. I contacted an old friend, a higher-up still in the military. He wasn't supposed to say anything, but he confirmed Russia attacked the USA."

"So, beyond the outage, we're safe here?"

"Safe? Hardly. It's tough to comprehend the extent of the damage after that last earthquake."

"That I felt."

"Yeah, well, don't expect it to be the last one you feel. We've gleaned through the emergency radio system that volcanoes are erupting all around the Ring of Fire, and fault lines have split. The San Andreas, Hayward, Cascadia, the New Madrid that runs through five states, and Ramapo on the East Coast have been affected. To what extent, that's to be determined, but San Francisco is gone, that's for sure. We've already seen the Columbia River overflowing from the surge. The flooding is crazy along the eastern part of Oregon. If it wasn't for the Oregon Range, we might not be having this conversation." He stopped talking and looked off toward the people. "Most of these people have no idea. If we can, it will take years to bounce back from this." He looked at Bryce. "Is Oregon home for you?"

"Bryson City, North Carolina."

"That's a long way. What brings you here?"

"A brother."

"Was he the one injured or the other one?"

"No. No, my brother is back at home." He didn't want to

get into details or have to answer further questions. However, the mention of Chad reminded him of returning to bury him. In all the drama unfolding, he hadn't had a moment to think, let alone grieve.

The officer's radio crackled, and a voice came over it, calling him away. "Well, hey, stay safe out there. Duty calls."

He fist-bumped the officer before watching him haul his ass through the crowd to deal with a fight that had broken out. It was just a taste of what would come as people struggled to get what they wanted. Society would eventually face the choice to help each other, turn away, or tear others down. He wondered if there would even be a choice.

"There you go. Though by the pain you're showing with your ribs, I would line up and get that checked out at the ER," the Red Cross volunteer said.

Bryce smiled and thanked her before grimacing as he rose from his seat, still clutching his ribs. The sky looked darker than usual; the stench of smoke lingered, causing many to cough. "Would you have something to cover over my mouth?"

She handed him an N90 mask. It wasn't great, but it might help with the smoke. As Bryce worked his way through the crowd, threading around vehicles, his eyes locked onto the area where he'd parked a few rows away. Relief washed over him. But then, as his steps closed the distance, his heart sank. A cold sweat broke out on his forehead, and his eyes widened in disbelief.

The window on the driver's side had been smashed, glass shards glinting maliciously on the pavement like shattered dreams. "No," Bryce muttered, his voice a mix of frustration and shock. He took hesitant steps closer, his heart heavy with dread, praying it wasn't as bad as it looked.

But his worst fears were realized as he reached the front.

The hood was unlocked. He propped it up, its metal frame rising like a gaping maw, only to find a wreck. Wires dangled from their sockets like the entrails of some mechanical beast torn apart by a cruel hand.

Bryce looked around, his hands clenched into fists, his knuckles turning white. "Bastards," he muttered, his voice full of anger as he realized who'd done it. All four tires were punctured.

Then his eyes fell upon the white graffiti spray-painted on the side of his truck, stark and mocking in its message. "If we can't have it, neither can you!" The words screamed at him in jagged letters, a cruel taunt that cut through his frustration like a knife. His brows furrowed, his teeth grinding together as he tried to comprehend the audacity of the act.

Unable to find the keys and steal it, they ensured he couldn't use it either.

He took a deep breath, his anger coiling tightly within him.

Just as he turned to return to the hospital, a familiar voice called out to him through the crowd, a hand rising.

"Bryce," Colton said, running toward him. "Jackson wants to speak to you, and I was wondering..." He trailed off as his eyes saw the truck.

12

Tennessee

T he early hours of the Fourth of July saw a veil of darkness shrouding Gatlinburg, Tennessee. The once-bustling town lay paralyzed after the colossal power outage that had plunged it into silence. Dante stood among the ruins, weariness etched on his face as he gazed at the desolation. The night had been relentless, full of flames, embers, and people hurrying to extinguish the fires.

Beside him, Natalie stood motionless, her eyes bloodshot and expression full of exhaustion, as did the teens from the group home. Together and with the entire community, they'd battled the fires that raged like vengeful demons sparked by the earthquake that had shaken the very foundation of the town. The sky had been a canvas of terror as planes plummeted from on high, setting the landscape ablaze.

"I haven't seen this much devastation since the 2016 fires. But this was different, more sinister, deliberate even."

"We don't know that."

"Sure we do," Natalie said, turning away from the tree line that resembled charred toothpicks. "Come on, let's go."

"Natalie," Wendy Bowers said, waving to her and hurrying over. Wendy was one of five elected city commissioners who oversaw the function of the city, its ordinances, resolutions, and policies. She'd been a longtime friend since Natalie had taken the supervisor role at the group home. "Thank you for helping. All of you."

"Seems we weren't the only ones."

"That's what gives us hope. Look, did Jackson go on that run out west?"

"He did."

"Shoot." She ran a hand around her neck. All of their faces were blackened by smoke, hers no less. That was one thing about the city's leaders: they weren't ones to sit on the sidelines giving out orders. Natalie had seen all of them out there, sleeves rolled up, carrying buckets of water from the stream and passing them along a line to put out the fire.

"Is there something I can help you with?"

"I was hoping to speak with your husband."

"About?"

"The use of the trailer. It's built for cold storage. Obviously, there's no power, but the container might be effective if... well, it's just that with the power out, we're already looking at ways to grow more produce."

"Grow? Hold on a second. So, you anticipate the power being down longer than a couple of weeks?"

Wendy took a deep breath. "If the rest of the United States is anything like Gatlinburg, I don't anticipate it turning back on any time soon. The workers here in the city are hamstrung. The fire has torn through what little infrastructure we had, and there currently needs to be more communication established. Our hands are full. It's our job to try and get ahead of this. Now, some in the town have ideas, a way to keep our heads above water."

"How?"

"Vertical farming."

"That's great, but that requires an extensive amount of power. Electricity."

"Correct. Darren Waitman from the board said he knows another way it can be done using solar and wind energy."

Natalie brought her hands up to the side of her face. "Back up the train a second. Wait. We've barely finished the night, and you are thinking about creating long-term produce?" She took a second to catch her breath.

"Creating. Saving. Look, I'm sorry, I'm jumping ahead here. But that's what we do. Every town has an emergency response plan that must be put into action for the safety of everyone. I've been placed in charge of food supplies."

"And..."

"I'm running my mouth like usual. Look. They will hold a town hall meeting in the next twenty-four hours to address immediate concerns so everyone is on the same page. I was just hoping Jackson was still here."

"No. He's not."

Wendy placed a hand on her shoulder. "Okay. We'll speak later."

With that said, she turned away.

"That was strange," Dante said.

"You're telling me. How many people would begin to think about these kinds of things on a day like this? If I'm not mistaken, I would wonder if the town was privy to something like this coming down the pipeline. But if that was so, why wouldn't they tell anyone?"

As the first rays of dawn began to pierce the blackness of night, the once-vibrant town of Gatlinburg was now a landscape of blackened ruins and smoldering wreckage. The community had rallied together and fought bravely, extinguishing the flames that had threatened to consume everything in their path, but the victory had come at a staggering cost. Buildings lay in ruins, and lives had been forever altered.

As they trudged back to the group home, the atmosphere between them was quiet. They passed many others in town, each seeking respite from the sudden and unusual events.

They followed the road through the untouched woodland threading the town. Her gaze shifted towards the group home, at least to where it would have been.

His throat dropped into his stomach.

The place that had provided solace and shelter for the teens now stood as a charred skeleton, a stark reminder of the night's horrors. What perplexed him was that the surrounding structures remained untouched by the inferno. It was as if a selective force had honed in on their haven and left the rest unchanged. A chill slithered down his spine as he contemplated the implications and recounted the evening's events, the run-in with Jordan's father.

"No. NO!" Natalie said, running ahead of him, her shock evident. She stopped and stared at what was left — nothing more than an ashen landscape. Each step felt like a journey through a nightmare as they struggled to comprehend the magnitude of the destruction.

"How can this be," she muttered.

Across the debris and soot, Dante spotted a figure

standing by the roadside. Natalie eyed him and, with determined steps, made her way towards him.

"Trevor. Hi," she called out to their neighbor.

His gaze drifted from the smoldering mess to Natalie's soot-streaked face, an acknowledgment of the trial they had all endured. "Natalie," his voice was heavy with emotion.

"Did you see what happened?" she inquired.

"Not exactly," he admitted, his tone guarded. "I saw a vehicle pull away, that's all."

Natalie's brow furrowed in confusion. "A vehicle?" She touched her chest. "Mine?"

"I don't know."

"When?"

"A few hours ago."

"But why would anyone—"

Before she could finish her sentence, the truth of the situation hung heavy in the air. Someone had ignited this nightmare intentionally.

"I thought it was you. The flames were already chewing through the house. I thought you'd evacuated."

"Because of the town fires."

He nodded.

"Except no other buildings on this street have been touched," she said. Natalie looked at Dante in a way that made him wonder if she was thinking the same as him.

"Natalie," he said, reaching for her. She brushed him away.

"It was him, wasn't it?" Jordan said. "Son of a bitch."

"We don't know that," Natalie responded.

"Of course we do." Jordan lowered his head. "This is my fault. I should have gone with him. You should have just let me go."

"Hey. Hey!" Natalie said, taking hold of him before he spiraled down. They'd already seen what came of that. "You did nothing wrong. If this was your father, that's on him, not you. And it should make you realize even more why they had to take you out of that situation. It's not safe. He's not safe."

"And this is?" Jordan said, pointing to the ruins.

"We'll find somewhere else to go in the meantime until—"

"Until what? You heard that woman from the council. They aren't expecting this to get any better. And now this. If this was my father, then chances are he won't stop here. You need to let me go. If this had happened when we were here. I..."

"Don't you go blaming yourself. Don't you let him put that on you!"

"But..."

Dante could see why Natalie was good at her work. She had a way of talking the kids down when their minds ran rampant. As she was talking to Jordan, Selena was walking among the ashes.

"Selena. Come on out of there," Natalie called.

Selena reached down and picked up a black chain only to drop it. "Everything is gone," she said. "Everything I had."

The teens had minimal personal belongings, but what they had meant a lot.

"What matters is we are all alive and safe. Okay? Possessions can be replaced. Now we'll head to my house."

"Might be better if we go to mine," Dante said. "If this was Clyde, who knows if he's scoping out your house? I'm new. He has no clue about me."

"You hope," Liam remarked, kicking some of the ashes and shaking his head.

DANTE LIVED a few streets east of the group home in a two-story house just off Ellis Ogle Drive. It was set back from the road, nestled in the woodland, shielded from prying eyes. It was meant to be a house he would stay in for the next twenty years, but after his fiancée left, he had decided to sell it. The sign was still outside. In the same place it had been for the past nine months. Trying to sell the house had become a full-time job in itself. Keeping it clean, ready for buyers to see it.

"You're moving?" Natalie asked.

"Only within the town. This is too big for just me. However, the way things were going, I was planning on taking it off the market as I've had hardly anyone come through."

"How so? It's beautiful," she said as the six of them strode up the driveway. The residence exuded a timeless allure, blending harmoniously with the surrounding nature. The exterior was rustic with its wooden siding that looked weathered by time. It gave it a warm and inviting appearance. A quaint porch stretched across the front, adorned with a swing that swayed gently in the breeze, beckoning anyone to pause and relish the world around it. The porch was adorned with potted plants, vibrant blooms contrasting against the earthy wood tones.

"Two rate rises in the past year. Buyers are cautious about spending. And let's face it, Gatlinburg might attract tourists wanting to visit the Smoky Mountains, but it's not Knoxville."

Dante twisted the key in the lock, opening the door and beckoning the others to enter. They strolled in and looked around, taking in the sight of the minimalistic home.

"I have to apologize for the lack of furniture. I moved most of it into storage and the rest April took with her."

"That was her name?"

"Yeah."

He tossed his keys into a bowl.

Off to his right was a medium-sized living room. At the back was a good-sized kitchen with state-of-the-art appliances. "Upstairs, there are three bedrooms. Selena can take one; Jordan, Daniel and Liam, you'll have to share, and Natalie, you have my room."

She looked at him, and her eyebrow shot up.

"I'm sleeping on the couch downstairs," he said to clarify.

"No, I meant it's your home. I'll take the couch."

"Guests get the bedrooms. Besides, I sleep downstairs more than I do up — too many memories."

Liam strode into the living room. "You got any alcohol, Mr. A?"

"If I did, you wouldn't have any. And call me Dante."

Selena picked up a framed photo. "Who's this?" she asked, turning the frame around and showing him.

"My sister."

"You always keep pictures of young girls around?" Liam added with a smirk.

"I do when that's the only one I have."

His reply took a moment to sink in before they realized.

"When did she pass?" Natalie asked.

"Twenty-one years ago. Drunk driver." He took the photo frame from Selena and set it back down again. "We should all get some sleep. It's been a long day," he said.

Natalie nodded and gestured for them all to head upstairs.

"Mr. A," Liam said.

"Dante."

"I prefer the other. A little odd."

"Whatever."

"Sorry about your loss," he said before heading up. Jordan glanced over but said nothing. Selena gave a strained smile.

"I'll be up in a minute," Natalie said. She waited until they were gone. "I wanted to say thanks for putting everyone up."

"It's all right."

"No. The other folks who work at the home wouldn't have done it. I can barely get them to work the hours they're supposed to."

"Don't mention it," he said, crossing to a liquor cabinet and taking out a bottle of bourbon. "You want some?"

"I... I don't drink. I mean. I used to, but... well, let's say that when I get started, I don't have a shut-off valve."

"Got it," he said, putting the cap back on.

"But you go ahead. Don't deprive yourself for the sake of me." He set the bottle back in the cabinet, not answering that, and closed it. The last thing he wanted to do was drink in front of her, even though he could have downed multiple glasses after the day they'd had.

"Night," she said. He gave a smile and listened to her head up the steps.

He took a seat for a moment, staring out the window at the smoke rising at the break of dawn. His thoughts ran rampant, his mind circling back to the encounter with Clyde and his cousins. Getting up, he went to the liquor cabinet, reached into the back, and pulled out a box. He opened it to reveal a revolver. He loaded it, poured a drink, and returned to his seat. A few sips, and he felt the warm embrace of alcohol blot out the memory of the night before.

He spun the revolver a few times as he had many a night and brought the gun to the side of his head, tapping it ever so slightly. Dante glanced at the photo of his sister, remembering that night, the drunk driver, and the incident that led to his arrest and dismissal as an EMT in Bryson City.

It was easier to lie.

Easier for Natalie. Easier for the teens.

But now he was in deeper than he wanted.

13

Oregon

Blood was on his hands — literally.

When daylight came, Foster Bennett felt the total weight of guilt and responsibility weighing heavy on his shoulders. It wasn't just the look in Talis' eyes after he'd told him his brother was dead; it was how the others viewed him.

He'd lost their respect.

They didn't need to say anything, he could tell they judged him, and rightfully so, he would have done the same. He was among the older generation, the ones the new blood looked up to. Since the early '90s, he'd stood shoulder to shoulder with those who had died years before they formed the Proud Boys.

In days gone by, he would have taken a bullet for Ryland O'Brien.

But after the birth of his second child, his view of the group had changed. Age had played an enormous factor. At fifty, he wasn't getting any younger. Wisdom came with age, and what once was seen as an exciting form of rebellion, a means of creating a militant organization that would change the country, even the world — no longer held his interest. He wanted to be around to see his kids grow up, and he sure as hell didn't want them following in his footsteps.

Despite its name, he wasn't proud of what he'd done — whether that was violence at rallies or the kidnap and torture of those behind the scenes.

It was no life for a child.

Indeed, it wasn't something to aspire to.

No, he had no illusions about it. If it wasn't for his many years with the Proud Boys and being one of the founding members, Talis and the others may have deemed his escape as cowardice and turned on him.

Deep in the woods, a short distance from the farm, Foster drove the shovel into the ground, scooping out heaps of soil. He refused to let anyone else bury his brothers in arms. He certainly wouldn't make their final resting place the property where they fell. Instead, he'd suggested burying them in the woodland near the river. All of them had grown up along the banks and had spent many a sleepy summer in their teenage years swimming in the water.

Ryland was the only one who wouldn't be buried there. Talis planned to take his body home after he'd enacted vengeance on Bryce Mitchell.

After burying the last one, he hammered a cross into the earth, said a short prayer before heading back, and told them he'd one day see them on the other side.

Foster's heavy footsteps crunched against the under-brush. The memory of the fallen lingered in his mind — those final moments and the events that led up to it.

Ryland, much like his brother Talis, was bull-headed. Once he got something in his mind to do, there was no swaying him from it.

Foster recalled the phone call to his friend.

They'd been planning for the July Fourth rally when Ryland's phone jangled. He'd nodded a few times, asked some questions, then agreed. After getting off the phone, he'd told them that an old military pal of his wanted a favor. Foster had learned that this pal was locked up, so he couldn't do it himself, but he'd wanted to send a clear message to someone living in their neck of the woods.

"Torture and kill him?"

"Uh-huh," Ryland said, swigging from a bottle of bourbon like the request was nothing more than an order to pick up fast food.

"Who is this guy?"

"Does it matter? Every person we've ever harmed has had it coming to them."

"So, they're antifa?"

"Nope, but they might as well be."

"Because?"

"Because, Foster, I say so."

"You know there was a time you didn't just jump to every request."

"Jump?" Ryland asked, looking up from his pad of paper. "I know this man. I owe him."

"But do I? Do the others?"

"What is good for one is good for all."

Foster chuckled, shaking his head.

"You want to stay back on this one?" Ryland asked.

"I want more details."

"And if I can't give you them..."

Foster stared at him. "How long have I known you, Ryland?"

"A long time."

"Since we were kids. And I've always had your back."

"As I have had yours," he shot back.

"Then tell me."

"I can't."

"Why not?"

"Because I don't know myself."

Foster stepped back, struggling to make sense of what he was saying. "Let me get this right. You've agreed to go and torture and kill a man, and you have no idea what they did wrong?"

"I never said torture and kill. You said that."

"Please. I hardly think you are just there to scare the man."

"That's exactly what we're there to do. And like I said. I owe him."

Foster shifted from one foot to the next. "And you owe us."

"Owe?"

"We deserve to know. I don't know about you, Ryland, but I want to know why I place my life on the line. I want to know why this guy deserves to die."

"He's not going to die."

"Yeah. Yeah. You've said that. Who is this for?"

"An old military buddy."

"Not good enough. You go alone on this one, and that goes for the others."

That got Ryland's attention. He tossed the pad of paper

and pen on the table and got up nose to nose with Foster. "You speak for the others now, do you? Because I'm pretty sure you don't run this show."

"I formed this with you. You're damn right I do. If you are leading us into the unknown and jeopardizing our lives, then yeah, I'm speaking for the others."

Ryland smiled. "This wouldn't have anything to do with Bella putting pressure on you, would it?"

"What's that supposed to mean?"

"Oh, I don't know. Actually, strike that. I do. You've lost your balls."

Foster waved a finger in his face. He was the only one who could get away with it. Any other would be put on the ground in an instant. "Or maybe I've found them. Have you ever thought that maybe it's time for us to get out?"

"Get out? We're in this for life."

"Now, who is speaking for us all?"

Ryland stared at him. "All right. I'll get more details. And if you want to hang back. So be it. You can stay in the car. Like I said, we're just going over there to talk with the man and maybe scare him a little."

"No murder, right?"

"Right."

Foster had been adamant that he didn't want any part of it. He'd also told Ryland it would be the last time he attended a rally with him. That night was meant to be his final night as a Proud Boy.

Foster shook his head as he emerged from the dense tree line, his heart still heavy, when suddenly a cacophony of voices reached his ears.

His instincts kicked in, the years of combat training reflexively propelling him into action. He dropped the shovel he'd been carrying and swiftly pulled his weapon from the holster. With brisk determination, he hurried toward the source of the commotion, his eyes scanning for any signs of danger.

The voices grew louder as he approached the old farmhouse, taking shape as distinct words. "Hold on," he muttered, mentally preparing for whatever threat awaited.

But as he rounded the corner of the house, his trigger finger tense, he was met with an unexpected sight.

Chris stood at the forefront of the tense scene. The other group members had formed a half-circle around two young figures. Foster's brows furrowed in confusion as he eased his grip on the weapon, though his guard remained up. "What's going on?" he demanded, his voice low and commanding.

Chris turned towards Foster. "Found them on the road," he explained, his eyes darting between the newcomers and Foster. "Tell them what you told me."

The first of the youths stepped forward, his posture a blend of street-smart confidence and visible unease. His dark eyes held a glint of defiance, yet his fingers trembled with fear. His leather jacket was worn, the edges frayed, and his jeans had seen better days. A bandana tied around his head revealed a hint of rebellion.

The second one was slightly shorter, no less intense. She stood a step behind the first. Her gaze was fixed on the ground, her fingers fidgeting with the hem of an oversized hoodie. A riot of colorful hair, streaks of blue and pink, peeked out from under the hood. Her lips were pressed into a thin line.

"Go on!" Chris gave the guy a shove.

He stumbled a little, scowling at him.

"We saw two men and a girl. The guy was injured. Over at Rusty's wreckers."

"The injury?" Foster asked.

"It looked like his leg was bandaged up."

Foster glanced at Talis and then back at the kid.

"What were you doing out there?"

"Collecting some parts for my old man's vehicle. I figured with the power out, we could snag a few items. That old fart has tons of items there. He overcharged and ripped off my old man. Anyway, the guy has a friend of ours."

"Ah, now tell him why he does."

"We left him behind."

Talis slapped the kid on the back, grinning. "Looks like you're not the only one to leave friends in the dust," Talis said, glancing at Foster. "How about you tell us where they went?"

The kid shrugged. "I don't know. They took off in an old truck from the yard — no idea how they got it working. But Rusty's still back there. I'm sure he knows where they went. But you'd be a fool to go in there and find out. That old-timer has lost his marbles. He set his dogs on us and fired several rounds. Isn't that right, Skylar?"

The girl nodded.

"Is that so? Well, I'm sure he can be reasoned with. What do you think, Foster?" Talis said. It wasn't as much a question as it was a statement — an expectation he had for him to put his own life on the line to make up for the death of Ryland.

MINUTES LATER, outside the house, Foster got into it with Talis. "You're staying here?"

"Someone has to be here just in case the brother returns. I'm not missing that window. If you find him before then, bring him here. Simple."

Foster nodded. "Look, I get it. You're pissed because I survived and your brother didn't. But it could have easily gone the other way."

"Could it?" Talis said with skepticism. "It didn't, so now it's upon you to right that wrong. Of course, unless you would prefer to step down and tell the rest of our group what happened here."

It was a form of blackmail. Plain and simple. If he refused, he knew where it would end. More than likely, he would go free. At least it would look that way, and then, at some point in the days and weeks ahead, an accident would happen to him and his family. A fire at home, a vehicle brake malfunction. It would look natural. Unlike the way they dealt with those who crossed them, they didn't want detectives sniffing around. Besides, he was already on the government's radar.

"There was a time you would have never spoken out of turn."

"And there was a time when you wouldn't have run," Talis shot back. "The ball is in your court, Foster." He turned and went back inside. On the way in, he thumbed over his shoulder. "Pete, Chris. Go with him. Sawyer and Jagger, you stay."

Having them go with him was as much about ensuring he returned with Bryce Mitchell as it was ensuring that Foster didn't have a change of heart.

～

As the morning sun cast its soft golden hue over Rusty's wrecker's yard, Foster, Pete, and Chris strode to the closed gate. They exchanged glances. Foster's hand rapped against the metal, echoing through the quiet yard. When they got no response, he did it again.

"We'll go another way," Chris said, taking the lead.

"Hold on, Chris. He might…"

He wasn't paying attention and began skirting around the fence to see if they could find a way in. They slipped over the top one by one, their boots touching the uneven ground. The yard was a graveyard of vehicles, a sea of rusted hulks and twisted metal.

"This place stinks," Pete said, as smells of oil and decay mingled with the distant sound of chirping birds. Their eyes scanned the area as they moved toward the trailer at the center of the yard. It was hard to see it. Aisles of stacked vehicles blocked most of their view and, in turn, made it hard to see what would happen next.

"Remember. We don't kill him," Foster reminded, his voice firm yet cautioning. "We find out where they are and leave."

"That's how you think this will play out," Chris retorted.

Foster grabbed him. "Ryland might be gone, but you will still show me some respect."

"You lost that, old man, the moment you ran. Now get your fucking hands off me."

He shrugged him off. So much had changed in their group. The attitudes. The respect. Ryland was at fault for that, but in some ways, so was he. How could they expect them to improve without showing them another way?

They continued. Their footsteps crunched on the gravel as they advanced, their senses alert for any sign of movement. But their caution was interrupted by a sudden commotion — the swift and fierce bark of dogs. Foster's heart quickened as two pit bulls charged toward them, teeth bared and muscles tense. Before they could lunge, Chris unleashed a barrage of gunfire, the loud cracks of the shots echoing through the yard. The pit bulls skidded to a halt, yelping and retreating until they fell dead.

"I told you we were not to..." Foster began, but Chris cut him off, his voice edged with urgency.

"You've got your orders. We've got ours."

The urgency of the mission remained as they pressed on, adrenaline coursing through their veins. Rusty's voice called out, a mixture of concern and anger, as they rounded a corner. He stood before them, a shotgun at the ready. His eyes narrowed with suspicion.

"Who the hell are you? Where are my dogs?"

"Easy, old-timer."

"Get off my property now!" His voice cracked harshly as his grip on the shotgun remained unyielding.

Foster raised a calming hand, his voice steady. "We'll leave, but I need to know where Bryce went."

Rusty's gaze narrowed; confusion evident. "Who?"

Pete exchanged a glance with Foster, frustration mounting. "Don't play around, old man. Bryce Mitchell was here with an injured man and a girl. You gave them a truck and sent them on their way."

Rusty's expression shifted as recognition flickered in his eyes, but the hostility remained. "Yeah, and I'm going to send you fools on your way."

A blur of motion surged from the side before Rusty could follow through with his threat. Chris had skirted around earlier before they'd rounded the bend and now had launched himself at the old-timer, his pistol swung with precision. It connected with a sickening thud, and Rusty crumpled to the ground, his shotgun slipping from his grasp. Chris wrenched the firearm away from the fallen man.

Foster charged into Chris' side, his breath coming from ragged gasps. "That's enough!" he exclaimed, his voice sharp with reprimand. The chaotic energy hung in the air as they stared down at Rusty.

"Where is he?"

"Fuck you!" Rusty said.

Chris didn't waste any time thrusting his foot into Rusty's face.

Foster pushed him back. "I told you."

"And Talis told you," Chris growled. "Now stop messing around."

Foster dropped down beside Rusty. "Look. We'll get out of your hair, but we need to know."

Cupping his bloody face, Rusty replied, "Where do you think an injured man goes? The hospital. The same place I'll have to visit after this fool—"

"You..." Chris said before Foster raised a hand to stop him.

"Which one?" Foster asked.

"How the fuck would I know?"

Chris raised his leg in a threatening manner to repeat the same punishment.

Foster moved between him and Rusty to prevent him from doing it.

"Just tell us. Please."

The tension in the yard momentarily subsided as Rusty reluctantly divulged the information they sought.

"The closest one — dummy!" Rusty shot back before spitting a wad of blood. "You killed my dogs. Didn't you?" he muttered, his defiance now replaced with an air of resignation.

None of them answered, but it was clear.

Foster nodded in gratitude, acknowledging the help. He turned to head into the trailer to fetch a cloth for Rusty's face, his footsteps echoing in the sudden silence.

Inside the trailer, the dim light filtered through the dusty windows as Foster rummaged through a drawer, searching for a piece of cloth. His heart still raced from the confrontation, the adrenaline refusing to ebb away. He heard the distant chirping outside, starkly contrasting the violence that had just unfolded. With the cloth in hand, he took a deep breath and steadied himself before heading back out.

But a sharp crack sounded as he stepped toward the door. His heart clenched with a terrible premonition, and he rushed outside without a second thought. The sight that met his eyes sent a shockwave through his being. Rusty lay on the ground, a gruesome wound on his forehead, his life snuffed out instantly. Chris stood nearby, his handgun held loosely at his side, his expression unreadable.

Foster's voice caught in his throat, anger swirling. "What the hell have you done? He wasn't a threat. He told us what we needed."

Chris met his gaze, eyes cold and unwavering. He nodded in reply, the weight of his actions clear. "Yeah, and now we can leave."

The enormity of the situation crashed down upon Foster. Pete hovered at Chris' side. Foster's eyes darted between them, his mind racing to make sense of the sudden turn of events.

For a moment, he stood frozen, his mind grappling with the choices that had led them to this point. Then, he slowly crouched beside Rusty's lifeless form, his fingers brushing over the old-timer's rough features. In sadness and reverence, he gently closed Rusty's vacant eyes, a final act of respect for a life that ended too soon.

The yard remained deathly silent as they exited.

14

Virginia

Continuity of government was paramount.

There were numerous places President Sam Devro could escape to if faced with an attack on America — the PEOC under the White House; Raven Rock, North Carolina; Mount Weather in Virginia; Green Brier Resort in West Virginia; Denver International Airport; Cheyenne Mountain in Colorado; an aircraft carrier; or even in the E-4B, aka the Doomsday Plane. The decision on where wouldn't be made by him but by Homeland Security, based on his whereabouts at the time. However, he wasn't ushered to any of these locations when Russia attacked.

Instead, he found himself in the Appalachian Mountains of Virginia, in a less-known retreat called Peters Mountain.

Under the guise of an AT&T logo, a helicopter pad was built on top of the mountain. Few would question that it was used for anything more than ease of transportation for wealthy CEOs who would frequent the project offices.

In reality, what had begun as a department-store-sized bunker buried far below in the 1950s was now ground zero for intelligence agencies and key figures from Washington. Thousands of employees and private citizens viewed as vital to maintaining the continuity of government were housed there in what amounted to a self-sustaining underground city with a power plant, heating and cooling system, and water supply.

Sam sat in his dimly lit office. The dull hum of the bunker's ventilation system provided a constant backdrop to his thoughts. His weary eyes glanced at the large wooden desk before him, adorned with scattered documents, a half-empty glass of bourbon, and a world map that now seemed to hold a weight heavier than the globe itself.

A knock reverberated through the room as if on cue, shattering the fragile tranquility.

"Come in," Sam uttered, his tone carrying a hint of annoyance. Since arriving several days ago, he'd had less than five minutes to himself. He got more time in the shitter than outside, so he'd reverted to frequent bathroom breaks.

The heavy steel door swung open, revealing Vice President, Matt Stephens. With a practiced ease, Matt entered the room, placing a stack of paperwork on his desk before taking a seat across from Sam. Their eyes met briefly, a silent exchange encompassing years of camaraderie and shared burdens.

Ice clinked softly within Sam's glass as his fingers moved to scoop up the paperwork. He'd been waiting to get a breakdown of the devastation. They'd relied on satellite imagery to get a bird's-eye view. It would be years before they got an accurate death count. Sam scanned the contents, the lines, images, and numbers blurring as his mind grappled with the magnitude. "God. This is a disaster on so many levels," he muttered, his voice full of anguish.

Matt leaned forward, his voice cutting in, each word measured and heavy. "We weren't the only ones they hit. It was a coordinated attack on our allies. The UK, Canada, Australia, France, Germany, Italy, Japan — you name it — have been decimated in one way or another." His gaze remained steady, delivering news that would change history. "The UK is gone."

Sam's head whipped around, his eyes narrowing in disbelief. "Gone?" he echoed the word.

Matt nodded solemnly, his expression mirroring the gravity of the situation. "At least in terms of their ability to assist. Sam, this wasn't just an attack by the *Belgorod* on the USA. Russia made good on that promise of having thirty Poseidon torpedoes. Combined with them using hypersonic ballistic missiles, the world as we know it is in the dark."

"And China?"

Matt shrugged. "Radio silence."

"Of course," he muttered. Sam's papers slipped from his grasp, fluttering like dying leaves as he sank into a chair. It was a posture of defeat that Matt had witnessed only rarely in the man who had shouldered the nation's burdens. "We're done. I'm done," Sam's voice trembled, displaying his vulnerability. "I should have followed your advice, but everyone around me said take the diplomatic approach — that Putin wouldn't do it, that it would be pure madness. But everything that occurred before this was exactly that — madness. The invasion of Ukraine, the threats, and the positioning of subs were all red flags. We didn't want to believe that this day would arrive."

Matt rose, moving purposefully around the desk beside his old friend. "You did what you thought was best for America. If you had sent our boys to war, the public would have crucified you, and if we were the first to nuke them, the whole world would have been against us. There was no way anyone would win in this scenario." Matt's voice was full of conviction. "It's a chess game. You know that. Every conversation, every meeting, and policy is all done in the hopes of avoiding, but some things can't be avoided."

Perching on the edge of the desk, Matt placed a hand on Sam's shoulder, a gesture of solidarity. "Besides Roosevelt, you are the only president to have made it into a third term."

A scoff escaped Sam's lips, tinged with bitterness. "Not by choice. I should have been out if this event hadn't happened. I wish—"

Matt finished the sentence that hung in the air. "... that you had gotten out after two terms? Well, you didn't, Sam. Look. I understand more than anyone how you must be feeling."

"Don't patronize me."

"I'm not. This could have happened at any time. Hell, in the '80s with the Cold War. But fate dumped it in your lap. Your job is to find out why. But let me remind you of something you told me many years ago. It's not where you are when anything ends that defines you. It's who you are with and what you do next. Now, we have a chance to turn this around."

"This? Nothing is left, Matt! This isn't the war in the Middle East that we can govern through words and sending in troops. We have been hamstrung, reduced, and our numbers are dwindling by the hour. Once the lights don't come back on. When the people see help is not coming. When the young and old perish from disease and malnutrition, and the rest question whether they should press on... God help us."

Matt faced Sam head-on as if daring him to embrace the challenge. Sam's resistance was palpable, his skepticism evident.

"Sam. We can rebuild."

"Rebuild? Are you kidding me? They have crippled the infrastructure, practically wiped out most of the West Coast, and set off a chain of events around the Ring of Fire and the world. Even the countries that didn't want to be involved are now. We will see the fallout of this event for decades to come."

"Nuclear fallout?"

"You know what I'm talking about."

Matt lifted both hands. "I'm just trying to remain optimistic."

"Well, forgive me if I can't find that optimism. It's not you who will be remembered for this shit show."

Matt snorted and turned away.

Sam shook his head. "You know what I mean."

"That's the thing, I do know. I've always known. I've always been here by your side through it all. But here's the thing. You and I are alive. A vast majority of America is still alive. No one wanted it to come to this, but we are where we are. What we do now is what we will be remembered for."

Sam's bitter chuckle punctuated the room, accompanied by the final gulp of his drink. He got up and picked up a framed photo of his family. "Two girls. A wife I barely have time for. The only time we're together is for media photo ops and a vacation once a year to Martha's Vineyard to give the illusion that everything is good on the family front. But it isn't. Is it?" he said, looking at Matt. "Do you know Jillian has been a stone's throw away from separating from me? My children. I barely know them. Nannies have raised them. This wasn't ever what I imagined serving my country would look like, Matt, but then, is anything ever the way it looks?"

"No. But there is a cost, and when this is over, they'll remember what you did to help."

"And how are we going to help?" He set the photo down and sighed. "Where are we at, Matt? How many fleets of aircraft carriers do we have out there to fight this war? How many Americans expect us to swoop in and provide them with supplies and resources when we barely have enough for ourselves? That Russian knew what he was doing. I should have considered every angle, and I didn't. An attack on America from the sky or land would have been futile, but an attack below the sea was like knocking down the first of thousands of dominoes. He only needed to topple one, and he achieved that. The rest will fall by themselves."

"So, it's set us back. They survived in the 1800s, and so will we."

"The Ring of Fire hadn't erupted back then," he said, bending down and picking up one of the sheets of paper that gave him a breakdown of what might be the worst possible outcome. Sam crossed the room and poured himself another drink. "Can I get you one?"

Matt dipped his chin.

"Oh, for goodness' sake," he said, taking out another glass. "I hardly think anyone gives a shit if you stink of alcohol. I've passed multiple officials today who smell like a distillery." He poured him a glass and continued to read. "The

Ring of Fire passes through fifteen countries; it's home to 90 percent of the world's earthquakes and 75 percent of the world's volcanoes."

"Yeah, the Kamchatka Peninsula in Russia is a part of that."

"So, they shot themselves in the foot. We warned him."

"The UN did. His officials didn't."

"Or maybe it was a mistake, a miscalculation," he replied.

"I hardly think a man with an arsenal of nukes makes miscalculations."

"Other dictators have before, and they will again," Sam said, handing him his drink. Matt took a large gulp, his hand trembling.

"These 452 volcanoes. Could they all erupt from this?"

"No. And anyone who says otherwise is full of shit, fear-mongering, or trying to profit from the worst possible outcome. The Poseidon that hit the coast was far more powerful than Hiroshima but not powerful enough to trigger all the volcanoes. Our experts said it would take an enormous tectonic event, like forming a new supercontinent, to cause them all to erupt. Then it wouldn't matter. It would be game over. No one would survive. The air would be filled with pollutants reflecting the sunlight into space and sending us into a nuclear winter for decades. The atmosphere would be full of so much toxic gas that few would survive, if any. The ocean and lakes would become too acidic to yield life, and... the rest would succumb to *Lord of the Flies* mentality. However, like you said, all it takes is one domino to fall. We don't need all of them to erupt for the world to suffer. My greatest concern is that the people will kill each other to secure medicine, water, and food, never mind all the other creature comforts they want to get their hands on. It's going to be chaos, sir."

Sam nodded. "This is where we see what America is made of."

"I don't think this is an American thing anymore, sir." Matt glanced at the satellite imagery. Many more volcanoes had erupted along fault lines around the nation, killing thousands, but Matt was right; it was far from the worst outcome.

"At least tell me this is manageable?"

"It's too early to tell. We'll know more in the coming weeks, but until then, we'll stay locked down, communicate with the other bunkers, and see what tomorrow brings. The National Guard, FEMA, the Red Cross, and other agencies are busy assisting civilians, at least those they can contact and reach. However, with the grid down, transportation reduced to older vehicles, and communication hamstrung, it's much harder to rally the troops together, so to speak, sir. A lot of the strength of towns will be found within the strength of the community, the emergency plans they have in place, and those willing to chip in and help."

"God help them," he muttered. With a heavy sigh, Sam turned away from Matt; his shoulders weighed down by regret and the uncertain path ahead.

AN HOUR LATER, Matt exited the president's office, his mind packed with a list of to-dos. Having served for many years in the Navy, he had a better grasp of the situation than most. He'd held back much of the actual disaster from Sam, knowing that what he shared was all he'd be able to handle.

As his footsteps echoed down the hallway, he took a

breath, allowing himself to realize that he was one of the lucky few who would ride out the following years in the lap of luxury. Whereas towns and cities would crumble under the strain of failed infrastructure, Peters Mountain would sustain some of the most intelligent people in America.

The 24/7/365 days Response Operation Center would continue to provide situational awareness and crisis support using a network of underground bunkers nationwide.

Few knew of their locations, and even fewer understood their purpose.

Hundreds of contractors had worked on the underground tunnels, connecting them nationwide. Work began during the Cold War when fears of Russian attack were at the fore-front of their minds.

The solution was simple.

Build cities, towns, and villages under the ground, with tunnels that would connect and allow America to continue to operate even if the world above ceased to exist. Billions of dollars in the U.S. so-called black budget had already been spent on the top five agencies — CIA, NSA, NRO, NGIP, and GDIP. The American people didn't know that billions more had been allocated to the continuity of a New America.

Not even Sam was privy to it. He knew just enough.

In many ways, Sam was just a puppet, a spokesman, a face for America — the fall guy for when things went wrong, the hero for when situations got better.

He was America's distraction, a political pawn used to keep the hearts and minds of the people engaged in anything else but the truth.

In his mind, the budget existed for only five reasons: to warn U.S. leaders about critical events, combat terrorism, stop the spread of illicit weapons, conduct cyber operations, and defend against foreign espionage.

However, an alternative budget had to be in place to win. That meant using covert action programs like armed drone operations, paramilitary organizations, and plants inside international politics to incite a war, foment terrorism in foreign countries, spread illicit weapons, and attack countries through cyber operations.

There was what the ordinary person heard in the news and the politician read in a memo, and then there was what existed off the books.

War was profit.

And profit was all over this, though only a few could see it.

Matt pulled out a phone explicitly designed to work beneath the surface. "Tim. He's been brought up to speed."

"Good. And if he doesn't go through with it?"

"He will."

"But if he doesn't."

"Then we will go with plan B," Matt said, and hung up.

He made his way around a bend in the narrow corridor and waited.

How long would it take? Would it occur?

The country had become too settled and diplomatic, and nothing significant came out of peace.

Minutes passed.

Crack! The sound echoed.

A gun planted by Sam and a nudge in the right direction was all it took.

Soldiers hurried, their boots clacking against the polished corridor. For all their effort, service to the country, and the hopes of America rising from the ashes, nothing could have prepared them to find the president of the United States dead from a self-inflicted gunshot wound to the head.

Back pressed to the wall, Matt prepared to take on the role. "You were right and wrong, my friend; they will remember you as a coward. And me? The one who lifted us out of the mire."

15

Oregon

The doctors made no promises.

Jackson's life hung in the balance for more reasons than one. Under the strain of an event that had pushed everyone to exhaustion, patients were left for hours without anyone checking on them. It was a given, especially with the steady influx of people needing critical care.

Fluorescent lights made a humming noise above. Jackson lay motionless on the bed; a thin veil of medication-induced haze shrouded his consciousness. His leg was swathed in bandages covering the bloody wound. Nearby, curled up in a chair, Zoe was fast asleep.

The hospital's environment was tense with the whirring industrial-style generators, the only steady companion against the silence that enveloped the room. Outside, the world was gripped by a country-wide power outage, and its turmoil was mirrored within the hospital's walls as doctors and nurses moved like shadows, their faces etched with tiredness.

"Shitty job," Colton said.

"Someone's got to do it," the janitor replied.

"You do realize the country has come under attack."

"And?"

"We're here because of an injury, but you..."

"Hmm. All right. What? You expect me to drop what I'm doing and run for the hills?"

"Well, yeah," Colton replied. He was holding two cups of coffee he'd gotten from a room set up to offer something warm for the staff and patients.

"And go where?"

"Wherever there's no trouble."

"And then what?"

Colton gave him a puzzled expression.

"You see, that's the trouble with America. Everyone thinks the situation will get better if they run for the hills. But no one thinks about the trouble waiting for them there, you know, the other morons doing the same thing. Think about it. Who do you think you will run into?" He paused for effect. "That's right. More scared and freaked-out individuals. Nope. As I see it, you hunker down where it makes sense, pick your battles, and don't run until you need to. You see, right now, this place has power. My apartment doesn't."

"You raise a good point. How does this place still have the lights on?" Colton said to the janitor, who was mopping up a puddle of blood. "Everywhere else has gone dark."

"Shielded generators," the guy replied, leaning against the blood-soaked mop.

"Shielded what?"

"Brand-new shielding. They spent more money on that than they did on the generator. Go figure, right!? Anyway, they're kept in the bowels of the hospital. Another move they said was crucial. Something to do with a nuclear deterrent, you know, when they say shelter in place, they tell you to go to your basement."

"Okay, and how does that work?"

"Going to your basement?"

"No. The generator."

"Oh. Right. Well. If the power goes out. Those suckers kick in within ten seconds. All diesel generated, of course. The hospital made a big thing about it a few years back. I did some video online demonstrating it kicking in. Some marketing rep from the company was here with cameras. They kept harping on about how it could withstand an EMP. I needed to figure out what he was talking about. I know now. That's what everyone is calling this."

"I heard," Colton muttered, glancing over at Bryce, who had given him the breakdown, in Jackson's room.

"Any hoot, the hospital said they are leading the way. They made it part of their marketing scheme, I guess, to attract more people here. Stability and whatnot. I've yet to see a cent in a pay raise." He returned to mopping the floor. "But I have seen a lot of blood spilled."

Colton pulled a face. "I bet," Colton said, opening the curtain wide and walking back in, handing Bryce his brew.

He took a sip. It tasted like ash, but it was a welcome sight after the shit they'd been through.

The morning had arrived, casting its tentative light through the curtained windows. Bryce, the interloper in the somber scene, had returned to the hospital at the behest of Jackson only to find him in a drug-induced haze. He'd sat there for several hours waiting for him to wake up. It wasn't like he could go anywhere. The event of the previous night, woven with violence and sabotage, had left its mark on everyone present.

Bryce's gaze lingered on Colton, who nursed his cup of coffee. It was a simple gesture, a beacon of normalcy in a world that had gone awry. Although the hospital temporarily had power, the TV wasn't playing anything. All the stations were down. Whatever the horror that had befallen the nation was, it was widespread and wasn't removing its grip anytime soon.

"Why were you at the wrecker's?" Bryce asked, breaking the silence, probing for answers.

Colton's gaze shifted from the cup to Bryce. "What does it matter to you?" he retorted defensively.

Bryce smiled; his response was tinged with a touch of irony. "Kid, that old-timer would have put two in your chest if it wasn't for me. Come on, twenty years old, late at night, after an earthquake and power outage. What would be so valuable that you would risk your life?"

"Who said I was risking my life?"

"You never knocked. You climbed the fence when there were clearly no trespassing signs, and after what happened, he would have been within his rights to shoot you."

Colton's fingers traced the rim of his Styrofoam cup, a nervous gesture that betrayed his façade. He shifted uncomfortably, a tell-tale sign that Bryce wasn't willing to overlook. "Collecting parts for my friend's old man's vehicle," Colton finally confessed, his words punctuated by a shrug.

Bryce's stare remained unwavering; a challenge laid bare. "Bullshit," he stated flatly, unyielding in his skepticism.

Undeterred, Colton offered a wry chuckle. "It's true," he insisted.

A tense silence hovered between them; a battle of wills concealed the truth. Colton's discomfort didn't go unnoticed by Bryce, who seized upon the opening. "You know, I've met many a liar. They all have the same tell-tale signs. Shifty eyes. Unable to give you a straight answer. Some bullshit story. How about you start again?"

Colton's chuckle was met with a raised eyebrow from Bryce, who seemed uninterested in backing down. "You've been watching too many episodes of *Columbo*," Colton quipped, his tone attempting to diffuse the tension. "Why do you care?"

Bryce's motivations were apparent in his response. "Because I don't think you wanted to be there."

"What gave you that impression?"

"You're not hurrying to return, which makes me wonder why."

"That's simple. I took a knock to the head. Figured I would stick around, just in case."

"Is that so... and yet a nurse told me you refused treatment."

"I feel fine."

"Feeling fine and being fine can be worlds apart. Could it be you're on something, and it might show up in your blood work?" His words hung in the air, a challenge Colton couldn't easily dismiss.

"Whatever, man. Believe what you want." He rose from his seat and discarded the empty cup with a careless toss before drawing back the curtain and allowing daylight to stream in. Bryce, however, wasn't ready to let it go. He moved closer, his grip firm as he took hold of Colton's arm.

"What the—"

Colton's protest was met with determination, a request that became more compelling with the passing seconds. "What the hell? What are you doing?" His voice carried confusion and irritation.

Bryce's resolve was unyielding. "Take a walk with me. I'm sure you need a cigarette, right?" A pack emerged from Bryce's pocket, a tangible offering in a time of uncertainty.

"Hold on a second. Those are mine."

"Exactly."

Colton's initial resistance faltered as they moved past the nurses' station, a mundane encounter that barely registered against the backdrop of their conversation.

"Sir, you can't smoke in here."

Colton's laughter was a release of tension. "All this time, we've been waiting for an update, and you haven't piped up. I walk by with a cigarette on my lips, and you get all bent out of shape. Relax. It's not lit."

They pressed on.

Outside, daylight had transformed the surroundings — the once-hostile night had given way to a brighter reality, though the chaos outside remained palpable. A lighter sparked to life, and Colton's cigarette flared with the promise of a momentary reprieve.

"You in the habit of stealing people's property?" Colton asked, eyeing him through a plume of smoke before offering him one from the pack.

"Stealing would imply I took them from you. They fell out of your pocket when you were being a jackass at the wrecker's yard. So why were you there?"

"Why are you so interested? I mean, Zoe is Jackson's

daughter. So, what does that make you? And how did you end up there?" Colton asked.

Bryce's response was swift, unadorned by unnecessary details. "They gave me a ride after I got out of military prison," he admitted, a confession that lingered.

A hint of surprise marked Colton's acknowledgment. "Shit. You were in the can? Now, that's something you don't come across too often. Sure, I know people who are doing time, but that's in the county jail. What are you... army, Marine, SEAL?" His curiosity painted the scene.

"Marine."

"So, what did you do? Refuse to jerk off your commander? Go AWOL? Or... I know... you screwed the wrong person, right?"

Bryce's gaze remained steady. "Murder."

Colton's reaction was visceral, a stumble born of shock and disbelief. He took a few steps back; the distance between them was a physical manifestation of the gulf that separated them. The cigarette ember glowed in the morning light. He eyed him. "You're shitting me."

"No."

"Do the other two know?"

"Nope. And I would like to keep it that way as much as you want to keep whatever secret you have to yourself."

"Then why did you tell me?"

"Because you remind me of myself."

Colton nodded, taking another hit on his cigarette. He glanced over his shoulder toward the front of the building, where officers still held a tide of people at bay. The need was even more significant than the night before. "I wasn't there to get parts for my friend's old man."

"Why did you lie?" Bryce asked.

"For the same reason you probably did before you got sent away. Self-preservation."

"From what?"

Colton blew out smoke. "Not what. From who." He took another drag, letting it burn a bright orange. "You ever heard of auto parts trafficking?"

Bryce narrowed his eyes, his interest piqued. "The selling of stolen parts?"

"Right. The two friends I was with are part of... well, let's call it an auto theft ring. That's how we made our livelihood. Or let's say that's how we helped Rusty make his livelihood."

Bryce's brow furrowed in confusion. "You worked with him?"

"For him."

"And yet he acted like he never knew you."

"As far as he was concerned, he didn't. That old bastard screwed us over. Sold us a line and then failed to deliver on it."

"How so?"

"Ah, man, like I said, it doesn't matter. Fucking world has gone to shit. You have better things to think about now than me."

"My brother is dead, my ride is destroyed, and the man who was supposed to give me a job when I got out, you're now telling me, wasn't on the straight and narrow."

Colton blew smoke his way before laughing. "Old Rusty was supposed to give you a job? That's funny. I wonder what angle he was looking for this time," he said, eyeing Bryce. "I'd say you dodged a bullet there, my friend. That would have been a one-way ticket back to the clink – of that, I'm sure."

"Why?"

"No, forget it. You don't have time to hear my shit."

"Until I speak to Jackson, I've got nothing but time." Bryce leaned up against the wall. Colton stared at him, dropped the remainder of his cigarette, and twisted his foot to put it out. He immediately fired up another one.

"All right. You want the short or the long story?"

"Whatever you want, but don't lie."

"A murderer with a conscience. Now that's funny." He took a hit on his cigarette. "From age fourteen, I was surfing from couch to couch. Didn't exactly have a good upbringing, if you get my gist." He eyed the cops as if they could hear or were interested, then continued. "At some point, I ended up hooking up with Skylar Morgan and Dominick Rodriguez. The two people I was with last night. At first, it was just petty crime in and around Portland. Smash and grabs. We'd pull up to some vehicle, smash out the window, and grab whatever we could see. From there, we graduated up to taking a few for joy rides. Then it dawned on us that we could make a good amount of cash selling some of those stolen cars to salvage yards. That's where Rusty comes into it. That old coot is smarter than he looks. He clued in that we weren't working for some used car dealership. You know, Dominic's old man. That was what we told him. Instead of turning us over to the cops, he gave us a proposition. Initially, he told us he would pay top dollar for auto parts. We would steal wheels, catalytic converters, tailgates, batteries, seats, airbags, you name it. If we couldn't get the vehicle, we collected parts. Next, he upped the ante. He offered us more money than we could imagine for entire vehicles. He would strip out the parts, dismantle, crush, and dispose of the frames with all the traceable vehicle IDs. He would then sell the parts. It was working well. Really well. He even let us stay in his trailer. Gave us a roof over our heads. I mean three meals a day, a warm bed, more money than we could shake a flea at. What more could you ask for?"

"So, what changed?"

Colton dipped his head. "The old man wasn't just into paying for car parts." Colton's eyes reddened. The shame he saw in his eyes. That's what he recognized. It was what he had in his eyes as a child.

"He touched you?"

"Fuck you, man. Forget it. I shouldn't have."

"You think you're the only one that's happened to?" Bryce asked.

Colton stopped with his hand on the door, about to enter the hospital.

"Three years. Three years a guy I knew abused me as a teenager. I get it."

Colton released his grip; he seemed at a loss for words.

"I bounced around the foster system," Bryce said. "I know what it's like."

Colton sniffed hard, trying to put on a brave front. "I'm not a faggot, man."

"Never said you were."

"Anyway," Colton was quick to change the subject. "Dominick figured out a way we could make even more money and leave that old dirty bastard behind. You see, because he never gave us the full amount of money. That's how he did it. We bore all the risk, and he threw us just enough to get by, but we still needed him. Dominick realized that we could steal the VINs from Rusty and place them on new stolen cars. He discovered that the DMV showed very little information on a wrecked car. He'd get someone to file paperwork with the DMV claiming that they had gotten it from a wrecker's yard and restored the vehicle to work. Registration fees were paid, the car did a road test, and then it gained a legal title, and it's sold on to a buyer who has no idea that the vehicle was stolen. It was simple — money in the bank. We cut out the middleman. Rusty didn't like that. He also didn't like us climbing over his fence and stealing the VINs. That's why he got those dogs."

Bryce nodded. "So, you were there to steal VINs because you knew he wouldn't go to the cops otherwise..."

"He would risk exposing himself for other fraudulent behavior. Yeah," Colton said.

"And your reason for not wanting to go back?"

"Dominick. You could say our friendship hasn't been what it once was. Once he realized the kind of money that could be made, he figured he would set himself up a bit like Rusty. You know, taking the lion's share of profits but taking the least amount of risk." He sighed. "Look, please don't tell the others."

"You got it."

16

Tennessee

The survival instinct was ingrained in the fabric of human DNA, but only a few would ever see it, let alone understand it, until they were given no other option.

But she had lived it in one form or another.

In her years of running a group home for teenagers, Natalie had witnessed the walls of life closing in, the extremes that consumed and forced teens into life-or-death decisions.

Few made it out in one piece.

Those that did were funneled into the system with not much more than hope and a prayer.

Teens bounced around the foster system like cattle on a farm — some made it, others fell by the wayside, and the rest were lucky if they squeaked through to their eighteenth birthday without taking their lives.

The truth of existence was hard for those not born into a good family. The way it affected their minds and forced them to grow up faster than most was a case study in and of itself.

Still, there was a flip side to everything

While they were resilient, she knew all too well they would have traded that newfound strength for something stable.

No, survival was their reality.

People abandoning them.

Being let down more than lifted up.

Disappointment, not hope.

That's why she knew if anyone could make it through this, it was the teens in her group.

Still, it was upon her to be the stability until society caught up.

That began by making sure they had supplies and plenty of them.

When Natalie opened her eyes, medication, food, and water were high on the to-do list. She groaned and rolled over, the events of the previous evening flooding in, looking to overwhelm and paralyze her. It all seemed like a nightmare, but waking up in Dante's home only reminded her it was the new reality.

"One, two, three, four, five. Go!"

More than once, she applied the five-second rule on days she wanted to stay in bed.

Natalie pawed at her eyes, flipped the covers back, and set her feet on the carpet. She slipped into her jeans and buttoned up a shirt, but not before sniffing it. It stank of smoke. That was another thing they would need. Clothes.

Fresh clothes and lots of them. Striding out of the room, she caught the faint smell of coffee.

Without thinking, Natalie ventured into the bathroom and went to use the toilet. It flushed, emptying what little water was in the tank behind it, but there was no sound coming from the pipes of water pumping back in.

She tried the wash basin. It spluttered to life momentarily as the water in the pipe drained out. "Great."

Natalie went down the stairs, turned, and headed into the kitchen, where she found Dante fiddling with a device on the counter.

"Morning."

He glanced back. "Hey. Coffee?"

"Would love some. By the way, the water is not working."

"I know. I had to fill up this using bottled water," he said, gesturing to a pack on the counter. That's when Natalie noticed he had a Coleman stove on the counter and was making coffee in a Moka Press. She took a seat at a round table. "I was thinking of cooking a big breakfast for everyone with what I've got in the fridge before it goes off. It won't last long."

"So, you think she was right."

"Who?" he asked, pouring out a coffee and then handing it to her.

"Wendy Bowers. One of the city commissioners."

Natalie smelled the milk carton.

"It's fine. For now," he said.

She poured some into her drink and stirred, then took a sip. Dante continued to stay busy, pulling out several pans and then collecting a carton of eggs.

"As for your question, I don't know. You know her better than I do. What do you think?"

Natalie squinted. "It's odd. She seemed convinced this would last weeks and it only happened last night. Tell me if I'm overthinking here, but that makes no sense, right? Talking about dealing with produce, vertical farming, and whatnot."

He shrugged. "The writing is on the wall."

"What's that supposed to mean?"

"If your vehicle breaks down, you don't wait a couple of days before calling a tow truck — you get on it immediately. Everyone is different in how they cope with stress. For some, they cower back and do nothing; others observe and follow suit, and some rush to solve the situation even if it doesn't call for an immediate solution."

Natalie nodded. "I guess. It just seems odd to me. Almost like she knew this event was going to happen."

"Hardly. How can you know planes will fall out of the sky or the grid will shut down?"

"I know, but then there was all that talk about Darren Waitman knowing someone who could assist. How do you assist with this situation? Whatever this situation is..." She paused. "By the way, do you have a radio?"

"No. Why?"

"I expect the government will be broadcasting some message over the radio. I want to stay up to date on what is happening."

"I'm sure we'll get updated on what measures are in place today, what with that meeting Wendy mentioned." He cracked a few eggs, tossed some bacon into the pan, ignited the Coleman burner, and quickly filled the kitchen with the smell of heaven.

"I meant California."

"Right. Your husband and daughter." Dante went to the

doorway. "Hey guys! Breakfast will be ready shortly. Time to get up!"

He glanced at Natalie on the way back.

"You know I appreciate all of this," she said.

"You already said that last night."

"I know but... it's worth saying again. I want you to know I don't plan to put you out longer than a day."

"What do you mean?"

"Well, I'll have to head back to my place today, if only to get some fresh clothes. These stink," she muttered.

"Natalie. I want to think that the group home was unlucky, that some random spark sailed through the air and landed, causing the fire, but you heard what your neighbor saw and Jordan's father said."

"What's that about my father?" Jordan asked, striding into the kitchen and running a hand over his face.

"We were just talking about last night. How did you sleep?" Dante asked.

Jordan scratched his head. "Like a log. It must have been all that work we did. I don't think I've worked that hard in years. All those buckets of water. We were lucky to put out what we did."

"You're right about that."

Shortly after Jordan entered, Selena and the other two came in and sat at the table. Dante busied himself cracking more eggs. Liam laid his head on the table; Daniel leaned back in his seat with his hood up and said, "Oh, um, everyone. Heads up. I took a dump in the toilet. It didn't flush. My bad."

Dante glanced at Natalie, and she shrugged, grinning. "We'll have to use buckets of water from here on out to force it down or you can use the great outdoors."

Selena's brow furrowed. "Buckets?"

"Yeah, the water plants are powered by electricity. Until it comes back on, you'll have to bathe in the river."

"Story of my life," Liam said, as someone who had spent much time living out of a car with his mother before he was finally funneled into the system.

The following hour was spent in conversation, eating breakfast, and discussing plans for the day.

"You think I could get a moment of your time?" Natalie said, stepping out the back.

Dante followed her. "What is it?"

"I know you think that Jordan's father was responsible for the fire at the group home, and it's possible. More than likely after the bullshit that happened last night, but I think it would be better if you stayed here with the teens while I head over and get what I need."

"Hell no."

"Dante. I appreciate you wanting to help, but I can care for myself."

"I'm sure you can, but against three men?"

She grumbled. "I hardly think they know where I live."

"Clyde knew where you were last night."

"Because he's been watching the group home. That's how he managed to show up. No. I appreciate the offer, but if you want to help. Stay with them."

"Okay. But if you're going over, let me get you something."

Dante went back into the house. Natalie breathed in the air. It still stank of smoke, and she could see the entrails in the distance. "Here," Dante said, emerging and extending a Glock to her.

She chuckled, taking a step back and lifting her hands. "I'm not taking that."

"It will give me peace of mind."

"It will give me nightmares. Come on, Clyde might be pushing his luck, but that's taking things to the extreme."

"Look around you, Natalie. We're in the extreme."

She glanced at it. "Well. I don't even know how to use one."

"You've never fired a gun?"

"Never held one. Had no need or desire."

"Well, it's pretty simple. Look, I can show you," he said, stepping forward. "You just..."

She shoved him back. "I told you I don't want it. Okay?"

Dante stared at her. Her reaction was unusual. "All right. All right."

She folded her arms and looked off into the distance. "Sorry. Can you just take it away?"

He nodded and headed back inside. While he was upstairs, Natalie ducked into the house. The teens were still around the table. "Hey, guys. I'm just going out for half an hour. I'll be back soon."

"Where you heading, Mrs. Reid?"

"Home. I'll grab a few things for this evening. Just stay put." She wagged a finger. "And Jordan. Listen to Dante. No playing games."

He offered back a deadpan expression as she exited and went out the rear door. Natalie's property was just a short distance from Dante's place. She lived a little further east off Mountain Breeze Way. She'd have to cut through the forest and cross East Parkway.

Pressing through the woodland at the back of Dante's property, she noticed through the trees a slew of people working their way south and north on the main highway, backpacks on, dragging suitcases behind them. Single people and families, many of whom had to evacuate their homes and seek accommodation at one of the many hotels and motels in the area. It was a quick fix for those who had suffered losses. Many didn't get the chance to collect their belongings.

She could only hope her home was still there.

The closer Natalie got to her home, the more her conversation with Dante replayed in her mind. She didn't want to think that Clyde would have gone to that extent to get back at her, but that seed of doubt had been planted. Could he have found out where she lived? And why would he have targeted her? She was nothing more than a supervisor at the group home and certainly wasn't the one who called the shots or sent Jordan there. Her job was to oversee the kids, nothing more.

Still, she'd seen the way he looked at her with malice in his gaze.

Relief flooded her chest as she saw her neighborhood had been spared from the fires. Several of her neighbors were outside, conversing, probably talking about what was happening or what could be done.

The way she saw it, there was very little that anyone could do.

They were like every other town in America, at the mercy of the state.

Natalie slowed her pace, thinking about Clyde.

Not taking any chances, she skirted around some of her neighbors' houses and positioned herself on the far side of Mountain Breeze Way.

Tucked into the woodland, Natalie peered out. It was hard to see because of all the foliage, and if Clyde was over at her place, she didn't want him seeing her first.

Nat glanced up at the enormous trees and reached up,

taking hold of a low-hanging branch. She climbed, and worked her way up until she had a clear view of her home.

Initially, nothing looked out of the ordinary.

The street was quiet, barring a few neighbors pointing toward the fires in the north.

Natalie had turned to get out of the tree when, out of the corner of her eye, she spotted something she didn't notice the first time. It was hardly noticeable. Anyone else might have overlooked it. Not her. The curtains in the top bedroom were drawn together. Not entirely, but enough to block the glare of light. She knew damn well those curtains had been open.

It was the one thing she did before she left each morning.

It allowed the house to catch rays of sunlight and helped warm each room — a simple hack that reduced her heating bill. Jackson would often joke that she was a miser, but she never saw it like that. It was all about being thrifty. She'd saved hundreds each year doing that.

Natalie squinted. It was then she wished she had some binoculars.

"Shit." Some part of her just wanted to leave and return to Dante, but he would only say I told you so. Police were out of the question. By the time she made it there and back, Clyde might be gone — then she'd look like an absolute fool.

A fiery anger rose up in her.

The reality was, she didn't even know if he was in the house.

Someone could have broken in, one of the many families who had been forced out of their homes by the fires. It was possible that some, those with small children who couldn't find a place to stay, knocked on doors until they found one where no one answered and then had broken in.

Then, it dawned on her what to do.

Natalie climbed down, worked through the thick under-brush, and double-timed it to Leo Sullivan's home. He was a long-time neighbor of hers, a patriot through and through. She'd often see him outside in the morning raising an American flag and saluting it or lifting a rifle and firing off a few rounds. The cops had been called out a few times over that. He never harmed anyone, but that wasn't to say that he wasn't outspoken. He made a name for himself at town hall meetings, recording and posting the sessions online to hold them accountable.

With Jackson away from home, he'd often come over and offer to help mow the lawn. Jackson would joke that Leo had a thing for her, but it wasn't that. Now that he'd retired, he was alone and just enjoyed the company.

Natalie skirted around to his front door and knocked, glancing back over her shoulder at her house across the street, a few doors down. There was no answer. She knocked again, a little harder.

"Okay. Okay."

There was movement on the other side, and then the door opened.

"Natalie?"

"Leo. Can I come in?"

"Sure. I was just thinking about you," he said. "I mean. I was wondering how you were getting on with the fires. I didn't see your truck in the driveway this morning. I was hoping you hadn't got caught up in those fires. What do you make of that?" he said, strolling into his living room and taking a seat on his La-Z-Boy. He had multiple rifles laid out on the table in front of him and had been cleaning one.

"Preparing for war, Leo?"

"Always. I figured it would come to this. Those damn

Russians have been biding their time," he said as he lifted a Mossberg shotgun. "Got this one last week. What do you think? Good timing, huh?"

Natalie nodded. "Uh-huh," she said, glancing at her window.

He sniffed hard. "I reckon it will be a week before we see boots on the ground. Jackson will probably get drafted, as will the rest of the town."

He stood up, holding his rifle by his side. "I'm not as spry as I once was, but I figure they'll take me. What do you think?" He lifted one leg and drove it to the floor, demonstrating his ability to take orders. "Yes, sir!"

She smirked. "If you go to war, who will protect this street?"

"Good point."

Natalie turned away from the window. "I'm wondering if boots are already on the ground."

"What do you mean?"

"You know, infiltration and whatnot."

"You think the Russians are already here?"

"There were those mass arrests a few years back."

"Sleeper cells? But that was in New York."

"Who's to say they don't have a few in this town."

He raised his rifle, and she stepped to one side. "If they are, they won't last long, especially with some of the hollers. We'd soon sniff them out."

"That's why I came over. I noticed someone had pulled my drapes together last night. Did you see anything?" she asked, knowing that it was common to see him on his porch at night, smoking a cigar and keeping an eye on the neighborhood like he was some old-time sheriff.

"Can't say I did. Why? You think someone's in your house?"

She nodded. Without saying another word, he marched to the front door and swung it open, striding forward with his shotgun at the ready. "Hey, uh, Leo. Just in case it's a family..."

"I've got my finger off the trigger. Don't you worry, love."

As they crossed the street, Oscar Chambers, two doors down, couldn't help but chime in. "Problem?"

"Nothing we can't handle."

Before Leo was within 100 yards of the house, he held his shotgun high and unloaded two rounds. "All right, you scummy bastards. This is your warning. You better be out of that house by the time I land on that porch, or I'm going to..."

Natalie squeezed her eyes shut, momentarily realizing it had been a bad idea. There was a downside to everything. The downside with Leo was a person never really knew what state of mind he was in at any given moment. What with the pills he was taking and his frequent use of the devil's lettuce, he could be chilled or on edge.

"Well, if the neighbors aren't up. They are now," Oscar said, getting out of his chair and standing on his porch to take in the entertainment. One door down from him, Alice Brooks, a recent divorcee, came outside wearing nothing more than a nightgown. She glanced over at Oscar. He tipped his baseball cap to her. "Alice."

"What is he doing?" Alice said.

"Dealing with an infestation problem by the looks of it."

Leo made it to the front door of Natalie's home and fired off another round. "Last chance!"

Although it wasn't the situation she had in mind, it was attracting additional attention, which was the purpose. "All right, Leo. I think we're good."

"I'll be the judge of that," he said. "Open the door. I'll clear the rooms before you come in."

Natalie stuck a key in the lock and gave it a turn. She listened for a second before Leo charged in all balls and glory. "Just don't fire a round in my house. Please."

"Like I would," he said before working through the house like he was part of a one-person SWAT team. Natalie remained outside, now joined by three more neighbors, all keen to know what was happening. Her biggest concern was the upstairs. Leo disappeared up the stairs, back to the wall, barking out orders that he would shoot and then, if they were still alive, ask questions after.

Fortunately, she never heard a gunshot.

"Natalie."

"Yeah?" she said, poking her head inside.

"It's all clear, but I think you should see this," he said. Natalie excused herself and entered the house, hurrying up the steps. She turned onto the landing and entered the bedroom. Spray-painted all across the back wall behind her bed was the word BITCH!

The duvet cover was bunched up in a mound and soaked in what looked like blood. It almost looked like it was alive.

"Do you want me to?"

She nodded. Leo crossed to the bed and lifted the duvet with the tip of his barrel. As soon as the blanket fell away, they were met with the sight of snakes swirling around a dead cat. Her cat.

Natalie turned and rushed into the bathroom to vomit in the sink.

17

Portland

The sight of barriers and angry people only made him smile.

They were stonewalling people. Loved ones, friends, even the sick. This wasn't what Chris and Pete wanted to encounter. On the other hand, it was precisely what he'd hoped to find. It gave him a solid reason to turn around and return.

The journey down had been relatively short and uneventful; the sight of stalled vehicles and people on foot had only bolstered his reasoning.

Foster had tried to convince the other two that they were wasting their time. The chances of finding Bryce were next to none. He'd suggested heading north to the hospital further away, but Chris refused to believe they would have gone that far — citing what the old-timer had said.

Foster thought that part had slipped over his head. Chris had always been hard of hearing, but now he realized it was more selective hearing. The two were cardboard cutouts of what Ryland and Foster were twenty years ago. Back then, they didn't take no for an answer and sure as hell put nothing before loyalty.

How times had changed.

Chris had his feet up on the truck's dashboard. The vehicle didn't belong to them. They'd commandeered it. Well, hijacked was the better term. Jagger had shot a man driving it along a stretch of road outside Rusty's wrecker's. After almost every vehicle ground to a halt, the older models were easier to spot. They were far and few between. Talis had said it was because they didn't have the electrical components that new models had.

Had they not seen the vehicle, there was a chance they wouldn't have made it this far.

"I'm telling you we should split. Forget this," Foster said.

"I don't get you, Foster," Chris muttered. "You used to champion the cause of us Proud Boys, and now you want to shy away from what any of us would have done for you had you been lying there."

"So, we find this guy, and Talis kills him. Then what?"

"We go back to doing what we've always done."

"Look around you, Chris. You ever seen this in your lifetime?"

"Plenty of disasters happen every year in America."

"Like this?"

He puffed on a cigarette, all relaxed. "No, not like this, but give it a few days, and they'll have this in the bag and deliver a fairly normal reason why."

"You can't be that naïve after what happened at the

Capitol riots. Do you think the government has anyone's best interest in mind? Wake up!"

Chris looked over at him. "You need to relax."

The truck wound its way down into the vicinity of the hospital. "Don't park in the lot. I don't want to lose this vehicle," Chris said, pointing to a grove of trees. They parked and got out, making their way toward the hospital. One look and it was clear they weren't getting in.

"I told you," Foster said.

"Shit, he's right, we aren't getting through that," Pete added.

"That's what people said at the Capitol, and look who got people in."

"Yeah, and what was the outcome?" Foster added.

"I swear, Foster. If you weren't one of the OG's, I would put you in your place."

"Sure you would," Foster replied.

"But that's not to say Talis won't if we don't bring Bryce back."

They strolled down a steep grassy incline toward the crowd. "And if we don't bring him back? What are you going to tell him? Huh? I'm telling you, finding this man doesn't matter. Ryland knew the risk when he agreed to kill that mans brother. Trust me on that. I tried to change his mind."

"You tried to talk him out of it?"

"Damn right. He was repaying a favor. It had nothing to do with our values."

It was the first time Chris had listened to him. He thought he might reply with some sarcastic comment, but he didn't. They pressed on toward the barrier, getting close to the main doors.

Beyond the barrier, the hospital's sterile corridor buzzed with fluorescent lights as the double doors opened and closed, and patients came and went. Its harsh glare contrasted sharply with the tension etched into the faces of the three men standing at the entrance.

Foster's expression hardened as he shifted uncomfortably on his feet. He didn't want to be here. Flanked by those who wouldn't take no for an answer.

Foster glanced at Pete, a burly figure with a steely resolve, matched only by Chris, a hulk of a man with a strong will. Foster cleared his throat as he approached the barrier where a pair of uniformed police officers conversed with someone looking to gain entry.

Pete's eyes darted nervously between the officers. "Let's find another way in."

Chris, ever the risk-taker, had a different idea. "And search for the next hour? Forget it. Maybe they know where he is," he whispered. "Let me handle this."

Foster's anxiety deepened, but he reluctantly agreed, watching Chris confidently approach the officers. "Excuse me," he began.

"Be right with you."

Chris looked back at Pete and then continued. "Sorry. Do you mind if..."

"I said we will be right with you," the officer barked.

"It's just that we're looking for someone. A man who might have been brought in with a leg injury."

The younger officer, a woman with a stern expression, regarded him with an annoyed look. "Name?"

Chris hesitated for a moment, then replied, "Bryce."

The older officer exchanged a knowing look with his

partner before addressing him. "Sorry, pal," he said with a stern tone. "Can't help you unless you have a surname."

Pete, lurking nearby, couldn't help but chime in. "Let's not waste any more time."

Chris nodded reluctantly. "Yeah. These assholes aren't helping," he said, his voice tinged with frustration. As they turned away, Foster quickly rubbed salt into the wound.

"This is a sign. Let's leave."

"You want to pussy out like you did back at the cabin. By all means. But once Talis gets wind, you'll have to deal with him."

"He doesn't scare me."

"Never said he did," Chris responded, glancing at him. "However, when you deal with him, you deal with all of us." It was clear what he was saying. That was another reason why he'd been looking for a way out. The politics around the group had tightened over the past few years, with some calling for a heavy hand on those who didn't toe the line. It was different from when he was their age. If someone wanted out, they just left the group. It was simple. Not now.

Chris led them to a side exit, but none were open. Tired of waiting any longer, Chris took out his handgun and used the butt of it to smash a window in the rear of the hospital. "Give me a boost up," he said, placing a hand on Pete's shoulder and launching himself through the window.

"All right. Foster. You're next," Chris said with a grin.

Foster glanced around him, looking for cops before he entered. "This is a bad idea."

"And yet here we are," Chris said, clutching his hand and pulling him inside. Pete followed after. Once inside, they worked their way through a labyrinth of corridors.

"All this for one man."

"See, that's the thing with you, Foster. You think we're doing this for Ryland, but we're not. It wasn't just Ryland who lost his life, or have you so quickly forgotten in your haste to distance yourself from it?" He paused, allowing the words to sink in. "We let this slide; how many others will think they can walk over us?"

"Walk over us? There is no us anymore. Don't you get it? The sentences given to some of our group for the raid on the Capitol made that loud and clear. And now this. The sooner you wake up, the sooner you start living outside this bullshit we have bought into."

Chris shook his head. "There was a time I used to look up to you. It was a time when you wouldn't bat an eye to take a bullet for the rest of the brotherhood. Now look at you," he said. "Can you even call yourself a Proud Boy? Or better still, do you even want to be one of us?"

Foster remained quiet. There was no point getting into it with him. He didn't understand. None of them did. Time. Age. Family. That's what put things in perspective. One day, if Chris lived long enough, he'd realize.

"I say we split up," Pete said.

"No, I'm the only one who knows what Bryce looks like."

Pete's eyes bore into Foster's. "We don't need to know. We just need to find someone with an injury to the leg who's with a guy and a girl."

"Yeah, and how do you expect to do that? You saw how many were outside. People have overrun this hospital. We could be looking for hours."

A vigilant security guard spotted them before they could put a plan into action. "Excuse me," he said firmly, his tone challenging. "You're not supposed to be back here."

Chris shot Foster a mischievous grin, ignoring Foster's

frantic gestures to leave. Instead, he approached the security guard. "I'm sorry," he began smoothly, "this place is a maze. I was looking for the X-ray department."

The security guard's face tensed with suspicion. "Can I see your tags?"

Chris shrugged. "They're only given out to patients, we're visiting."

"I don't know how you got in here, but you'll have to either show me some tags or leave now."

Chris nodded with feigned confidence. "Sure. Sorry, I..."

Instantly, Chris drew a knife from his pocket and thrust it under the security guard's ribcage. The guard's eyes widened in shock, and Chris swiftly clamped a hand over his mouth. He dragged the gurgling man into a nearby room, the muffled sounds of a deadly struggle echoing in the space.

Pete watched from the doorway, his expression a mix of awe and horror, while Foster paced. "Are you fucking serious?" Foster hissed. "There are cops outside."

"Never stopped us before. He would have raised the alarm. Now stop whining and hand me that sheet."

Foster grabbed up a bed sheet and tossed it to him. He laid it out on the ground and rolled the guard into it before rolling him up like a giant burrito and then dragging his body into a storage cupboard. "Now, let's go find Bryce."

After disposing of the security guard's body, Foster, Pete, and Chris went to a bustling nurses' station, a central hub in the hospital's heart. It was a chaotic scene with a vast number of people waiting anxiously. Some lay on gurneys in the hallways, while every room and holding area seemed filled. Doctors and nurses scurried back and forth between the station and patients, their faces etched with weariness and urgency.

The cacophony of the hospital was overwhelming. Groans of pain and cries for assistance and the constant hum of medical equipment blended into a dissonant symphony of suffering. It was a place where hope and despair coexisted, where life and death hung in the balance.

Chris leaned in close to Pete and whispered, "Go around to the other side of the nurses' station and ask for details about three people who came in, one with an injured leg. Tell them it's your cousin." He wanted to see how the nurse would react when searching for the information.

Foster and Chris waited on the opposite side of the station, watching as Pete approached one of the nurses. He engaged in a hushed conversation, and the nurse furrowed her brows in concentration. She turned and spoke to another nurse who pointed to a tray nearby. She thumbed through several clipboards, sorting through multiple patient records. After a moment, she muttered something to Pete.

Pete gestured for them to join him, and as they did, Pete reached over and snagged the clipboard the woman had been holding and handed it to Chris while he pointed out something to the nurse. Chris glanced at it. "Jackson Reid. Does that name ring a bell?" he asked Foster.

Foster nodded, recalling the name he'd heard.

"He's in zone three," Chris said decisively before placing the clipboard back over. One of the nurses saw him and scowled.

"Excuse me."

"Sorry. I thought..." he trailed off, walking away.

They wasted no time, heading toward zone three, navigating the crowded corridors, and passing the rooms filled with patients. Upon reaching the designated room number for Jackson, Chris pulled back the curtain, revealing an older woman lying in the bed. "Do you mind?" the woman said, clearly startled.

"Sorry. Wrong room," Chris muttered, closing the curtain hastily. "Shit. Where are they?" He glanced off to his right and noticed a hospital cleaner, emptying a trash can. "Hey pal, room six. The guy with the injured leg. Do you know where they've taken him?"

The cleaner shot back without any hesitation, "Yeah, they were off to get discharged. They treated the leg and sent him on his way about five minutes ago. We can't keep anyone here long because..."

Chris didn't even wait to hear the last part; he slapped Pete on the shoulder, and they all sprinted toward the main exit, their hearts pounding with urgency. Bursting outside, they elbowed their way through the crowd, just in time for Foster to catch a fleeting glimpse of Bryce getting into an old '70s Dodge Warlock.

He pointed desperately, but the van roared to life and sped away, disappearing into the chaotic cityscape.

Chris shoved his way through the crowd, causing a scene.

"Hey! That's my father you pushed." Someone cracked him on the chin before he could leave the crowd.

He went down hard, and Foster watched from the sidelines as multiple people swarmed and began kicking him. The crowd turned into a mosh pit as cops came around the barrier and surged into the midst of them, trying to get everyone to stop.

Pete did the intelligent thing and fired off a round into the air.

Several women screamed. The crowd dispersed in every direction. The cops had no idea who fired it. It all happened so fast. Foster reached into the midst of everyone and grabbed Chris' arm. He pulled him up and dragged him toward the truck, his face cut and bruised.

18

Tennessee

It was all a disaster in his mind.

Earthquakes, planes falling out of the sky, and the grid going down didn't change the situation one damn iota. Come to think of it, it only bolstered his reasons and offered more opportunities to get his son back without police involvement.

Of course, there was no denying he was having fun doing it.

Eight months he'd been waiting, wondering, searching, trying to find out where they'd taken Jordan. And now he knew, and if it were the last thing he did, he would get him back.

"I'm just saying, killing the cat was a little extreme," Bobby said.

"Bobby, do you know how many young men will be sent

off to fight this war who will die within days of their boots hitting the ground?"

He shrugged. "I don't know."

"Hundreds, thousands even. And do you think, besides the family and friends of those young ones, anyone in this country will weep?"

"But that's not the point—"

"Of course, it is. There are always casualties of war. Pain is exchanged for pain. In war, the playing field is leveled. Everything is off the table. Anything goes. What we are doing here is no different. We are fighting for our blood, for freedom, for the very thing the State took away from me — my son. So, one cat dies? Big fucking deal. Cows and fish are slaughtered daily for meat; you don't bat an eye driving through a fast-food joint. So, drop the self-righteous crap, it just makes you sound ignorant. The truth is every act of murder is villainized or justified based on a person's opinions and beliefs at that moment in time. In war, we call those murderers heroes. In everyday life, animals. I don't fuckin' care what you think. Okay? The only thing I give a shit about right now is Jordan."

He sank the remainder of a warm beer, watching from a home across the street while a couple lay dead near his feet. The homeowners had objected to his request to use their living room for a little low-key surveillance. It wouldn't have been long — twenty-four hours at the most. But no. Community was a slogan slapped on a town sign, an excuse given when people wanted others to give their time for nothing in return. It didn't exist, at least not how it was pitched. People helping people. Please, give me a break, he thought. Those days were long gone. At one time, Clyde wanted to believe what his mother had said. He tried to think that way, but life had taught him differently.

Nosy neighbors had gotten involved in his business.

The same ones had sent police to his door demanding entry.

A warrant was out for his arrest, and the State took away his kid.

His mother might have ended up with Jordan if it wasn't for her illicit behavior. As much as she liked to think she was the mother of the Smoky Mountains, the police saw her like any other, a common criminal. No, community only existed if he was willing to dot his i's and cross his t's, but that was so fucking tiring.

Clyde glanced down at the dead couple.

They looked so relaxed, so sweet. Better off.

When the couple had protested, and Clyde barged in, he tried to quiet the old man's yelling by placing a hand over his mouth and nose. He'd given him a chance. A chance to shut the hell up. But he wouldn't listen. Oh no, he thought he could keep yakking. It wasn't his fault that the old boy had a heart attack or that they had to put a round in his wife's head because her screams would have attracted the neighbors.

Besides, they were in their late seventies, aged to perfection by life's bullshit, and probably would have been first in line to die anyway if the situation they were in now continued beyond a few months.

"She's smart," Ricky said.

"Everyone thinks they are smart."

"No, Clyde. She didn't go waltzing into that house alone. She didn't show up here with Jordan and the others. Something tipped her off."

"I told you not to close the curtains."

"I had to make it darker. Had the plan fully worked out, she might have stumbled into that room and plopped herself into her bed, which would have been her end. Then you would have sung a different tune. Anyway, that ship has sailed. So, what now?"

Ricky released the curtain he'd held open, took out a pack of Marlboro Lights, and tapped one out. He handed one to Clyde and lit it for him. Clyde blew smoke toward the window. "Maybe you're right. Maybe that bitch is smart. But I'm smarter. We follow her. She couldn't have left them at the group home. That's gone. And that fellow isn't with her. I figure he's watching over them."

"So, I can't jump her before she returns?" Ricky asked. "She sure looks good."

"You'll get your chance. For now, we observe. Bobby, get me another beer."

"Why can't Ricky?"

Clyde screwed up his face. "Because I asked you."

Bobby grumbled, walking into the kitchen. He returned with three beers and tossed one to each of them. Clyde cracked his open and took a hard chug before wiping his lips with his sleeve.

"We're going to need more food," Bobby said.

"We've got it in the cupboards," Ricky added.

"No, I mean if this drags out."

"Would you two, shut up! We have the Smoky Mountains National Forest. That is more abundant than any grocery store," Clyde said, turning away from the window. Bobby was sitting in the recliner chair. "Go on. Get out of there. That's mine."

"But you weren't sitting here."

"Nor were you until we arrived."

Bobby grumbled as he got up. Clyde's cousins were simple folk. They all were. They came from a long line of coal miners, but instead of going into the same soul-destroying business, they'd opted to earn their living selling meth and pills throughout the hollers. It was either that or do the whole moonshine still. But that was old school —something his mother had always handled. No, drugs were where the money was to be made. Keeping people dumbed down, hooked on a line. It was a lot harder to get off meth than moonshine. Contrary to what some believed, the days of meth houses were long gone. The cartel had become the number one source for what was hitting the market, and he and his cousins had been at the forefront of its distribution.

"You got something to say, Bobby?" Clyde asked, eyeing him over his beer.

"I was sitting there. Why do you always take what I have?"

He chuckled, swigging his beer. "Take? You know what, Bobby, if it weren't for me, you would be down in those mines, coughing up black dust and working every hour under the sun. So, you're damn right, I will take what I want when I want, how I want. Got it?"

He reminded them of where they would be whenever they pushed their luck. It was true. Few had opportunities around these parts, and they were too damn dumb to seek them out elsewhere. Of course, that wasn't a generalization of Appalachian folk. Oh no, they would be hard-working, good people who would give the shirt off their backs. But these two a-holes. They were ignorant pieces of shit that tested his patience every day. Sometimes, he wondered whether it wasn't worth his while putting two in their heads and burying them in a shallow grave.

He grinned at Bobby. "Sit your ass down over there and put a sock in it."

Ricky inhaled deeply as he sat on the edge of a chair,

keeping an eye on the window but addressing Clyde. "If we get him back..."

"If?" Clyde asked.

"When," Ricky replied, correcting himself. "You want to head over to Pikeville?"

"And why would I do that?"

"You know, to stay low for a while. I'm sure she'll inform the police."

"That would imply she'd have a tongue to do so," he replied, grinning and taking a large knife from a sheath on his leg and holding it up, allowing the light of day outside to glint off the steel. "Like I told her, she made a big mistake, and I'm going to make sure she remembers it."

"You going to kill her, Clyde?" Bobby asked.

"No. Where would the fun be in that? Her colleague. Sure. But her. No, I'm going to introduce her to a few of the old Appalachian ways," he replied, referring to his knife. He sat there thinking about a story his grandfather had told him about a man who had crossed him in a bar. "I ever tell you about Martin Winslow?"

"Everyone knows about him. It's one of the sad tales of the mountains," Ricky replied. "He entered the woods and got lost. A bear mauled him."

Clyde stared at his knife, seeing his reflection on it as he puffed away on a cigarette. "Yes and no. That was a version they would have you believe. Hell, the bear population has been blamed for all manner of things. The truth is Elroy Parker was responsible."

"Your grandfather?"

Clyde nodded. "Back when I was twelve and being beaten on by some jackass in the neighborhood. I came home one day with a busted-up lip and a black eye. I got into trouble with my mother for fighting. A few days later, Elroy got wind of it. He took me out into the woods to go camping. A man-to-man. You know, what with my father being locked up. He thought I'd lost my way." He took a swig of his beer, staring into the blade, reliving that time in his mind. "Anyway, he takes me out to Grotto Falls. We pitch a tent. We fish a little. He never caught anything. But it didn't matter. He then has me follow him past the waterfall to a spot just above it, a stone area. That's where he killed him."

Bobby spat out his beer. "Elroy told you that?"

Clyde nodded. "He said this man Winslow made him look a fool in front of a woman he liked. You know — in town at one of the bars. Became the laughingstock of the town. He said he would have let it slide if the guy swung by and apologized, but it was clear he wouldn't get that apology. So, he jumped him."

Ricky leaned forward. "No way."

"Yes, way. As he got into his vehicle after one too many, my grandfather dragged him to his truck, knocked his ass out, and drove him to the Great Smoky Mountains. He took him to the falls, stripped him of his clothes, and then splashed water in his face to wake him up. He said he gave him a fair chance."

"Naked in the woods. Doesn't sound fair to me," Bobby muttered.

"He set this knife down. This is the exact one. Right in front of him. About ten feet. Elroy stepped back ten feet. The distance was equal. He told him he'd have a fighting chance if he could reach that knife before him."

"What happened?"

"Winslow laughed. Figured it was one big prank. You know — what with him drinking and all. He called out the names of his friends, expecting them to emerge from the forest. When it was still silent, he realized what was about to happen."

Clyde took another heavy drag on his cigarette, allowing the smoke to slowly slide out the corner of his mouth up into his eye. He squinted, turning the knife in his hand.

"Well? What happened?" Bobby asked, eager to know.

"Winslow went for it. My grandfather stood there and did nothing. Winslow snatched it up and came at him. Elroy kicked him in the nuts. He was naked, right?" Clyde grinned. "The nuts were the most direct target. Now, had Winslow been smart and made a dash for it, he might have had a fighting chance. So yeah. It was fair. Anyway, Winslow buckles without even getting one chance to stick my grandfather. Elroy pried that knife out of his grasp while Winslow was writhing on the ground in pain, and he silenced him." Clyde got up from his seat, went over to Bobby, and grabbed hold of his face. "Stick out your tongue."

"What?"

Ricky intervened. "Clyde. Come on, man."

"Stick out your tongue!" he shouted, squeezing his face until Bobby did it.

Clyde brought the knife down on his tongue, letting the edge touch the skin. "Elroy took his tongue that night, then gouged his eyes out," he said, taking the tip to Bobby's eye socket before he gently slapped Bobby on the side of the face and shoved him away, chuckling. "My grandfather left him there to find his way back. So, yeah, the park rangers were right, a bear got him. But not before my grandfather did."

Bobby stared back, fear in his eyes.

It was the small things Clyde did that kept people on their

toes. His unpredictability to fly off the handle at any minute made them wary.

"He kept the knife?" Ricky asked.

"Not exactly."

"So, the cops didn't know?"

"They had suspicions, but you can't argue with claw marks and bear bites, right? Anyway, he gave me this knife that day at the falls. No pig will ask a twelve-year-old boy about a hunting knife."

Clyde tossed his can on the floor and went and got another one, leaving them speechless. "So no, I'm not going to kill her; the wilderness will do that." He emerged from the kitchen, cracking open the can. "But I'm going to make sure she never messes with our kin again."

19

Oregon

"Thanks for the ride." Bryce slammed the door on the '70s Dodge Warlock and walked around to the other side. The event had crippled the police department's modern-day transportation, forcing them to take extreme measures. To continue offering even bare-bones service, someone had been smart enough to commandeer a few older models within the day from wrecker's yards and the general public.

"It was the least I could do," Officer Saunders said fist-bumping him through the window. "Oorah! Stay safe out there, brother. No telling what the future holds."

It was at that moment that Bryce felt a deep ache. He felt like a sham not telling him that he'd received a dishonorable discharge. Serving in the Marines had always been his dream since he was a young child. The camaraderie he found was next to none. He'd never envisioned his life playing out this way. He only wished it could have ended differently.

Bryce turned to Jackson as the Dodge Warlock rolled away, its tires crunching over gravel.

No two gunshot wounds were alike. Distance when fired, location of entry, the type and extent of the wound, medical history, meds, and condition at the time all factored into how soon a patient could be released.

With the hospital bursting at the seams, they didn't have the luxury of keeping a person in bed for days. It was a matter of assessment, treatment, and then release.

It certainly wasn't ideal, but they had no choice — beds needed to be freed up.

Jackson had been fortunate that no internal organs, major muscle groups, or appendage had been blown away, and no bone had been broken. It looked worse than it was. He'd bled badly, but the gunshot wound was treated almost like a deep laceration. After giving him blood and stitching the wound, they discharged him with antibiotics and painkillers and told him to take it easy for the next two to six weeks.

It was only then that Bryce told the others about the truck being sabotaged. Fortunately, Officer Saunders was returning to Portland PD to collect more officers for a shift change, and he offered them a ride.

"The perks of being in the military, aye," Colton said, patting him on the shoulder.

"Yeah. I guess," he replied, thinking of all the downsides he'd experienced. Had he ended up in a different platoon, the outcome would likely have been better.

"Well, come on in," Colton said, leading them into a two-story home off Newell Ridge Drive. The neighborhood backed up to Newell Creek Canyon Nature Park, a sprawling forest full of creeks and falls.

Jackson hobbled in on crutches. Zoe kept a firm grip on him.

"You own this place?" Jackson asked.

"Own? No. We rent. After we went our separate ways, Skylar and Dominick thought it would be good if we got a place. Something in a good, quiet neighborhood."

"Must have cost a lot."

"We've made good money."

"Illegally," Zoe added.

"Albeit illegally, but nowadays, is anyone doing anything above board? Car dealers, dentists, vets, realtors, you name it, there are tons of people ripping people off, and no one bats an eye."

"That's slightly different from outright stealing cars or parts," Zoe said.

"Maybe," he replied, closing the door behind them.

The home was modest, a typical suburban two-story on a winding street full of cookie-cutter homes made for families.

"So, you're sharing with your friends?" Bryce asked, entering the living room. It reminded him of his college days — a frat house where the party rarely stopped. The coffee table was covered in bottles of alcohol, bongs, and all manner of weed. Colton darted in, seemingly embarrassed, and began scooping up items and stuffing them behind the couch.

"Excuse the mess. We rarely get guests."

"About that. Are you sure your friends will be okay with this?" Jackson asked.

"Well, you can't exactly return to the other place, right?" Colton asked, looking at Bryce.

Bryce exhaled hard. "Not without putting them at risk."

"So, it's settled. You stay here. Until your leg is healed, and you're ready to journey back to Tennessee."

Jackson hobbled over to the couch and plunked himself down, groaning as Zoe lifted his leg and laid it out. "I'm fine, honey. I just need to rest. Pain meds are helping, but it will be a while before I'm ready to do much more than rest."

"You good?" Bryce asked.

Jackson nodded. Bryce could tell there was some animosity there. He couldn't exactly fault him for it, but then again, he didn't expect to be much more than a passenger for a short trip back to Oregon.

Colton went into the kitchen, and Bryce followed him in. Colton turned on the faucet, and barring what was left in the pipe, nothing more came out. "Ugh. That's not good."

"Colton."

"Yeah?"

"Are you sure about this? I mean, after what happened back at the wrecker's. I don't understand why you would go out on a limb for us."

"It wasn't you who hit me in the head, right?"

"No."

"And you all didn't know the situation between us and Rusty, correct?"

Bryce nodded.

"Then there you go. I appreciated you taking me to the hospital to get checked out and from the looks of Jackson, he's in no state to travel even if you could get another vehicle from Rusty."

"Well, look. We'll be sure to pull our weight in the meantime."

Colton laughed. "Jackson can barely pull his leg off the ground."

"You know what I mean."

Colton nodded, smiling.

"How did you pull this off, anyway? This place, I mean?"

"Dominick. Not sure exactly. I wasn't there when he signed the contract."

"And so, you just pay a portion of the rent?"

"You got it," he replied, stepping out the back to an enclosed yard and taking out his smokes. He stuck one between his lips and lit it.

"They won't have any problem with us being here, will they?"

"I pay rent. This is a four-bedroom house. More than enough room."

"I thought you didn't want to come back."

"I didn't say I didn't want to. I just..." he trailed off. "Wasn't in a rush to do so."

Bryce stepped outside and took in the privacy. The house was one of the few that backed onto the forest. "So, no family?"

"None that wanted me around. You?"

"They wanted me around and enjoyed using me as a punching bag. But that was a long time ago."

"Where are they now?"

"Tennessee. I ended up in the foster system, then in a group home before I came of age, went to college, then joined the military."

"I thought of joining," he said. "But I never was one for taking orders." He grinned, blowing out smoke. The front door opened, and Colton looked over his shoulder.

"What the... who the hell are you and—?"

"Dominick," Colton said, entering the house and raising a hand. "They're with me." A guy stood in the entranceway; his long hair pulled back tightly. There was a tattoo of a scorpion on the side of his neck. In his shadow behind him was a young woman with colorful hair, streaks of blue and pink peeking out from under a hoodie.

"Is that so."

Colton gestured toward them. "They're friends of mine."

"Friends? Really, Colton? Because they sure as hell look like the same people that shot at us and knocked you unconscious."

"That was Rusty, and you know it."

"Well, they were with him," he replied, eyeing them suspiciously. Bryce entered the house, getting the attention of both of them. Dominick pointed at him. "And him. Oh, hell no. You need to go and now."

"They're staying!"

"Like hell they are," he said, opening the front door again and gesturing for them to leave. Colton stepped forward and closed it.

"I pay rent."

"For one person."

"It's just for a short while."

Dominick stared at him, grabbed him by the arm, and led him out the rear door. Bryce observed the girl walk past him, narrowing her eyes but saying nothing. She joined them and closed the door so they could have some privacy. He could see Dominick getting all theatrical through the glass, raising his voice. It was clear they didn't want them to stay, even if it was for a few hours.

Bryce glanced over at Jackson. "We should leave," Jackson said.

"And go where?"

"That's not their problem."

"No, but it is mine."

"It's not yours either."

"If it weren't for me, you wouldn't be lying here."

"You know that's not true," Jackson muttered.

"Anyway, what kind of friend would I be to Natalie if I let you and her daughter walk out of here?" He scoffed. "Walk," he said again before chuckling. "You can't even do that."

"I can move."

"More like hobble," Zoe said, touching her father's shoulder.

Before Bryce could even consider other options, Dominick charged back into the house; he glared at Bryce before heading out the front door with Skylar directly behind him. She slammed the door hard. Bryce looked to the rear to see Colton step back inside, waving it off. "Ah, it's fine," he said. "It will just take a day or two for them to get used to it. Take a seat. Relax."

"I wish I could," Bryce replied. "Look, I really need to swing by my brother's and bury him. And I figure Rusty might have another vehicle."

"Yeah, best of luck with that. That cheap ass will expect you to pay for the other one."

Bryce frowned. "But I didn't ruin it; it was a piece of shit."

Colton shrugged. "Doesn't matter. That's Rusty for you. All he cares about is the bottom line. The mighty dollar." He paused. "Listen, I'll go with you."

"Nah, probably best you stay, what with the other two liable to show up again. Which reminds me." Bryce hurried to the front door just in time to see an old Jeep pulling away with the two of them in it. He called out to them, but they didn't stop. Skylar, though, did hear him as she glanced his way. A smirk danced on her face. "Shit. We could have gotten a ride."

"Not from Dominick. He's made it clear that he wants nothing to do with you. But he said you can stay for now."

"Really?"

Colton ran a finger across his chest and stomach, creating the cross symbol. "God's truth."

"Are you sure?" Bryce asked, noticing Colton's demeanor change.

"Positive."

"You going somewhere?" Zoe asked, approaching them at the door.

"I have to get some supplies, bury my brother, obtain a ride back to Tennessee. Not essentially in that order."

She raised her eyebrows. "Back to Tennessee?"

"There's nothing here for me anymore. Besides, it's the least I can do after everything. There's no way Jackson is going to be up to driving. And you said you don't drive yet."

"I didn't get around to it. I may never get around to it by the looks of it," Zoe said.

"I just need my leg to heal," Jackson said, overhearing him.

"And you will. A few days should help, and then we can pile you into a vehicle and head east. Besides, it's best to be close to that hospital if anything goes wrong in the next few days."

"You expect things to go wrong?" Zoe asked.

He never answered that.

Colton patted Bryce on the chest. "Look, I really need to go and get some food. There's a grocery outlet nearby. Dominick told me that if you're staying, I'm responsible for ensuring you don't eat into our supplies, which I might add..." he trailed off. "Isn't much. We tend to eat out," he replied, glancing at Zoe. "Cooking is not exactly our thing."

Zoe stepped forward. "I'll go with you."

Bryce lifted a hand. "No, stay with your father."

"I don't need babysitting," Jackson replied.

Zoe was persistent. "No. I want to get some air anyway."

Bryce looked at her and then Jackson. "Hey, it's not my decision."

Jackson frowned.

Colton was quick to interject. "I'll make sure she's safe."

Zoe looked embarrassed. "I'm twenty-one years of age. I think I'll be good."

There was a debate between her and Jackson before he reluctantly agreed. "Look, there's some beer in the pantry. Warm, but it's better than nothing. Also, some bottles of water. If you want the harder stuff..." Colton pointed to a cabinet.

"Thanks."

"We won't be long," Zoe said.

Zoe and Colton headed out on foot while he remained at the window, observing them until they vanished around a bend. Bryce went over to the cabinet and opened it to find bottles and bottles of bourbon. He took one out and glanced at it. "You want one?" he asked.

"Is a pig pink?" Jackson replied.

Bryce grinned as he took out two glasses and filled them. He handed one to Jackson and took a seat nearby. "Oh, that's a nice burn," Jackson remarked.

"Sure is. Hits the spot." Bryce studied him. "I imagine she must be worried out of her mind," he said.

"Natalie?"

Bryce nodded. "She's a mother. All mothers worry."

Jackson nodded, looking at him thoughtfully. "You know, you never said how you came to know Natalie."

"We grew up together."

"And?" His brow shot up.

"That's it. We grew up together," he repeated.

"I got that part. I meant, how did you connect? She didn't have the best upbringing, at least from what she told me, and she's from Gatlinburg, and you're from Bryson."

He nodded. "What did she tell you?"

"Bryce," Jackson said, looking down into his glass. "Be straight with me. When was the last time you spoke to my wife?"

"A day ago."

"I meant before that?"

Bryce could tell that Jackson was uncomfortable. "Roughly twenty years ago."

"So, you had her number all that time?"

"No."

"So why did you call her out of the blue? We all have people we grew up with, but calling them so many years later. A little odd, don't you think?"

Bryce regarded him through narrowed eyes. "We have a connection." He took a breath. "What did Natalie tell you about her upbringing? I mean, family and so on?"

"That they no longer talk."

Bryce nodded. "So, how did you meet her?"

"Through a friend. She was single at the time. I'd just come out of a bad relationship. We went out together a few times and hit it off."

"And you never met her parents?"

"No."

"She never showed you any photos of them?"

"Never." When he didn't reply fast enough, Jackson probed deeper. "Bryce. Am I missing something here?"

"Jackson. Natalie and I grew up together in a group home."

"She was in a group home?" His eyes widened; it was clear he had no idea.

20

Portland

Chris cursed loudly as he nursed a bloody nose while Foster drove, returning to deliver the bad news to Talis. The engine's roar sounded louder than usual, with only a few vehicles on the road.

"There was nothing you could do. It is what it is. Besides, it's probably better this way," Foster said, gripping the wheel tightly.

Chris turned toward him, stunned. "And how do you figure that?"

"Maybe now we can focus on surviving this event."

"Surviving? Is that all you can think about?" Chris said, lowering a bloody tissue. He was furious that he'd come so close, yet Bryce slipped through his fingers. All the young ones were like that. Overly zealous. They berated themselves or others if they dropped the ball instead of taking it in their stride. It was all ego — a chasing after that which could never be satisfied. "We came this close," he said, holding up a bloody thumb and finger. His face was a mess after being stomped multiple times by the crowd.

"It wasn't meant to be," Foster replied.

"The hell it was. We are not done."

"Have you considered that maybe it's done with you?"

"What the fuck is that supposed to mean?"

"You're fighting what isn't meant to be. Stop. We came. We tried. It didn't work out. Now I get it. You want Talis to feel some sense of satisfaction by bringing him that man who killed his brother and the others, but I'm telling you, it won't bring closure."

"And you would know?"

Foster shot him a sideways glance while white-knuckling it back on the winding road full of stalled vehicles. "Kid, I attended rallies while you were still shitting in diapers."

"First, don't call me kid, old man. Second, the Proud Boys haven't been around that long."

"No. No, they haven't. But other movements have and others will long after the Proud Boys become a thing of the past."

"Oh, now the truth comes out," he said, looking at him. "I knew you didn't want to be one."

"After what's happened, is that so bad?"

"It's a pussy move. Anyway, that won't happen."

"Oh, wake up, Chris, it's already happened with Ryland's death and the others. Do you think any of those guys thought they would be dead by now? Please. It's time to realize that ship has sailed."

Chris scoffed. "Maybe for you."

Foster narrowed his gaze "Let me tell you something: the

enemy isn't antifa or any of the groups out there that you disagree with. That's a fool's game. And it's one I bought into for far too long. No. The war is within you. The fight begins and eventually ends there."

"Now you are making no sense."

Even Pete looked over, a little baffled.

"I've lost people too. Good friends. Close brothers." Foster paused, recalling those early days when he and Ryland had associated with some of the worst of society. Groups that, too, thought they could change the world. They never did. "Killing those who kill or killing those who don't believe the same doesn't change anything. It just keeps perpetuating the same bullshit cycle of insanity. Don't you get that?"

Chris chuckled. "Oh, I get it, old man. And like Talis said, I think you've lost your balls in your old age," Chris replied, blowing his nose into another tissue and spraying it red.

"Then you'll learn the hard way. We all do."

As they rounded a bend, another vehicle was coming in the other direction. It shot by, and Chris looked over his shoulder. "Whoa! Stop. Turn around!"

"Why?"

He thumbed over his shoulder. "That was the cop."

"How would you know? It shot by too fast."

"How many other Dodge Warlocks are on the road right now? Now turn around." Foster ignored him for a moment. Chris had to bring out his gun before he agreed. It wasn't that he didn't believe him. He did. He'd hoped the two hadn't registered it as the vehicle shot by quickly.

Foster did a U-turn and floored it back the other way.

Once they saw the Dodge, Chris told him to ease off the gas. They kept their distance as the truck veered into the hospital, and several officers piled out and made their way over to the barriers.

"What now, smart ass?" Foster said, allowing the truck to idle at the top of the hill. Chris leaned forward, tapping the gun against his leg. Foster wasn't scared of the kid. He certainly wouldn't have put it past him to shoot if push came to shove, but he had a wife and child at home he had to think about now.

"He's getting back in," Pete said, a grin forming.

"Perfect. Follow him."

"You know he's going to see us in his rearview mirror."

"Exactly. I want you to pull up beside him. Get him to pull over."

Foster laughed. "Oh yeah, the nation has gone to shit, and you expect a cop to pull over?" Chris stared back at him. Foster could tell he was chewing it over. Logically, it made no sense. The cops were already on their back foot with how the situation had changed.

"Just follow him."

Foster sighed, shaking his head. He waited until the officer drove out of the hospital parking lot before he pulled in behind him. They observed him glancing in his rearview mirror at them as the officer pulled onto Route 213 and headed south.

"What are you hoping to achieve?" Foster asked impatiently.

"Close the gap."

"I'm not bumping him off the road."

"I never said we would. Pull beside him. Pete, bring the window down."

"Are you going to shoot him?"

"Foster. Calm yourself. I know you've lost the plot, but some of us know what we're doing. Now give it some gas!"

The engine growled, and the truck roared forward. On a lonely stretch past Newell Creek, Foster accelerated hard. As they got closer, Pete brought the window down. Chris motioned to the officer to bring his window down. The officer looked ahead, then at them, and did so. "Pull over!" Chris hollered over the wind.

"Why?"

Chris motioned with a thumb behind him. He purposely replied in a quieter voice, saying, "It's back there."

The officer shrugged, but Chris persisted.

Now, whether it was because the cop was wet behind the ears, convinced that nothing bad would happen, or he still thought that wearing a uniform meant something, he veered off to the edge of the road.

"See," Chris muttered with a smile. They pulled in behind him, and Chris hopped out, stuffing his handgun into the back of his jeans. The officer got out but had the good sense to keep his hand on his weapon. He lifted the other ahead of him as Chris made his way over.

"That's far enough. What do you need?"

"It's not what we need. We heard the police needed vehicles. We wanted to help. Give you ours. If you need it," Chris said, laying it on thick that he gave a shit.

"What happened to your face?"

"Back at the hospital. It got a little wild. I was caught in the middle."

"You should get that looked at," the officer said, his gaze bouncing between them. "As for the vehicle. That's much appreciated. As you can imagine, we are hamstrung regarding transportation. There are only so many older working vehicles. If you want to return to the hospital, you can approach any officer there. They'll take your details so it can be returned later."

"Right. Okay," Chris said. He thumbed behind him. "We'll just get going then."

As he went to turn, he stopped and looked back at the officer. "Oh, uh, one last thing. You gave a group of people a ride earlier from the hospital. You wouldn't know where you dropped them off?"

"Why do you want to know that?" the officer replied, taking a forward step.

Foster had to give Chris credit; he replied calmly and smoothly as if he was used to pulling the wool over people's eyes. "Back at the hospital. They left a bag. I told the nurse we'd give it to them. We saw you leave with them. Well..."

"So that's why you were following."

"Yeah. Hey, sorry to spook you. I'll get the bag for you," he said. "You can give it to them."

The officer nodded. "Sure. That's appreciated."

Chris turned back to the truck, and Foster could already tell where this was heading. The officer, still cautious, remained where he was, hand still hovering over his sidearm. Chris came to the passenger side and scooped up a small backpack that belonged to the previous owner. It still had blood from where Chris had shot the gun, and the owner had slumped over the passenger side.

"Chris."

Chris didn't say a word. He removed his firearm from the back of his jeans in one smooth motion. His hand was hidden from view of the officer by the open door. He placed the gun behind the bag and met Foster's gaze for but a second. There was no smile. No words were spoken. But as he returned to the officer, he returned to his routine. "It's crazy out on the roads. We were nearly jacked for our vehicle. I figure the truck is safer with the police department than us," he said. "Anyway, tell the owner that we didn't take anything. Everything is there," he said as he got closer and extended his arm to hand off the bag. Naturally, the officer reached for it. Even though he didn't use the hand hovering over his firearm, there was little he could have done to prevent what came next.

Crack.

Chris fired through the bag, striking the officer in the knee.

The officer collapsed, and Chris was on him before he could pull his sidearm. He drove a hard foot down on the officer's wrist. Pete rushed in and disarmed the officer.

Chris dropped to a crouch. "Fucking pig. Did you honestly think I was here to help?" He chuckled, glancing back at Foster. "See, Foster. This is why the Proud Boys will continue long after you are gone. We get shit done!" He turned back to the officer. "Where are they?"

"Who?"

That was the worst thing to say. Chris pistol-whipped the officer across the face. "Don't fuck with me. The three men and the young woman. Where did you drop them off?"

"Go fuck yourself."

Chris laughed before beating him multiple times with the gun barrel on the face.

"Let's try that again, shall we? Where are they?"

The officer spat blood and it trickled down the side of his face.

"Chris. Enough."

Chris turned the gun on Foster. "Back the fuck up. We are

in this mess because of you. People are dead because of you."
He glared before turning back to the officer. Chris cracked his
head again from side to side. "Again. Where are they?" he
said slowly, each word through gritted teeth.

The officer, struggling to breathe with all the blood
coming out of his mouth, motioned for Chris to come closer
so he could tell him.

Chris leaned over. "What?"

The officer spat in his face and offered back a toothy grin,
his teeth dripping red.

Foster saw his ghost long before the bullet left the
chamber of Chris' gun.

He stuck it under the officer's chin, screaming an
obscenity in his face before squeezing the trigger. The
gunshot echoed loudly.

"Let's go. Chris. Let's go!" Pete shouted, looking nervously
around him.

Chris got up and hurried back to the truck; he got in and
looked at Foster.

"Good one," Foster said sarcastically. "Now, who fucked
up?" Foster hit the gas, and the truck squealed away.

21

Tennessee

Disturbed was an understatement. After changing out of her smoke-drenched clothes, she spent half an hour peering out the window for any sign of Clyde. Now, she wished she'd taken Bryce up on the offer of taking the gun with her.

It wasn't using a gun that bothered her, but the use of one on her back in her youth that had instilled fear. As Natalie looked out the window, her thoughts drifted. A child of domestic abuse, she'd been caught in an argument more than once. Whereas other parents might have tossed around words, her stepfather habitually threw her mother around.

Years of it had beaten down her spirit, and one day she snapped.

Her mother had snatched up one of her stepfather's rifles. Multiple rounds were fired. However, due to her mother's lack of experience, he was a little quicker than her and managed to duck out of the room and grab one of his handguns. Instead of firing at her, he grabbed Natalie and used her like a shield, a pawn in his game, to get her to drop the rifle. She remembered the sound of the gun cocking beside her ear, his firm grip on the back of her collar, and the yelling match that ensued.

She recalled urine trickling down her twelve-year-old leg.

And then the gunshot rang out when her mother finally laid down the rifle.

Her stepfather shot her mother and then left the house, leaving Natalie frozen by fear. A neighbor had been the one to call the police. Ten minutes later, they barged into the place to find her kneeling in her mother's blood, holding her hand.

Her stepfather was later caught one state over and sentenced to life, leaving her to be funneled into a group home.

That kind of event left a significant imprint on a kid's mind.

She spent years reliving it, waking up in the middle of the night with cold sweats and having to talk about it with a therapist. That's why she understood the youth in the group home better than even the most well-trained therapist. Living through trauma taught a person something that couldn't be gained in a class. It was a hands-on, boots-on-the-ground, real-life-in-the-trenches experience, and the kids picked up on it. They knew when a staff member was just rattling off what they'd been taught.

Maybe that's what scared her and pissed her off about Clyde.

He embodied her stepfather, a man given to alcohol-fueled outbursts and dangerous behavior. She didn't want to see Jordan suffer through that.

"Are you expecting Jackson to roll down the street?" Leo asked from the doorway.

"No. Just lost in the past."

"Well, I cleared out the room of all those snakes, and Oscar helped me search the rest of the house. It's all good."

"Thank you, Leo."

"Be honest with me, Natalie. Who do you think did that?"

"I don't know," she said. The truth was she didn't. It would have been easy to jump to conclusions, to point the finger at Clyde. He was the most obvious suspect, but over the past year, she'd had multiple threats from family members who found out their kids were in the group home. A disgruntled staff member had posted the kids' names online with the address of the group home. She had been days away from hiring a full-time security guard when the event happened. So, many people came to mind when she saw the home burnt to the ground and snakes in her bed. Like the movie *The Purge,* a situation like this presented an opportunity unlike any time in history. Now, anyone with a chip on their shoulder could get away with murder.

"Anything else I can help you with?"

"I think she wants her privacy," Oscar said, walking into the room and glancing around. "You know, I always thought this place was like mine. I mean, it looks the same on the outside, but you have a lot more room in the rear." He paused for a second. "Okay, that came out wrong."

Natalie chuckled as Leo slapped Oscar on the arm. "Bonehead," Leo said.

"Ah, it's fine. Looks can be deceiving."

"So, you staying here tonight?" Leo asked.

"No. I'm staying elsewhere. The group home was burned down."

"Burned down. Ah, in the fires."

"Um. Not exactly."

Leo frowned.

She waved him off. Getting into it meant another half an hour of explaining, and she'd already spent long enough trying to sidestep the conversation around the snakes.

"So, where are you staying?"

"With a colleague. He's been kind enough to open up his house for the teens, and without any staff or a place to house them, it's down to me to watch out for their best interests."

Oscar took out his pipe.

"Don't light that in here," Leo said.

"I wasn't going to."

"Go ahead. I hardly think a little smoke will matter after all the smoke drifting across the town. The whole area smells like a bonfire." She walked past them and made her way downstairs. Natalie collected one of Jackson's long duffel bags and began loading it with as many cans of food as she could.

"So, where is this colleague's home?" Oscar asked.

"Over on Ellis Ogle Road."

"I know that place. My daughter used to live just around the corner from there," Leo said. "Nice. Very modern. Though I expect some of those houses will be the first ones they target."

"They?"

"The looters, the good-for-nothings, those who are seeing opportunity right now when others are seeing disaster." He leaned against the wall, watching her load the bag. "The mistake folks will make is thinking that this will all change in a week. It's not. Oh, no, this will be dragged out for months, maybe even years."

"That long?"

"Uh-huh," he said.

"Stop scaring the woman," Oscar said.

"I'm not. I'm preparing her. What happened upstairs is a wake-up call. That's just the tip of the iceberg. We are in the early days. If ever there was a time to get ready, it's now if you haven't already done so."

"Yeah? And how would you have prepared for this, smart ass?" Oscar said.

"How? By doing the very thing that people haven't done. Get ahead of the curve. Five years ago, I started squirreling away a few extra cans when I was grocery shopping, extra bags of rice, pasta, you name it. Add to that, I got myself a dual generator, one that takes both propane and gas. I ordered multiple portable power stations that can work off solar. I keep them inside the house in the basement. No one knows I have them."

"We do now," Oscar said grinning. Natalie chuckled.

"As I was saying," Leo said, scowling. "On top of that, I bought plenty of ammo, because you can be damn sure you'll need it to keep out assholes like whoever did this. Um, what else," he said, wandering around the kitchen.

Natalie observed him with interest. Neither she nor Jackson had done any of that. They were like the large majority of Americans living paycheck to paycheck. Scraping by on a prayer and a dream.

"Oh, medical supplies and water," he added, tapping they air with a finger.

"Water?"

"Yeah, bottled. Though that won't last, so I bought rain-water storage tanks."

"I thought you said they were for your yard?"

"They are. They have dual usage. Instead of running out now to dig around the grocery stores with what little cash I have on me, which is another thing you'll need, I'll get to that in a moment, I can just go out the back and turn on the tap, and boom, I've got fresh rainwater to stay clean and drink. How much have you got?"

Oscar shrugged. "Well, I don't. I didn't want those big ugly containers in my yard."

"Aha, see, that's the thing. Today's America is all about looks and not what will keep them alive. Anyway, where was I?"

"Cash," Natalie muttered.

"That's right. With the power out. No one is going to be taking debit or credit."

"I don't expect they'll be taking cash either," Oscar said. "So, you are in the same boat as us."

"Au contraire, mon ami," Leo said with a grin. "People right now think this event will blow over and all will be cleared up in a week, two at the most. Why? First, most of them don't have a way to find out. So, they are going to rely on the likes of our mayor, and he isn't going to be forthright. He will think of number one if he shows up at all. So, in the meantime, they are going to treat this like a regular power outage. Do you remember the last one we had?"

"Yep."

"You could still buy stuff as long as you had... cash."

"All right, but how much cash?"

"Well, that's the thing. Most say keep a hundred, three hundred at the most on hand." He laughed. "That is a pipe dream. The first thing these scallywags will do when they realize no one can buy anything on debit or credit is jack up the prices. That can of beans you got there," he said to Natalie. "How much that cost you?"

"Um. A dollar sixty, maybe less."

"Add another five, maybe even ten, hell, even twenty dollars on top."

Oscar laughed, slapping Leo on the back as he spotted a bottle of bourbon on the counter. "Do you mind, Natalie?"

"Go ahead," she said.

Leo continued. "What, you think I'm joking?"

"Leo. You always think the sky is falling. If I listened to you last year, I would be in a bunker right now playing tiddly-winks." He roared with laughter.

"Okay. Okay. Yuk it up, but let's see who's laughing in a few days."

"What's happening in a few days?"

"Chaos. Total and utter chaos. The average American only has enough food for a family for three days. Three days. You do the math. Once people get hungry, or should I say hangry, this town's atmosphere will become tense if it hasn't already. I expect a few boneheads have already got into fist fights. It doesn't take long for people to get freaked out. Take that event we had a few years back. What was everyone rushing out to buy?" He paused for effect, running his hand around the back of his ass. "Toilet paper. Can you imagine that? Out of all the things to hoard. Toilet paper. That's where the minds of the world are today — in the toilet. Yeah, we are not dealing with high-level thinkers here. Anyone with a lick of sense could have told you that as long as you had access to a river, you'd have a clean ass. But that's not America. Oh no, they are looking for creature comforts, the familiar, leaning on their regular habits. But the reality is that shit will get you killed faster than a New York minute. But not me," he said, sniffing the air and eyeing them both. "No, sir. I'm ahead of the game."

Oscar poured himself a glass and downed it, then looked at the bottle. "Damn that is awful."

"Jackson was given it as a gift a few years back. It's been sitting on the counter ever since."

"Ah, so he doesn't want it?" Oscar asked.

"No."

"Do you mind if I take it?"

"You said it was awful," she replied.

"Well, it's just if anything that Bear Grylls over there is spouting is true; beggars can't be choosers," he said, taking the bottle.

Natalie laughed. "You two are quite the pair."

"Don't be pairing me up with him," Leo mumbled.

She zipped up the bag. "You might have no choice. Anyway, guys, I would love to chat, but I've got to get moving."

"Right on," Oscar said. "I should get back before the old wifey starts accusing me of being too flirtatious with you." He laughed. He was old enough to be her father. "You should do the same," he said to Leo as they all piled out of the house, and Natalie turned to lock the door behind her. That's when she realized that something had changed. Before, she rarely needed to lock the doors. The town was small and friendly enough; she always had Leo and Oscar watching guard over the street like sentinels throughout the day.

"How did you get here?" Leo asked her.

"Cut through the woods."

"I'll walk you back."

"You don't have to do that."

"I want to, and I won't take no for an answer. Jackson isn't here. He'd want me to make sure you're safe."

She smiled and nodded. There was no point arguing with him; honestly, the whole snakes in the bed had unnerved her. "All right, I appreciate that."

"See you two later," Oscar said before strolling off.

Leo slung his rifle over his shoulder and glanced around before they ventured south. "You must have accumulated quite the stockpile if you've squirreled away items over the past five years," Natalie said.

"I have, however, some of the food I've had to rotate out because of the expiration dates. So, it's dwindled."

"I would have thought they were good to eat if they were sealed."

"Ah, even those canned goods can go bad. The expiration date has more to do with the taste and freshness. If push came to shove, I'd eat something past its expiration date as they figure it stays fresh for roughly a year to eighteen months, and then some can stay fresh as long as two to five years, but do you want to take that risk?"

She nodded. "I would if I'm hungry."

"By that point, if we are still in this mess, we'll be fishing, hunting, and growing our produce, not relying on canned goods."

"Talking of growing our own. Wendy Bowers was saying that they plan to do some vertical farming. I can't understand why they are talking about it so soon."

"I can," he said. She glanced at him. He looked back at her. "The Great Reset."

"The what?"

"You know, the global elite using whatever means necessary to dismantle capitalism and bring about social change. This whole shebang has probably been set up by the powers that be. You know, the top brass. Wendy and her cahoots probably already received the memo and were waiting for the pot to explode."

"You think they knew?"

"No, not everything. That's not how these A-holes work. Everything is kept on a need-to-know basis. Like a company that manufactures widgets but doesn't want people ripping them off. They outsource some of it to one guy, some of it to another. Everyone plays their part but never really can see the whole picture. You see, Natalie, no one is going to waltz into a new world order under normal conditions. Oh no, that requires something drastic to happen, multiple things to happen, actually. However, they did a great job this time. The bigger the shakeup, the easier it is. Kill a large chunk of society, and it gets easier."

"That sounds a lot like conspiracy. You don't believe that, do you?"

"What you just said is precisely the response they want. Disbelief leads to ridicule and inaction until they have a situation like this. Then it's too late. You watch. FEMA will roll into cities, spread out their plan to help, and they will. Oh, it will look all above board at first, like a fighter in a ring figuring out his opponent before he strikes the blow that ends him. It will be natural. But then you watch as they pull on the strings. And the sad part is people will go along with it. Why? Not because they are stupid but because they are already conditioned. It's the frog in the boiling pot syndrome. A frog will jump out to save himself if he thinks he will die, but place him in and slowly increase the temperature, and heck, he's going to believe it's a damn Jacuzzi. Have you ever slipped into an overly hot bath and then noticed how relaxed you have become to the point you can barely get out? It's the same thing. And it begins now with people like Wendy Bowers and her circle of clowns."

"She says there's a public town hall meeting tonight."

"More like a circle jerk."

"Leo. She's a good friend of mine."

"Like the old saying, keep your friends close and enemies closer. You going?"

"Yeah. You?"

"I won't be there."

"It's to update people on the situation. You really should go."

Leo laughed. "What are they going to tell us that we don't already know? You're in the dark? No shit, Einstein. No delivery trucks are coming. You think? Please. They are going to lay the groundwork for what comes next. FEMA, rules, enslavement. If I wanted an enema, I'd bend over and do it myself."

Natalie chuckled. "You sure do worry me at times, Leo."

"You'll worry soon enough when they bring in a one-world government. By that time, it will be too late to buy lube. No, not me. Not on my watch. I'm keeping my sphincter nice and tight."

They trudged on through the forest, the undergrowth crunching below their boots. Natalie pondered what he'd said while eyeing the shadows, wondering if those who had infiltrated her home were out there, watching, waiting to strike.

22

Portland

The parking lot at the Grocery Outlet looked like a mosh pit at a concert. People were shoving, fighting, and chasing after others. Shouts, screams, and the clatter of metal carts dominated. It was utter madness. Zoe had witnessed a few crazies at her local Walmart on Black Friday, but this didn't even compare. Looters had targeted the store at the corner of Molalla Avenue and Holmes Lane.

There was no order, line-up, or even police to step in. People clawed their way in and out through the main doors. Carts were scattered around the lot, torn bags and boxes the only sign of a battle. Those who had successfully managed to get in and out with goods didn't make it far. The craftiest individuals hung back like lions, just waiting to attack. It was easier that way — no scavenging shelves. No losing out. They got the pick of the crop.

"Holy shit," Zoe said as a man took a tire iron to someone's skull and then took off with one bag of groceries. The victim lay unconscious, bleeding out. But there was no mercy. People trampled over others as if they didn't exist. She saw others wounded and struggling to get up through the slew of legs, overwhelmed by the mob mentality.

"Stay close." Colton led the way, darting through an opening in the crowd.

"That's mine!" a woman yelled, getting into a tug-of-war with another woman. Bags of food burst, and produce scattered, apples and oranges rolling away only to be scooped up by the observant and desperate. The two women went head-to-head, clawing at each other's hair and taking the war to the ground.

At one point, someone decided that going it on foot was too risky and opted to drive their old pickup truck through the masses. She heard the thump of the bodies as the truck plowed them down. They disappeared below its wheels until the truck smashed into the doorway. After the driver got out, he never made it far; two men grabbed him and dragged him back into the crowd, to face their anger.

"This way," Colton shouted, heading into a side entrance that someone had left open. They'd stuck a small rock under the door to hold it in place. Inside, the picture wasn't much better. Shoppers raced down the aisles, scooping everything and anything into baskets and carts like they'd been told they would get it free but only had minutes to grab items.

As disturbing as it was, it paled compared to the terrifying blood smear down one aisle. A man lay crumpled into a ball.

Dead? As she went to shake him, Colton pulled her away. "No. You can't help him."

"But... but..."

"Zoe. Focus! Here, take this," he said, grabbing a basket. "Concentrate on light items, pasta, rice, granola bars."

"I would if there was any," she said, going down the aisle and gawking at the bare shelves.

"Fuck," Colton said. "Forget it, come with me. They usually keep the boxes out back. Everyone will be focused on this part."

They charged to the back of the store, entering through the frozen area. As soon as they were in the rear, it was clear they weren't the only ones with the same idea. Zoe and Colton slowed.

"I said put it down!" a gruff-sounding man said, holding another spindly looking man by the collar.

"There's enough for all of us here."

"That wasn't a question. Listen to him," another man said, cocking a gun and placing it on the side of the thinner man's temple. The guy dropped two bags of pasta. Colton coughed, and all three of them looked over.

"We're just..." Colton said, pointing to another area out the back. They changed direction and ran down an aisle of goods stacked on pallets. Boxes were open. Many of the goods were on the floor. "Come on, fill these up."

Zoe swallowed hard, not taking her eyes off the area where they'd seen the other men.

Multiple gunshots rang out from inside the grocery store. A jolt of fear went through her. "Hurry," Colton added. They filled two baskets with rice, pasta, and several cans of beans and chili. Zoe scooped up a few feminine pads she found in another area, and Colton threw in a few bottles of liquor.

"Really?" she asked.

"How else am I supposed to handle this shit?"

She shook her head as they turned to leave. They were met by the sight of even more looters as they headed for the loading doors, hoping to avoid the men. These guys, on the other hand, were a little smarter. They weren't content to endure the madness of the aisles by filling a cart. No, they had their eyes set on the prize — pallets of food.

Multiple guys were using pallet jacks to cart it out.

One of them had laid down a handgun on a stack of boxes. Colton scooped it into his basket and buried it under some pasta. "Colton."

He didn't care. They pressed on only to be stopped a few feet from the exit.

"Whoa, whoa, where do you two think you're going?"

"Man, we didn't see anything. We're just leaving."

"I didn't ask what you saw. I asked where you think you're going with all that."

Colton looked at his basket. "You're taking entire pallets and worried about two baskets?"

"Put it back."

"Or what?"

Several men stopped what they were doing and turned their attention toward them. "Colton, maybe we should just..." Zoe said, lowering her basket to the floor.

"That's it, do what she did and get the fuck out of here."

Colton nodded. "Um. Okay. Sure. Or..." Zoe's heart sank as he said that. Instantly, he pulled out the handgun and began waving it around like a crackhead. "Huh. Not so fucking tough now, are you? Now, Zoe, pick that up, and let's go!"

They backed out, jumping down from the loading docks.

"That's it, bitches. You stay there with your mouths shut like good little boys." He chuckled before bursting away from the grocery store.

Zoe's heart hammered in her chest as she struggled to carry the basket. "Are you out of your mind?" she said.

"Oh, for sure," he replied, not missing a beat. "And I love it. Did you see the look on their faces when I pulled it out? The one guy glanced over to the boxes and then realized. The others will be berating him around about now."

"Unless they're coming after us," she said, glancing over her shoulder to see four men on foot pursuing them. Colton didn't miss a beat. He stopped running, dropped his basket, lifted the gun, and opened fire. The men scattered, but this time, they didn't cower away; they returned fire.

"Oh shit." There was no chance of escaping with the weight of the baskets so they dropped them. Fortunately, the men were only intent on getting the goods.

They ran until they couldn't run anymore, disappearing into a surrounding neighborhood. Once Zoe was sure the coast was clear, she stopped to catch her breath, leaning over and placing both hands on her knees. Colton was laughing.

"You know you are bat shit crazy."

"Oh, come on. Don't tell me you didn't find that a little fun."

"Fun? We nearly died. They shot at us."

"Yeah. Shit aim." He cracked up laughing, and she back-handed him on the arm. A part of her couldn't help but find something amusing about the situation.

"See. I knew it," he said, pointing at her.

"We lost everything."

"A few bags, cans, and some female diapers."

"They weren't diapers, moron."

He laughed.

"Anyway, I hope you know the way back."

"I have no idea where we are."

"Colton. Don't fuck with me."

"I'm not. You just kept running. I followed you."

She stared back at him. She flung her arms up in the air when he showed no sign of laughing. "Oh, that's great. Fucking great."

She glanced off, shaking her head, before looking at him.

A smirk formed.

"You do know where we are, don't you?" she said.

He nodded, unable to keep in his laughter.

"Son of a bitch!" She started to chuckle, too, while shaking her head.

"Come on. Forget it. Dominick will find something. Until then, we have enough food. He'll have to deal with the situation."

They trekked back through a suburban neighborhood, observing the many cracks in the ground, fissures from where the earthquake had torn it apart. "You know your friends could have turned on you because of us. Why did you risk it? It's not like Bryce had your best interest at heart when he was in the wrecker's yard."

"I don't know. It just felt like the right thing to do. Like what Bryce did after. Besides..." He looked at her. "Maybe I like the company."

The corner of her lip went up. "All right. Though you're still an ass."

He smiled.

They walked for a good ten minutes, taking in the devastation. Water from the rivers and creeks in the area had flooded much of the terrain, turning the ground into a soggy mess.

"So, your mother is back in Tennessee?" he asked.

"Yeah. Yours?"

"Couldn't tell you. Maybe she's in a crack house somewhere with a needle in her arm. Things didn't exactly work out well. I left home early."

"Why?"

"Not much choice. It was either that or starve. There was rarely food in the cupboards. If my mother were around, she would have been dead to the world with all the drugs in her system. I used to see people coming and going through our house like it belonged to them. A steady flow of strangers. I just decided I had enough and left."

"Your mother never asked the cops to look for you?"

He shrugged. "If she did, they never came looking."

"And Skylar and Dominick?"

"The only real family I've had, but the dynamics have changed over the years. You know, with money flooding in. When we were at Rusty's, the guy who owns the wrecker's yard, we were closer. Everything changed as soon as Dominick realized he could make money without Rusty."

"Will you be staying in Oregon?"

"I guess. Nowhere else to go."

She nodded. "But it could get worse here."

"My life has been nothing but worse. I'll take my chances. By the way, sorry about your old man. He seems like a decent guy barring the shit luck."

"Yeah," she muttered, replaying the minutes before he was shot.

As they rounded a corner of the neighborhood, the conversation was cut short by the sight of the same men they'd seen at the grocery store, except now they were with a larger group, carting food into a two-story house. Colton pulled Zoe back behind a wall and peered out. "Huh, well, look at that," he said.

"I'd prefer not. Let's go the other way."

"Hold up."

She looked past him, watching as the men carted in food, and then closed the house door.

"Who says opportunity doesn't knock twice."

"Colton."

"It's a goldmine. No one is fighting over it."

"No. No. I'm not doing it."

"Come on, take a look. They're heading back to the store. They won't be back for at least thirty minutes. I can be in and out in less than five. We grab a few things and..." He looked back at her as she folded her arms. "Ugh. All right. Forget it. We'll leave it, but don't be surprised if Dominick decides to kick you all out. I had a hard time convincing him to let you stay."

He turned to leave, and Zoe stood there, eyeing the property, the wheels of her mind spinning over. She let out a sigh. "Okay. But I'm staying here. You go in. I'll alert you if I see anyone."

23

The risk of shit going south was high, but the reward was far more significant.

For Colton, this was just another day. He'd spent the better part of his teenage years stealing. It's how he survived. It wasn't like one day he just decided to become a thief and steal cars, but with no support system, no one to guide him in the right direction, and only himself to rely on for many years, there wasn't much choice.

On the other hand, Zoe seemed to have had life handed to her on a plate.

Sure, she didn't strike him as someone who had known nothing but a silver spoon in her mouth, but she might as well have. Good parents. A stable home. University all paid for. She was part of the fortunate. The lucky few would often look down on others and question their decisions.

But take it all away, and what would they do to stay alive?

Darting across the street, Colton skirted around the back of the home, climbed up a wooden fence, and peered over to check there wasn't a guard dog. It was a common tactic that allowed groups like them to continue to operate. Surround a home with ferocious Rottweilers or pit bulls and a couple of cameras, and they could leave without fear.

It worked for Rusty.

Except now, with the power out, the surveillance cameras he saw were useless.

He grinned and high-tailed it over, landing quietly on the balls of his feet.

He figured the house would be locked up tight. A quick turn of the handle and pull on the windows confirmed it. So, he did the next best thing. Sliding credit cards between locks rarely worked anymore. He didn't have his lock kit, but he did have the old-school method.

Colton removed his jacket and picked up a rock.

He placed the jacket on the window and struck it as hard as possible.

The glass shattered, but the coat deadened the sound. Within seconds, he reached in, unlocked the door, and was in. No guard dog came scampering toward him, so he felt relatively safe venturing inside.

The first order of business was to see what they had on aisle-free. He chuckled, wondering what they would say when they returned to find they'd been duped. Of course, he couldn't take it all. There was too much to remove, but he could regain what they left behind and perhaps a little more.

Colton went to the front of the house, peered out the window, and saluted Zoe, who was across the street, keeping watch. Next, he opened several of the boxes. Rice, pasta, you name it, it was there for the taking.

Without wasting any time, he double-timed it up the steps, tore off a king-sized bed sheet from the main bedroom, and made his way back down. He laid it out and began tossing items into the middle.

All the while, he would glance out the window to check that no one was coming. He'd told Zoe that if she saw anyone coming down the street to double-time it over to the rear and give him a shout.

As he filled the sheet, he chewed over what Zoe had said about things getting worse. Many of the streets were flooded, the surge from the tsunami hitting the West Coast. He couldn't imagine how coastal towns had fared. That was the only upside to living in Oregon City; they were behind the Oregon Coast Range. It was God's natural buffer to disasters, Rusty would say.

He hadn't been at it more than a few minutes when Colton heard the sound of the front door unlocking. His heart skipped a beat. Frozen in spot for a second, he quickly reached for his handgun and ducked down behind the sofa. Shit, shit, shit, he muttered. Why didn't she alert me? he thought. Had they spotted her? Had she not seen this individual? Or worse, had she opted to leave?

There was a hard cough.

"Terry!?"

Colton's pulse ticked up as he tightened his grip on the handgun.

The stranger strolled past the living room, seemingly not noticing the sheet on the floor and his stockpile in the middle. He went into the kitchen. That's when Colton knew he was busted. "What the fuck?"

The movement was fast, footsteps heading back to the living room, where they had piles of boxes stacked up. The next sound was the cocking of a gun followed by footsteps that sounded like they went up the steps, except that wasn't true. Colton assumed he had gone upstairs to check each room so he ventured out, moving quietly.

As he peered into the hallway, he felt a shockingly cold gun barrel press against his temple.

"Drop the gun," the man said. "DROP IT!" he shouted.

"All right. Okay. Please, don't shoot." Colton dropped his handgun, and the man kicked it out of the way.

"Back into the living room and keep your hands where I can see them."

Colton had no choice but to do as he was told. He took a few steps back, and then the man came into view. He was clean-shaven, very ordinary. Nothing about him looked menacing. He reminded Colton of any other suburban dad. A protruding pouch to his gut, a plaid shirt underneath a cream-colored coat, and khaki pants and boating shoes below that.

"Look, man, I just—"

"Wanted to take our stuff. You know I could shoot you where you stand."

"Then why haven't you?" Colton asked.

"Because I don't call the shots. Take a seat. We're going to wait for the others to return. They'll decide."

"Look. I'll leave."

"SIT YOUR ASS DOWN!" he shouted. "Or I will take the shot."

Colton tapped the air with both hands. "All right, man. Just go easy with that trigger finger."

The stranger regarded him through slitted eyes. "You in the habit of breaking into people's homes?"

"Not any more than you are of stealing from grocery stores."

"A smart ass."

"It's true, isn't it?"

The man stared him down as he used his free hand to take out a pack of cigarettes. He used his lips to remove one. Then he tossed the pack and lit it.

"You think I could get one of those?" Colton said.

The man chuckled. "You're a pushy little fuck."

"So that's a, no?"

The man regarded him, a smile forming.

"Sure."

That was the opportunity. This guy was no killer. Sure, he was waving a gun, but Colton could see it as clear as day. Holding his hands high, he inched over to the pack on the floor and scooped it up, taking one out. The stranger tossed a lighter to him but kept his distance. Colton inhaled deeply, allowing the nicotine to enter his bloodstream and take the edge off.

"So, anyone else with you?" the guy asked.

"Nope, just me." He took another hit on the cigarette. "My house was destroyed in the quake. Lost family," Colton said, testing the waters to see if he could elicit sympathy. "I was hungry. I hit the store, but it was already cleared out."

"And let me guess, you saw our crew and figured you'd wait until they were gone before you swooped in and stole it all from underneath our noses."

"Fella. I hardly think I could cart all of this out of the house. Hence, the sheet. I just needed enough for a few days to figure out what's happening."

"Well, that's simple. The nation is under attack."

"Then shouldn't we be helping each other instead of pointing guns at our own?"

The man laughed. "I see how you skated over the part about breaking the window and helping yourself."

"Desperate times call for desperate measures."

"Yeah, I'm not sure the others will buy that."

"They already have by taking this. You get it. You all do. The only difference is, you don't know me; I don't know you."

"To be fair. I barely know the others. The rest of the crew are homeowners on this street. We're not a gang. Just looking to take care of our own."

Colton blew out smoke from the corner of his mouth. "Yeah, I figured."

"What do you mean by that?"

"Well, you know, you don't exactly look like gang material."

"Is that so? And what do I look like?"

"Like someone's father who just returned from the country club after going 18 holes."

The man grinned and tapped his cigarette in Colton's direction.

Even though Colton felt like the guy wasn't a threat, that wasn't to say he wasn't stupid. Fear could make anyone perceive a situation as volatile. That couldn't have been any truer when he heard Zoe's voice.

"Put the gun down."

The guy turned his head. Zoe stepped into the frame, holding the gun the man had kicked away. At some point, she had sneaked in and approached quietly. Her shoes were off. Nothing but socks. Clever but unwarranted.

"Zoe."

"Put it down!" she said louder.

"Now go easy there, girl. No one needs to get hurt here."

"Zoe. No. Just..." Colton was about to try and explain that he had the situation under control. At least, he thought he did. He felt that he was only minutes away from the guy releasing him. Now this. This could change it all.

"I said put it down!"

"Okay. Okay." The guy began to lower his weapon, but then, in a sudden change of heart, he turned it toward her. Two rounds erupted, and the stranger dropped. A bullet had gone through his chest; the other had speared his forehead.

"Oh, for fuck's sake. What the..." Colton's gaze bounced between them. "He wasn't a threat."

"He had a gun on you."

"I know, but..."

That's when the situation got even worse. In his peripheral vision, he spotted the same group coming down the street, heading for the house. Colton darted to the front door and locked it. He jammed a chair behind the door handle. He grabbed the fallen man's gun and stuck it in his jeans. Next, he scooped up the sheet, tossing a few items to lighten it. "Go! Go! Out the back!" he said in a panicked state as he rushed toward the rear of the house.

THE JOURNEY back was one of silence. Although Colton wanted to question her motive, he knew the situation could have ended in many ways. It could have been him lying dead instead. Of course, the elephant was also in the room — how this would affect her now. Not even he had killed someone. Regardless of why it happened and the circumstances that led up to it, she now had to live with a new reality of knowing she'd taken a man's life.

As they entered the house, Bryce rose from his seat. "Hey, how did it go?"

Colton lowered the massive sheet full of food and showed him. "We got what we set out for. Not a lot, but as much as I could carry."

On the other hand, Zoe just glanced into the room before heading upstairs without a word.

"Zoe? Hey, Zoe!" Jackson asked.

"What?" she replied, looking at her father.

"You good?"

"Yeah. I'm just tired," she said quietly before retreating to a room upstairs. Bryce looked at Colton, as did Jackson.

He shrugged. "It was a long walk. There and back," he muttered before dragging the stockpile into the kitchen to begin unloading it, unsure whether he should have told them the truth. Then again, it wasn't his place to.

24

Tennessee

Conspiracy theories be damned, she thought, entering the city commission meeting that night. In all the years Natalie had lived there, she hadn't once attended. It wasn't that she didn't think voicing her concerns mattered, but she always thought no one truly listened. Three minutes. That was all anyone ever got to speak. Who could address anything in three minutes? It was absurd.

After the day's events, they all left that evening for the city hall building just off East Parkway, conveniently a part of the same building that housed the Gatlinburg Fire Department, Police Department, and City Court. The commission chambers were crammed with residents, all eager to hear news of the situation, learn what resources and supplies would be available, and voice their concerns.

"Quite the turnout," Dante said. "You get out to this much?"

She shook her head, observing the steady flow of people entering city hall.

Natalie had yet to tell Dante about the house. It would have just been one more thing to throw into the mix. They already had enough on their plate.

Inside, there was light, not just candlelight either. A generator could be heard churning away.

"Someone was forward-thinking," Dante said, motioning to the overhead bulbs.

Murmurs spread throughout the room as everyone waited for the meeting to start. Natalie eyed Wendy Bowers and Darren Waitman chatting at the front among the many other city officials in suits. Dotted around the room were several members of the police department to keep the peace. The whole room looked like a courtroom, with the commissioners on an elevated front platform, ready to judge and rule over everyone. She could see how Leo wouldn't have fit in here. He was known for being outspoken and not putting up with much nonsense. They probably would have had security drag him away from the mic.

Wendy acknowledged her with a wave.

Natalie gave a nod and smiled.

Truly, she was curious more than ever about how they intended to turn this around. So many families had been displaced.

Dan Nelson used a gavel to call the meeting to order. He hammered it hard, the noise cutting through the constant chatter. "You're officially called to order," Dan said. "Let's just do a quick roll call." He began. "Vice Mayor Barnhill."

"Here."

"Tricia Goodman."

"Here."

As they rattled off names, someone yelled from the back. "Can we just get on with it? We can see you're all here, you idiots."

A few laughed.

"Here, here!" others added.

Dan used the gavel again, striking it hard against the wood. "There will be order."

"Oh please, Dan, we left order behind over a day ago."

"Mr. James, I'd like to remind you—"

"Put a sock in it, Dan, and move on."

"Excuse me?"

"Don't you excuse me. I used to babysit you."

That garnered a few laughs.

"All right, Dan, I'll take it from here," Thomas Carter said, stepping up to the podium. Mayor Carter had held the position for as long as she could remember. Middle-aged, with a full head of black hair parted to one side and trimmed up nicely around the back and sides, he consistently presented himself as professional and confident. "Okay, welcome everyone. I'm glad you're here this evening and are interested in what is happening."

"What is going on?" Jake Barret yelled from the back. He and his family had a local butcher shop, and they prided themselves on delivering some of the best meat in the county. They were all there.

"Has FEMA been contacted?" a woman cried out.

Someone else stepped forward. "Should we be worried about nuclear fallout?"

"How can we get medicine? I have a mother that is…"

Carter lifted his hands. "Please. People. Before I address

that, I would like to take a moment of silence as we begin this meeting to honor those who we lost last night."

Everyone bowed their heads, even if a few muttered curse words at being shut down. When it was over, Carter said that anyone who wanted to address them would each get three minutes to speak, but anyone who had never signed up before the meeting wouldn't be given a chance and would have to see them after. That, of course, went over like a wet blanket.

"Now, to answer your question, Jake. It's early days right now. From what we have been able to glean before the power went out, the nation is under attack. From who? We don't know. From what? We don't know." He turned. "And Shelly, regarding nuclear fallout. We don't believe that poses a threat to us here. There are a lot of factors that come into play. It seems as if the West Coast has been hit as hard as the East. However, we will hand out potassium iodine tablets at the end of the meeting to anyone who wants them."

"Iodine? What's that for?"

"Protection against radioactive iodine. If it has been released into the air, it can be breathed in. But the pills don't help against other radioactive substances."

"So basically, they're useless!" Jake said.

"Something is better than nothing," Wendy Bowers added.

"Not exactly, Jake. It can block the absorption and reduce the risk of problems arising," Carter added.

"Arising?"

"Look, we are not scientists here. We are working from an emergency handbook. All I can tell you is—" He turned, and Wendy handed him a handbook. He flipped a few pages and put his glasses on. "Everyone is exposed to some form of radiation in their life, whether natural or artificial, through medical treatments, what we eat, and so on. The body can handle a good amount per year, but it's large doses that we are concerned about."

"And if we have been exposed? How would we know?"

"Symptoms are nausea, vomiting, diarrhea, headaches, and fever. These can appear from an hour to twenty-four hours after an event."

"So, we might not even know?" Jake said.

"Possibly," Carter replied.

"That's great. Really great," Shelly said, shaking her head.

"It can be longer than that," someone said. The voice was familiar. Natalie turned to see Leo edging his way through the crowd.

Dante leaned in. "I thought you said he wasn't coming."

"Must have changed his mind," Natalie replied.

Leo made his way forward to the front. He turned and addressed the room. "Two to four weeks. It can take that long for symptoms to show up."

"And how would you know?" Carter asked.

"Military background," Leo replied. "Fukushima is our best example. Everyone was evacuated within a 30-kilometer radius. Tokyo was told they were okay because they were four hours away from the release of radiation. However, that wasn't a bomb. It will depend on what ballistic missile erupted, if it was in the air or on the ground."

"Thank you, Leo," Carter said. "Look, folks. The situation we are in is not good. I'm not going to cherry-coat it. There is a lot about this that we don't know and won't know for a while. We are in the same boat together. We cannot address this power outage in the next few days or weeks. Our infrastructure relies upon a lot of factors. We are doing our best to try and find out more. The goal of this evening is to let you know that we are not standing by idly and hoping and praying that the federal government will step in and help. We have in place generators that were kept in a Faraday cage. That's what's powering this place right now. It's also what will allow our hospital to operate for a brief time. However, our resources are limited, so if there is fuel, food, water, medicine, or any supplies you have in excess that you think could help, I would ask that you see us after the meeting. This also applies to those who are good at hunting and fishing," he said, looking over to Jake. "We could use your expertise."

"You mean you could use us."

"Right."

"What if we don't want to be used?"

"I don't follow," Carter replied.

"Our time is valuable. How would we be compensated?" Jake asked.

A few others chimed in, glaring at his family and piping up. "Always thinking about yourself, Jake."

"Hey!" Jake pointed a finger. "I have yet to hear any of you offering to help. Just because we bring in fresh meat and fish doesn't mean we are here to offer our services for free. Event or not, our time is our time."

Mayor Carter tried to calm the crowd as they got worked up by Jake's comment. "Please. People. The only way we get through this is to remain calm and supportive of one another." Angry murmurs spread across the crowd, and a few people turned and walked out, tired of listening.

"What about the elderly?" Tanya Daniels asked.

"We will use the Gatlinburg Community Center for our disaster recovery location. You are free to bring anyone there who has been displaced. We are currently looking for more working generators. Many have been fried, so as you can imagine, the hospital, the police department, and the community center will use what we have. We will distribute candles, flashlights, water, food, and blankets on a case-by-case basis."

The room erupted. Many were angry, others defending the city and the hard decisions that lay before them.

"Case-by-case? Who makes that call?" Shelly asked. "I didn't pay thousands of dollars in taxes every year to be told my situation would be assessed. If I turn up and am denied, there will be hell to pay."

Others jeered, taking her side. Many nodded, jabbing fingers at Carter.

"Please, Shelly," Carter said.

"Don't you patronize us, Carter! You work for us. Don't forget it." That said, she turned and elbowed her way out of the building. It was clear the road ahead wasn't going to be easy. Not everyone was ready to roll up their sleeves and pitch in. The self-entitled, the angry, the ones who had lost family members, wanted to blame someone. It was easier to do that than to rally together and see how they could improve the situation.

"Listen, we will take this one day at a time. You are not the only ones who lost family, friends, and co-workers last night. Now, had it not been for the community, we may have lost many more. So, I want to make a point of thanking every one of you for helping last night. If anyone has any questions, my door is always open. Bring your ideas, concerns, and feedback, and we will take it seriously. We only rise from this through the strength of the Lord and together." He turned to Darren Waitman, and he stepped up to the podium.

"Hello, everyone. Um. Mayor Carter wanted me to share a

few things that may assist you right now. Without any power, any food you have in your freezers or fridges is liable to go bad within the next twenty-four to forty-eight hours. Unless it's necessary, keep them closed. It will help to keep the food frozen and cold for the next twenty-four to thirty-six hours. However, if you open them, pack any perishables into a cooler with ice."

"If we have any!" someone yelled. A few heads turned.

Darren cleared his throat and continued. "Please do not use BBQs, propane heaters, or portable generators indoors for safety reasons. The last thing we want is for you to die of carbon monoxide poisoning. If you see any downed power lines, stay at least 30 feet back from them. While we have no power, we are still establishing if a current is running through any of the downed ones."

"Let me answer that," Leo said. "There isn't. They hit the source."

"Who hit the source?" Jake asked.

"The Russians. That's who's behind this. But that's the least of our concerns right now. A shadow government, FEMA, even some of these folks might not have your best interests at heart."

"That's enough, Leo," Carter said, shaking his head.

He shrugged and stepped away, working his way through the crowd to Natalie.

"I thought you were staying home," she said quietly.

"And miss stirring the pot?" He grinned, folding his arms defiantly and looking out. Darren waited until the crowd calmed down as Leo's comments had fired up some of them, especially those who were trigger-happy nutcases just looking for a reason to go to war.

Darren continued, "To ensure that we keep everyone up

to date, we are handing out hand-crank radios and a flyer with all the information on a local frequency we'll be using daily to keep everyone up to date. Please know that we only have so many radios, so you must share them with people in your neighborhood. To ensure some order, we have created a city map and segmented off specific neighborhoods. Those who live in those areas, please see us if you are interested in being the one that conveys that information to neighbors on your street."

"And what about safety in the meantime? As there have been several break-ins. Looting and general chaos on the streets," an elderly woman asked.

Many agreed.

"We will continue to provide emergency service. Officers will be patrolling using bicycles, walking, and some old vehicles we've discovered work. Chief Patrick Donovan will address any questions that you have at the end. But please, I need you all to understand that we are currently working at a disadvantage. We will collect a list of names of those who want to volunteer to maintain order. The focus will be grocery stores, pharmacies, banks, and hospitals."

"A little too late," Giles Manson, a man known for being the town alcoholic, said. "The grocery stores were already raided, probably while you all had your thumbs up your asses."

Natalie shook her head. It was one thing after another. Tension was riding high, with it came a drive to speak their minds.

"And neighborhoods?" the elderly woman asked.

"Officers will patrol," the chief said.

"Patrol? Tell that to my neighbor who found snakes in her bed and her cat dead!" Leo shouted before Natalie could stop him. She closed her eyes and then felt a touch on her arm. She looked to her left to see Dante staring at her with his eyebrow raised.

"I was going to tell you," she said before Leo continued.

"Instead of handing out flashlights and radios, you should be handing out guns. People need to protect themselves."

"To be fair, Leo, most people own guns. So, that will not be a problem."

"Most people have been displaced. I'm talking about the ones that don't have guns. What about them? Unless a cop stays on the street. They aren't going to be able to help. A person could be mugged, raped, or killed before the boys in blue show up. No, you were asking for suggestions. Here's mine. We create a neighborhood watch. After all, this is a Stand Your Ground state, and we can open carry. I'm willing to step up to the plate in my neck of the woods. How about you all?" he asked, taking over in typical Leo fashion.

Jake's family responded enthusiastically to that. "Here, here. We're with you on that."

"There will be no vigilantes in the city," Carter said, rising from his chair. "People, allow us the chance to maintain order. That's what we are paid to do."

"Then you better get out there and start earning that wage," Jake yelled. "Because if you drop the ball for even a day. You're fired, and we take over."

Some burst out laughing, seeing it all as one big joke or needing to find a release for their worry, but it was clear that it was no joke. The writing was on the wall. People taking matters into their own hands. It had the potential to do a lot of good but could also be disastrous.

"That won't be necessary."

"You might not have much choice!" Jake replied.

Many of the people in the room agreed, storming out and ending the meeting before it was officially over. As the crowd dispersed and cops monitored and pulled out those who were problematic, Natalie glanced over the faces of her teens. "Selena, where's Jordan?" she asked.

"He stepped out to use the washroom."

"Without telling us?"

"You were busy talking. He tried to get your attention."

"I'm on it," Dante said, slipping through the crowd to check the washroom. Fear gripped her as she corralled the others together and ushered them into the foyer. Dante exited the bathroom at the far end of the hall and shook his head before darting outside. A cold chill came over Natalie as they ventured beyond the crowded foyer.

"Jordan!" she called out, hoping he'd left to get some air.

Frantically, her gaze bounced around, searching for any sign of him or Clyde.

There were too many people, and it was too dark to see.

Flashlights bounced on faces. "Jordan! Jordan!" Natalie shouted.

They all began to search the parking lot, calling out his name, but he never emerged.

25

Portland

The hot glow from a cigarette was the only light emanating from the darkened cabin as Foster rolled up the driveway and eased off the gas. Throughout the journey back, Chris had been trying to come up with different reasons for why they were returning empty-handed. None of them would suffice. Talis was much like his brother, hot-headed with a hair-trigger temper. Over the years, Foster had seen Ryland fly off the handle for something as simple as a man looking at him wrong.

But this.

This was far more personal.

The problem was there was no way of knowing who Talis would blame, how he would react, and the consequences. In years gone by, Foster wouldn't have given it a passing thought. His age, by default, meant he had earned a degree of respect from those younger than him; however, with Ryland now gone, there was no one to stop him.

"Let me do the talking," Chris said. "Don't say a damn word about that cop."

"By all means," Foster replied. If anyone got blamed, it would be him, but Chris was still reeling from killing the one person who could have led them to Bryce. In the chaos of the moment, he'd forgotten that Talis had sent Chris to watch over Foster. He had it all backward. But if he wanted to hang himself, who was he to stand in the way? The truck's doors echoed as they got out and made their way toward the cabin.

"The prodigal sons return," Talis muttered from the dark.

"A slight hiccup," Chris said. "We don't have Bryce, but there's a good reason."

"Oh, I'm interested to hear this," he said, leaning forward on a chair, only the glow of his cigarette illuminating his features.

"We found him. He was at the hospital. We arrived a little too late. Then the crowd went nuts outside, and I ended up getting clocked and stomped a few times," he said, turning his face from side to side and touching it to prove his point as if any of that would change the outcome.

"Huh. That's too bad," Talis replied calmly. Foster knew he was probably seething under the surface.

"But don't worry, I should know before the end of the day where he is."

"That's great, Chris. And you drove all this way to tell me that?"

There was a short pause.

Chris swallowed hard. "Well, not exactly. Um." Chris stumbled over his words and then looked behind him, hoping Foster or Pete might chime in and come to his rescue. But Pete knew better, and Foster remained silent.

Talis stepped out of the darkness like a monster, broad-shouldered, dark-faced and brooding. He stepped down from the porch, causing Chris to take a few steps back. Pete shifted from one foot to the next, nerves getting the better of him. It was always the way. One person calling the shots, the others following. Once Talis was gone, another would take his place, and the wheels on the bus would go round and round. It was the insanity of humanity. They were doomed to repeat the same illogical acts instead of learning from the past.

"By the end of the day, huh?" Talis said, walking toward him.

"Yeah. It relies on us finding those two that came by earlier."

"Oh, you mean these two?" He thumbed over his shoulder. "Jagger, bring out our guests."

Two youths were thrust out; a flashlight shone on their faces. Neither was injured, which was a good sign, but they didn't look happy.

"What the hell is this? I'm doing you all a favor," Dominick said.

"You found them?" Chris asked, looking perplexed.

"No, they returned, and with quite the story, isn't that right, Dominick?"

The young man nodded.

"Tell them what you told me."

"I know where they are. I can take you to them for the right price."

Talis smiled. "The right price. You hear that, Chris?"

Chris moved forward a little. "Where are they?"

Talis laughed. "Well, that's the million-dollar question. He knows, don't you, Dominick."

"Yep," he muttered. "But it's going to cost you."

Talis still hadn't taken his eyes off Chris except to glance at Foster. "And tell them what you want in return, Dominick."

"Anything we want."

Talis laughed. "You hear that? Have you ever heard anyone ask for anything they want?" He laughed again. "I mean, fuck, that is smart. The world has crumbled around us, and instead of restricting himself to food, medicine, guns, ammo, heck, even drugs, he keeps the door wide open with anything he wants." Talis chuckled, running a hand over his face.

"High-value target, high-value price," Dominick replied. "Seems fair to me."

Talis took another hit on his cigarette. "Couldn't have said it better myself." He sniffed hard. "I like this kid. I like you, I really do," Talis said, turning to Dominick. "Except you're asking the wrong people at the wrong time."

"What?" Dominick replied, confused.

Talis motioned with a wave of the finger. "Jagger."

Jagger grabbed Skylar.

"Get the fuck off me!"

Dominick went to react but stopped short when Sawyer pointed a gun at his head. "You see, Dominick. Here's the mistake you made. You never come into a man's camp and try negotiating if you're bringing something to lose. Now I've got something of yours. You see how that works. So, I've heard your proposition, and here's my counteroffer. You're going to take us to where they are, or Jagger here will take your girl back and have a little fun; you get my drift?"

"Like hell you are!" Skylar shouted, spitting at Talis before Jagger struck her across the face, knocking her down.

Dominick swallowed hard. "Come on, man. That's not what we agreed."

Talks never took his eyes off the kid. "Jagger, Sawyer, did I agree to anything?"

"Not that I heard," they both chimed.

"Fuck's sake," Dominick cursed.

Talis smiled. "So? Do we have a deal, or would you like to determine how far we can take this?"

Dominick lowered his chin and nodded. He waited a moment before he replied. "I'll take you to him, but she comes with us."

"No. She will be here when you return after I get what I want. You see, the first rule of negotiating is information is power. Had you not balked when Jagger grabbed her, maybe this might not have worked out as well, but clearly, you two have a thing going on. Am I right?"

Dominick glanced at Skylar, his jaw clenching.

"All right! We've got ourselves a deal!" Talis said, lifting his hands like he'd won the jackpot. He then stabbed a finger at Chris and Pete. "And you two, I'll deal with you later."

Talis glanced at Foster and scowled. He looked as if he wanted to say something, and maybe he did, but perhaps past respect for older people remained. Or he was biding his time, unsure of how to deal with someone who had left his brother to die.

Except that wasn't the truth.

His brother Ryland was already dead before he had a chance to react. And maybe deep down, Talis knew that.

26

Tennessee

The response from the Gatlinburg Police Department to the disappearance of Jordan was as expected. Nothing but apathy. They had bigger fish to fry than to deal with a troubled teen with a history of running away.

"Look, I know you're worried, but give it twenty-four hours," Chief Donovan said. "More than likely, he'll show up. Or one of our officers will run across him, and we'll return him. Most of the time, teens are just hanging out with friends, and then they return when they run out of money or get hungry."

"He doesn't have any money. Besides, it would be of no use to him now. Friends? Again, he's been in the system. The only people he knows are those from the house."

"And school?"

Natalie sighed. They felt it was a waste of resources to try and locate him when they already had him documented as having run away twice over the past year.

"Mrs. Reid, I'm not trying to be an ass here. Under normal circumstances, in 99 percent of cases, they return home unharmed when ready. You told me that he was upset a few days before the event and destroyed his bedroom. Could it be that he's gone off to find his father?"

"No. If you knew what his father did to him. You would know he wouldn't go back there."

"You'd be surprised how often I hear that only to see battered women return to husbands, children who've been abused make up excuses for their caregiver. Humans are complex creatures, Mrs. Reid."

"Don't I know. At least tell me where Clyde lives. That would be helpful, and I'll be on my way."

"I told you I don't have that information."

"Of course, you do. Why are you protecting him? We all know he's been arrested multiple times for drinking and driving, domestic abuse, and fighting at the local bar. The man is a danger to society."

"People change their address. They are supposed to update us, but they don't. They get rid of the phone; they sleep on a friend's couch. They can stay off the grid in many ways."

She shifted from one foot to the next and glanced beyond the glass inside the police station at Dante, standing by the rest of the teens. She sighed.

"Well, what about my cat, the snakes, the group home that was burned down?"

"Do you have any proof it was him?"

"No, but it's obvious. He made a threat yesterday. Said I would regret it."

"Not much I can do about that. It's his word against yours."

She chuckled. "You know, chief, this doesn't exactly build confidence."

"We can't just go arresting people without cause, Mrs. Reid. Already, our resources have been pushed to the maximum here. Now, if we come across Clyde, you have my word, I will speak to him. I will even go as far as to drop by his last known residence."

"So, you do know it."

"Last known."

"Which is?"

He looked at her without saying anything, and there was her answer.

"Of course, you can't tell me."

"Like the mayor said. We are not going to have any vigilante behavior."

"Really?" She folded her arms. "And, uh, how do you intend to stop it? It seems you couldn't stop this asshole from arson or murdering my pet; you sure as hell didn't stop him from kidnapping his son out from underneath your nose."

"My nose?"

"Oh, right. This is my fault. Of course, it is."

Chief Donovan sighed. "Mrs. Reid. I will get an officer on it. I will update you as soon as we come across him. You have my word on that. That's all I can offer you under the circumstances."

Natalie nodded. There was no point fighting with him. It wasn't like they could comb the streets quickly. "Thank you," she said, pushing the door open to take her into the lobby.

She pressed past a knot of people lined up, ready to voice their concerns or trouble. The police department had become a sanctuary for those with issues and fears.

"What did he say?" Dante asked as she walked past him and exited the building. Outside, those who had been displaced had pitched tents around the building like it was skid row. Families peered out; others cooked food over small camping stoves. It was a troubling sight. Not only were people in need, the police were under extreme pressure. All of which meant the chances of anyone finding Jordan or bringing in Clyde for questioning were slim to none.

"Hey, Natalie."

"What?"

"What did he say?" Dante asked again, catching up with her.

"That he can't help. Basically."

"But that's his job."

"Tell that to him. Look, he said he would put an officer on it, but look around you, Dante. Do you think they have an officer to spare? This is a powder keg that is just waiting to explode. More officers are positioned outside here than elsewhere to ensure people don't attack city officials. Forget the pharmacies, hospitals, banks, and grocery stores. And then what? Some are meant to be patrolling. Patrolling?!" She chuckled. "They might as well give them skateboards. It's useless."

"Mrs. Reid," Daniel said, walking up to her with Selena and Liam. "Any luck?"

"They'll start their search this evening," she said with a smile before glancing at Dante, realizing it contradicted what she said, but she didn't want them to worry. She turned back to Dante.

"So, they know where he might be?" Selena asked.

"Maybe. I don't know. I just hoped we could have found Clyde."

"Is that what that conversation was about?" Liam piped up.

"Liam. What have I told you?"

"All right. It's just that I know where he's at," Liam replied.

"Hold on. What?" she asked, turning around.

"I overheard him talking to Jordan the other day."

"But his father spoke to him on the phone, Liam."

Liam grinned.

She widened her eyes. "How often have I told you not to eavesdrop on other people's conversations?" They had a second phone in the house, and it was common to receive a call and shout upstairs where one of the other staff would pick up. She'd caught Liam listening in a few times. But then she smiled back. "So, what did he say?"

Liam laughed. "Yeah, I thought so. He wanted Jordan to come and stay with him. He gave him this whole spiel that he'd cleaned up his act, and he promised, yada, yada, yada, you know, the same bullcrap."

"Yeah. And?"

"He said he was holding down a job as a handyman at Bluegreen Vacations Mountain Loft Resort, and he had a room there."

"Son of a bitch. That is minutes from my house," Natalie said. "Look, could you take the teens back to your house and..."

"No. Not this time. Not after what happened. I'm going with you."

"We all are," Selena said.

"No. No, you're not."

"He's our friend, too," Daniel added.

"Dante."

"They have a point."

"Dante. We are responsible for them."

"Even more reason why we go together to get him back."

"He might not even be there, and if he is, and he sees all of us coming, he'll bounce," Natalie said. "No, I'll go by myself."

"Or I can go with you," a voice called out from the darkness. She knew who it was instantly. Leo stepped out of the dark.

"I thought you went home?"

"And I thought you had told them about your house."

"Oh, no, this is not happening."

"Look," Leo said, approaching her. "What happened at your house was on my street. When I said I would sign up to be drafted if called upon, you said, who would be here to protect the street."

"I was joking, Leo."

"Joke or not, if this boy's father is responsible for that mess back at your house, he is a threat to all of us."

Natalie sighed as she clenched her eyes shut and groaned.

"He has a point," Dante said.

"You're not helping the situation, Dante. If anything happens to these kids, I wouldn't know what to do with myself."

"Something already has, Natalie. And besides, if Leo is right and the nation has come under attack by Russia, and they invade, it won't be long before these teens will have no other choice but to grow up fast and fight."

Attempting to change their mind was a losing argument. No matter what she said, one of them had a good reason.

"Yeah, well, until then, I get to make that choice, not them. No. They go back to your place. I'll take Leo with me. Okay? He's armed. Hell, I'll even take that gun you offered me earlier."

"But you were adamant."

"I changed my mind."

He nodded, handing her his gun. "Hold on. How about this? I go with Leo. You stay with the teens."

"No."

"I don't have time to take you through how to use that gun. It's as much about safety as it is about point-and-shoot. You went last time. Let me go this time. If he's not there, we'll come back."

Natalie looked at the teens and then reluctantly said, "Fine."

"I have another gun you can use," Leo told Dante. "Save you going back. It's a good twenty-minute trek from here. We should leave now." Dante nodded and placed a hand on Natalie's shoulder. "I've got this."

27

Oregon

The staccato of gunfire wasn't cause for alarm; it was the long stretch of silence that followed. Since the grid had gone down, Bryce had heard the echo multiple times. He figured it was a response to looting, or warning shots from homeowners warding off home invaders. A couple of times, he'd approached the window and glanced out, hoping to see what was happening, but he never saw anything. As darkness fell over the street, gunshots became white noise, especially with his mind circling back to his brother.

"You okay, Bryce?" Jackson asked, now tucked inside a bed on the second floor.

Standing by the window, he glanced over his shoulder.

"I guess," he replied. "Just thinking about my brother. Tomorrow, I'll head back and bury him."

"Right." Jackson nodded, grimacing as he shifted his position in bed. "You said you were in the group home with Natalie. What about your brother?"

"He wasn't my biological brother. I ended up being placed with a family for a couple of years. We got close. The family had been trying for a child for a long time. They couldn't have one, so they adopted. Chad was the first. I came after that. So, we kind of had a lot in common. We bonded fast."

"Got it," Jackson replied. "Say, you still haven't told me why you ended up doing jail time."

Bryce slumped in a seat across from him and blew out his cheeks. "When I joined the military, I intended to serve my country. I just wanted to be of use and give back. You don't get to pick who you are put with in the military or who you serve under. A command is a command. You follow it, or people die. You learn fast that you might not make it home unless you get in line and work as a team. Out there, your brothers are everything." He pulled out a pack of smokes. "Do you mind?"

"Go ahead."

He tapped one out and lit it before continuing. "In war, whatever line existed between right and wrong blurs, especially when at any given moment, those beside you can be killed, or they can save you. Get saved enough times, and you feel indebted. That debt can be used against you." He closed his eyes, hearing and seeing it all play out in his mind. "The heat out there can make a man crazy. Combine that with hours of boredom and moments of sheer terror, and it can do a number on a man's mind. I guess that's why so many return with PTSD. The suicide rate is crazy. No one can ever understand that if they haven't put their boots on the ground out there, seen what we have, felt the fear we have." He paused as the raw emotion welled up inside him. Time inside had given him a chance to distance himself from it all, but it had taken years of pushing the past from his mind. Still, digging back into the archives of his memory quickly brought back the sting as if it had happened yesterday.

"You okay, Dad?" Zoe asked, pausing in the doorway. "I'm turning in for the night."

"Yeah. Sleep well."

She strode away. Jackson turned back to Bryce. "You were saying?"

"We were supposed to bring in a suspected insurgent bomber who had been arrested and released a couple of times. We couldn't find him. We searched so many properties that night. We had a few run-ins with families. You know — what you would expect from people pissed at seeing marines bursting into their house. Eventually, frustrations boiled over, accusations were made that families were lying, and our squad commander dragged this one man from his home to interrogate him. He clarified that the Afghan was related to the insurgent we were after. You have to understand that this wasn't our first time in this situation. People lie. They do. But it's the ones that don't, that stick with you." He paused for a second, swallowing hard. "Anyway, at some point, I had started to think that our squad commander cared less about the mission and more about inflicting harm on individuals, innocent or not. The thing is, he was likeable, you know, he had that charisma that made it easy to follow him. But it was all bullshit. I discovered days before that he was taking body parts as trophies like someone might collect antlers from a deer." He took a deep breath. "To cut a long story short, the guy we dragged out that night was shot, some of the guys played with his corpse, and then an AK47 and an IED were placed next to his body to make it look like he was a combatant."

Jackson looked stunned. "Then how did you end up in prison?"

"I killed one of the innocent men from a previous interrogation. It wasn't done in cold blood. There was a scuffle; he grabbed one of the guns from another marine and…"

"You shot."

He nodded. "Except when you put it all together, it doesn't matter. That killing, the others came under the same umbrella."

"But how did you all get arrested?"

"That was me. I recorded the last kill."

"You convicted yourself."

"I couldn't let it keep happening. I secretly recorded the death of the Afghan. It caught them placing the IED and gun beside the man. I then handed it over to the powers that be. We all went down; I was given a lighter sentence because of a plea bargain that gave more information on others involved in previous kills. I ended up doing five years and got a dishonorable discharge."

Jackson stared back at him.

"And the others?"

"They're still doing time. At least, I assume they are, unless they died in jail after the tsunami tore into the coast."

Silence stretched between them, but it wasn't because neither had anything to say; it was a change in the sound outside. Up until that point, they'd heard guns going off one after the other, an endless ruckus.

"Huh," Jackson said. "Maybe we will get some sleep after all."

"Yeah," Bryce replied, rising from his seat and going to the window. That's when he saw something odd. He squinted and noticed several of the homes along the streets were on fire. Under the glow of light, he saw a truck roll to a crawl outside. Six men got out; one being pushed forward.

Bryce squinted again. "Hey, uh, Colton."

No answer.

"Colton!" he cried out, shouting over his shoulder.

"What is it?" Colton asked, entering the room.

"Your friend is back, and it looks like he's brought company."

Colton rushed over to the window and peered out. "Son of a bitch."

Tennessee

The night lay in absolute darkness; the absence of light shrouding the Bluegreen Vacation Mountain Loft Resort was only made worse by the silence. Dante and Leo stood at the entrance, keenly attuned to their surroundings. A few gunshots nearby kept them on their toes.

"What apartment did he say?" Leo asked.

"29 D," Dante replied.

"You ready for this?"

"Depends what this is."

Leo snorted, walking past him. "War," he muttered.

The resort, a four-story clubhouse with vacation homes that resembled apartments, loomed like a monolithic shadow against the night. The dark wood and stone exterior blended seamlessly with the forest around it, rendering it almost invisible now that the sky was overcast and blocking the stars.

With weapons clutched in their hands, they advanced cautiously toward the doorway. The darkness clung to them like a shroud, and every step seemed to echo through the stillness.

Inside, they moved fast to reach the top of the stairs, their ascent punctuated only by the sound of their breaths. The air grew heavy with each step, tension mounting as they approached the fourth floor.

Leo stopped and glanced out along the narrow walkway.

"All good," he said before moving ahead. They went to the door, and Dante pressed his ear against it. In the impenetrable darkness, he strained to hear muffled voices from within. He exchanged a tense glance with Leo, the urgency of the situation pressing down on them.

"Wait a second," Leo said, taking his backpack off and unzipping it. He pulled out something.

"What is that?"

Leo grinned. "An Enola smoke grenade."

"Are you kidding me?"

"You should have seen the look on those kids' faces last Halloween after they toilet-papered my house. I caught them by surprise. I disoriented the little bastards. They were stumbling all over the place. I got it on video. I'll show you later."

Dante shook his head as he stepped back from the door. "Three, two, one."

Without any hesitation, he kicked the door open. It exploded inward, wood splintering and scattering across the floor inside. Leo tossed one of the smoke grenades inside, then pulled him out of the way. A gun erupted, followed by coughing.

"Follow my lead," Leo said, lifting his SIG Sauer and entering the smoke-filled darkness. Suddenly, from the inky blackness came the unmistakable sound of footsteps. Before they could react, gunshots shattered the silence; bullets whizzed past them. They returned fire, the flashes from their weapons temporarily illuminating the room like eerie, stroboscopic snapshots.

"Jordan!" Dante shouted.

"In here," a voice cried out.

Another round erupted, and then through the smoke, Dante saw the assailant escaping through a window, disappearing into the abyss of the night.

Dante carefully approached the window and looked out to find the man balancing precariously on a balcony ledge off to his left. Whoever the person was, a hoodie hid their face as they attempted to descend from the balcony to another.

"Hey!" Dante yelled.

Startled, the man slipped, his legs dangling over the edge. The gun tucked into the small of his back fell out, disappearing into the inky black.

"Don't be stupid. Come on up."

The man shook his head as Dante extended his hand even though he could have shot him. He had every reason to, but that wasn't his way. He could see the man was terrified, no doubt put in a situation he never wanted to be in.

"Give me your hand!" Dante said.

The man shook his head and tried to get his footing, but he couldn't.

"Listen to me. Give me your hand."

Whether he had a change of heart or fear got the better of him, the man tried to reach out as Dante leaned over. Dante was just able to touch his fingers. The man's toes scraped the wall, trying to stay up, but he was losing his grip.

"Push up! PUSH UP!" Dante shouted, trying to guide him.

The struggle was brief but intense, and then, in a horrifying twist of fate as the man tried one last time, he lost his grip and plummeted off the side of the four-story building to his death below.

Dante's stomach caught in his throat.

"Dante. Give me a hand," Leo said. Breathing heavily, Dante looked back to see Leo trying to shoulder the door.

"Let me do it."

Younger, a little stronger than Leo, he plowed into the door with his shoulder, causing it to burst open. Relief gripped him to find Jordan tied to the bed by his wrists. "Where's your father?" he asked as he crouched and cut the restraints loose.

"He went to your house."

"What?" Dante gasped

"He's going to kill Natalie."

Dante's heart clenched with dread.

29

Oregon

High-beam headlights flooded the interior of the house, blinding them. Bryce kept his back to the wall, peering out the upper window.

"How many of them?" Jackson asked.

"Six, including his pal."

Colton crouched and looked out. "Shit. I should have known he'd do this. Fucking guy is always looking for a way to screw over others. Look, I'll go out there. Find out what they want."

"Don't bother. I already know," Bryce replied. "It's me."

"You?"

"The men I killed back at my brother's farm. Probably related."

Zoe sat on the edge of the bed beside Jackson; worry masked her expression.

"Or maybe he ran into some trouble with someone else. I mean, that could be it. We've been hearing gunshots all night. Home invaders and shit like that," Colton said.

Bryce pointed to the east and west. "Homes a few doors down are on fire on either side."

"So, someone dropped a candle; we are in a blackout."

"Or they started it to drive people on this street away. Look at it. It's easier to do that than to barge into people's homes and kill them."

"But why?"

"Fewer distractions and people they have to deal with," Bryce muttered. "This place isn't some cabin in the woods. Folks on this street might not take too kindly to them showing up here armed."

Bryce pulled away from the window and made his way toward the door.

"Where are you going?"

"To find another way out," he replied.

"You're leaving?" Zoe asked.

"No. You and your father are."

"Bryce. I'm as much involved in this as you," Jackson said.

"No, you just happened to be in the wrong place at the wrong time. This is on me. This is Mason's doing."

"Your squad commander?"

He nodded, peering out at the forest behind the house. "Colton. What is that place to the rear?"

"Newell Creek Canyon Nature Park. The place is massive."

"And beyond that?"

"Trails End Highway."

Bryce nodded, pulled out his Glock, and checked how much ammo he had on him. "All right, here's what we're going to do. Colton, you go out there and speak with your pal. Don't get too close. Find out how they want to do this? It will buy Jackson and Zoe some time to head into the park."

"We're not leaving you here," Jackson said. "My wife would never forgive me for that."

"Your wife doesn't need to know," he replied. "All manner of shit has happened. As far as she knows, you gave me a ride to Oregon. That's it. Besides, I've been living on borrowed time. If it weren't these guys, it would be Mason and the others once they got out. Now, c'mon. We don't have much time. Colton. Head out there."

"Well. Um."

"What is it?"

He shrugged. "It's just now that you've told me. I mean, they could shoot me."

"Very possible," Bryce said, helping Zoe lift Jackson. "However, you could be shot anyway if they barge in here. At least this way, two of us get out alive."

Colton looked at Zoe. He nodded, scooping up the gun he'd found earlier that night and jamming it into the small of his back. Bryce and Zoe slowly made their way down the steps and then toward the rear of the house. Colton stood by the front door, waiting for them to leave out the back before he ventured out.

Bryce gave him the thumbs-up and opened the rear door. Darkness prevailed, making it hard to see if anyone else was lurking in the shadows. Jackson grimaced in pain as they made their way to the tree line.

"All right. You'll have to take him from here," Bryce said to Zoe.

"Come with us. Please. You don't need to stay. We could…"

"They'll follow. It's me they want. Go. Go now!" he said, urging them into the brush and dense forest.

Jackson gripped Bryce's arm tightly one last time. He nodded without saying anything, but he clearly appreciated him, or at least wanted him to be safe. But he was far from safe. Turning back toward the house, he hurried inside, locking the door behind him. He stuck a chair behind it and then approached the front window. Outside, he could hear the conversation but couldn't quite make out what they were saying.

Colton nodded, then backed up, heading into the house. He closed the door behind him. "Are they gone?" Colton asked

"Yeah."

Colton nodded; a strained expression passed over his features. "Like you said, all they want is you."

Bryce nodded. Fear coursed through him. He could have been shanked in prison any number of times. That's why this was no surprise to him. How he felt now was his default state. Bryce jerked his thumb over his shoulder. "If you go now, you can catch up with them," Bryce said. "I'm sure Zoe could use your support."

"And leave you here?"

"You want to live, don't you?"

"Yeah, if not for you, I could have died back at the wrecker's yard."

"Kid. You don't owe me or anyone anything. Go."

"I wish it were that easy," Colton said, taking out the gun from the small of his back and crossing to the window. "If you're staying. So am I."

Bryce stared at him and crossed the room. "Don't be a fool. You are younger than me. You have a life ahead of you."

"Oh, yeah, the future looks bright," Colton shot back. "If you haven't noticed, Bryce. The world has gone to hell in a handbasket. But frankly, I kind of like it. Because now I don't have to put up with everyone's shit. Like these assholes. They're just another Rusty in a different form. So no, I'm the one who says what I do from here on out."

Bryce sighed. "Suit yourself. It's your funeral, kid."

Colton grinned. "Well, let me be the one to give my eulogy." He took the butt of the gun and smashed one of the windows. "Hey, Dominick! I forgot to tell you what a betraying asshole you are!" Colton fired a round, and it struck him in the chest, knocking him down.

What followed immediately was a slew of gunfire that peppered the house.

30

Tennessee

nother gunshot rang out, startling her.

Her nerves were on edge. As the evening wrapped around Gatlinburg, casting an eerie pall over the town, Natalie approached Dante's house, a sense of dread settling in her chest. Not only had the power grid collapsed, throwing the city into chaos, but now she had to deal with a lunatic. With Selena, Daniel, and Liam by her side, she couldn't shake the feeling of walls closing in on her.

"Do you think that old man was right?" Selena asked.

"Leo?" Natalie asked.

The front porch lantern flickered as Natalie fumbled with the keys.

"Yeah. About the potential of us having to fight if Russia sends troops into the country."

She summoned a smile as the key caught, and the door

swung wide. "Leo was expecting a war before any of this happened. He's never gotten it out of his system. You don't have anything to worry about," she said, ushering them into the house. "You won't have to fight, honey."

"How can you be sure?" she asked, genuinely concerned, as Daniel hurried to collect some candles and light them.

"That's simple. I'll answer that," Liam piped up. "This is America. The greatest damn country in the world. All right, maybe those bastards hit the button before we did, but..."

Natalie's eyes widened. "Liam."

"Sorry, but it's true. Anyway, you can be damn sure our military won't take this attack sitting down. They'll make them regret it. I would say about now, Russia is probably shitting their pants, thinking, oh fuck, that was a big mistake."

"Curse words, Liam."

Liam grinned.

Daniel returned, holding three lit candles. "And if they're not?" he asked.

"Shit. I'm not even going to entertain that question, Daniel." Liam swiped one of the candles from his hand. "But! If I did, here's what I would say. Think about the logistics of it. The terrain of America alone presents massive problems to an invading nation. It's the third-largest country in the world, and we've got mountains, deserts, forests, plains, and vast coastlines. They would have to contend with the terrain, plus there would be the logistics of supply lines. And these morons just disabled our power grid. So, in essence, they just shot themselves in the foot. Add to that all the locals who are armed to the teeth, and you have got yourself a big problem if you think you will waltz on in here and occupy. Then, of course, there is the strength of our military. I mean, shit, we didn't create Rambo for no reason. He embodies the all-American soldier, and that doesn't even cover Arnold."

Daniel laughed. "Oh, Liam, you are so full of shit."

"All right, I'm screwing with you but look, here's the thing, they may have put one hell of a dent in our country right now with these earthquakes, a tsunami, and an EMP, but we operated quite well under these conditions back in the 1800s, and we will do it again."

"I think that is just wishful thinking," Selena added. "Look around you; we are floundering and barely know our ass from our head."

"Speak for yourself," Liam shot back.

"All right, all right, guys." Natalie held up a hand like a referee. "Let's not get into a spitting match," Natalie said. She'd seen how quickly conversations could spiral out of control more times in a group home than elsewhere. "Daniel, can you turn on the Coleman stove, and I'll get some water from the shed."

Dante had put the stacks of water bottles in the shed where it was colder.

"Liam, you can grab some rice from the pantry, and Selena, see what else Dante has in that cooler we can put together for supper."

Liam continued his rant as he collected the rice.

Natalie unlocked the rear door and took one of the candles. The flame flickered, casting shadows that danced ominously against the house as she closed the door behind her. The air outside felt heavy, holding the stench of smoke from homes still smoldering. An unsettled feeling came over her as she glanced into the darkest areas of the yard. Her heart pounded loudly in her chest, and her instincts screamed to be cautious.

She shook her head, willing herself to stop thinking of the worst.

Clyde had Jordan. He had what he wanted. He'd already burned down the group home and killed her cat; there was nothing more to worry about.

Natalie glanced over her shoulder at the three teens in the kitchen, talking among themselves as they prepared supper. She had to remain stoic, self-assured, and in control as they clung to her for guidance.

She was still determining what would become of the country or what would be required of any of them. Her thoughts turned to Jackson and Zoe and if they were still alive. Her unease had grown even more since hearing the update from city officials.

Pulling hard on the shed door, Natalie entered. She reached down and collected several bottles of water.

Just as she was about to head back inside, a cold, metallic object touched her chin, and a hand clasped her mouth. Natalie froze; her breath caught in her throat as she felt the unmistakable click of a gun being cocked.

"Don't scream," a sinister voice whispered into her ear. It was Clyde, his words laced with malice. "You scream, and Ricky here will go in that house and shoot those three teens. You wouldn't want that, would you?"

She let out a muffled cry. His grip tightened, as did his pushing of the barrel into her jaw. "Natalie. Confirm with a nod that you understand."

She nodded. The room seemed to spin around her as she realized the depth of the trap she had walked into. Her fears of guns and unfamiliarity with them led her straight into danger. Clyde's cruel chuckle echoed in her ear, drowning out the whispers of the pines outside and sealing her fate.

31

Oregon

"Anyone ever told you; you are one crazy sonofabitch!" Bryce said, positioned defiantly by the window with shards and pebbles of glass all over him.

Colton let out a chuckle. "All the time. But damn, that felt good." Colton rose slowly, craning to see the men below.

"You shot your friend, Colton."

"Dominick wasn't a friend. He tried to act like he was mine, but as soon as I stepped over the line and questioned his decisions, he showed his true colors. The fact is he left me back at that wrecker's yard. He didn't give two shits. No. Fuck him and Skylar. They only wanted me to be part of the crew, so he had someone to boss around and do his dirty work."

"Well, remind me never to ask you to help me."

Colton laughed before taking another look outside.

"There's five left," he muttered before shouting, "Hey, assholes. Step on up. Who wants to be next?" He roared with laughter, rubbing it in their face.

"Bastard! Fire!" someone yelled.

They opened up again just as Colton dived out of view. Drywall dust filled the air, chunks of debris skittered across the floor, and bullets speared the home, leaving gaping holes.

Bryce yelled. "You really do know how to stir the pot."

Staying low, squinting back at Bryce, he grinned. "Well, I figure if we die here, we might as well have some fun."

"The goal isn't to die."

"No, of course not, but it's inevitable unless you plan on going out there; then I can head out the back and join Zoe."

"I thought you wanted to stay."

"Yeah, long enough to pay back my debt to you. I'd say we're even now."

Bryce chuckled.

"Bryce. We've got more firepower than you. Give it up!" A voice from outside shouted.

Right then, they heard the sound of footsteps coming up the steps. Bryce scrambled toward the door, gun at his side. "They're inside. Get ready." He glanced at Colton. He aimed the gun at the door.

"Back me up," Bryce said.

Before the person reached the door, Bryce fired two rounds straight through it. "Whoa! Guys. It's me. Zoe. Don't shoot."

"Zoe?" Bryce asked with a touch of surprise as he pulled the door wide to find her crouching down. "What the hell are you doing back?"

She wasn't alone. There were two male strangers behind her, both carrying rifles. One was in his mid-fifties, with a thick beard and a thin jacket, the other in his early twenties, wearing nothing more than a T-shirt, jeans, and sneakers.

"Who are you?" Bryce asked.

"Neighbors," the older guy said. "Those men set our place on fire. We saw them do it to another home. They drove out most of us on the street. There were too many of them to stand up to alone. Besides, my wife is pregnant, and we have two other kids. We were cutting through the park. We saw this young gal and her father in the forest. She told us about you both. We figured that we could even the odds. So, you folks need a hand?" he asked.

"That's kind of you, but no," Bryce replied.

"Bryce," Colton said.

"No. I can't get any more people involved in this."

"We already are," said the man.

"Zoe," Bryce said. "Where is your father?"

"He's safe with my wife and kids," the man said. "The name's Scott Morgan. This is Mark, a neighbor of mine."

"Well, Scott, Mark. Thank you, but you should go back to your families. Especially you, Scott. Your wife wants you alive."

"She was the one that sent me."

Bryce stared back. He glanced at Zoe. "Fuck. Fuck!" he shouted, feeling the weight of responsibility. None of them would be in this if it weren't for Mason. This was all on him. And yet, the reality was it was the domino effect of giving up his brothers in arms.

From outside, they heard voices.

"This doesn't have to get any uglier than it already has. Just turn yourself over, Bryce."

"He wants you?" Scott asked.

This was the moment Bryce was hoping he could avoid.

"Seems so," Bryce replied. "Short story. I fucked over someone he knew. When I got out of prison..."

"I've already told him," Zoe said. "At least some of it."

"Again, last chance to leave," Bryce said.

"No, screw that," Scott said, marching over to the window and looking.

Colton grinned at Bryce. "Well, shit. Isn't that something? I'd say welcome to the neighborhood, and it's not usually this bad..." Colton peered out again. "But that would be a lie," he added before sticking out the barrel of his gun and opening fire again.

Bryce took one look at Zoe.

"I wish you hadn't come back," he said, taking her by the arm out of the room. "But thank you," he tacked on at the end.

"You're welcome. Where are you taking me?" she asked.

"To the forest."

"No. I'm staying. You're going to need me."

"Like hell you are."

"I'm twenty-one. I'm an adult."

"And so, then you know what is the logical thing to do here."

She pulled her arm away. "I'm not a child. Stop treating me like that."

"Look, I don't have time for this."

"Then give me a gun."

"You know how to shoot?"

"Don't tell my mother, but yeah. My father thought it best with me being out in California to know how to protect myself. He signed me up for some gun classes."

"Sure he did," he said.

She grabbed the Glock from his hand within seconds,

took out the mag, cleared the chamber, caught the round, and reassembled it. All the while keeping away from him, showing her understanding of safety. "Satisfied?"

"Geesh. All right, but you hang back. No going near windows. You watch the stairs, that means you watch their backs to ensure no one comes up. You stay right here."

"That's not much use!"

"That's the deal."

She narrowed her eyes. "Fine."

He took off his rifle. "Scott, Colton, you've got the top floor. Zoe is watching your back. We're going down to make sure they don't try to break in. Let's go, Mark."

They hurried down the steps and entered the living room. Bryce ensured the front and back doors were locked before they positioned themselves on either side of the house. "Colton! Don't waste your rounds."

Bryce and Mark took up position near the front of the house on either side of the window. It was hard to see anything outside. A couple of silhouettes rushed from one vehicle to another before muzzle flashes lit up the night.

Glass shattered.

"Is this really worth it, Bryce?" a voice called out.

Curious to know who was leading this, Bryce replied, "Who are you?"

"A brother," a voice responded. "Of a man you killed."

"Yeah? Was that the same one that killed my brother?"

"Doesn't change anything."

"Two wrongs don't make a right," Bryce shouted. While he wasn't so naïve as to think the man could be bargained with, the hope was there, even if it was a pipe dream. "This doesn't have to end in bloodshed. We've both lost."

"You piece of shit," the stranger replied. "You killed more

than my brother, and now you're going to have even more blood on your hands."

A staccato of gunfire raged, peppering the walls. Bryce and the others returned fire. A moment later, it went quiet. He peered out but couldn't quite make out what was happening. "Colton. Give me a sitrep."

"A what?"

"A situation report."

"Why didn't you just say that?"

He shook his head.

"I'm not sure what's going on. It's too damn dark out there."

That's when Bryce's eyes widened as he saw a glow, tongues of fire flickering, and then a figure ran into view and lobbed something in the air. "Molotov!" he shouted.

32

Tennessee

The Great Smoky National Park had always been a place of tranquility for Natalie, but now it was a nightmarish labyrinth of shadows and uncertainty. Grotto Falls was a good seven miles east of Dante's home. After parking an aging Ford truck at the start of the trailhead, Clyde yanked her out the passenger side by the back of the collar to begin the 3-mile trek to the 25-foot waterfall.

"Move it!"

"Clyde, please," Natalie implored, her voice quivering with fear. "Look, you don't have to do this. We can figure something out. There's got to be a better way."

She glanced back at him. Clyde's eyes were cold and unrelenting. They met hers briefly before he spat back, "Shut up, woman. Keep moving." He sneered at her. He and his cousin, Ricky, looked like demons under the limited moonlight.

Clyde stank of alcohol, and Ricky kept spitting wads of tobacco on the ground and wiping his mouth with the back of his hand. He was following closely behind, a rifle slung over his shoulder. He said nothing, his expression hidden in the shadows, but Natalie could sense his menace. They stank to high heaven of weed and were clearly on some substance as their eyes were bugging out.

They trudged on. Shrouded in inky darkness, the Trillium Gap Trail wound through the dense forest like a black ribbon. The only light came from the intermittent flickering of a flashlight in Clyde's hand, casting eerie shadows on the trees and the ground below.

"I don't get it. You already have what you want."

"Damn right I do."

"So why me? Was it what I said back in town?"

Clyde never replied; he kept nudging her forward with the barrel of his revolver. Natalie stumbled over gnarled roots and slick rocks, her heart pounding. Her wrists were tightly bound with a rough rope, and every step sent sharp pains shooting through her arms. She knew the fate that awaited her at Grotto Falls, so desperation fueled her voice, hoping to reason with him.

"I just don't get it. Why take Jordan back when you abused that child mercilessly?"

"He's my property."

"Property? He's a child. You're his father. You are supposed to protect, nurture, and meet all his needs, not treat him like a TV."

"Don't you tell me what I should do."

"What happened to you?" she asked. "Who hurt you so bad in your childhood that you need to act out this way now?"

"Don't psychoanalyze me, bitch. It won't work."

"I don't expect it to, but something drives you to do this. I mean, seriously. Think about it. So what? You're angry at the state for taking him, so this is your way of striking back?"

Again, he waited to reply.

"So, you kill me. Then what? Huh? How does that solve anything? A moment of anger. A brief flicker of getting the upper hand. Great. Then what? Someone else is going to take my place, Clyde. They'll return and take him back once they find out you've taken him."

"Not if they can't find him."

"You haven't changed anything. The state will continue to take away children from harmful situations."

"Not now, they won't," he replied. "The world has gone to shit, and the last thing on their mind is the welfare of Jordan."

"Why do you want him so badly?"

"He's my son!" Clyde shouted, shoving her again.

"And yet you treated him like common muck."

Clyde struck her in the back of the head, knocking her to the ground. He leaped over her, jamming the gun up under her chin. "Bitch, I will end you right here if I hear another word from your mouth. You are not better than me. You are not my judge."

"No, God is!" she yelled back. Natalie knew she would die in these dismal woods, but at least she would die on her terms.

"Where is God now?" he asked.

"He's here. He's here," she said with a sense of confidence.

He stared back at her with a mocking grin, like the devil himself. "Get up."

"No. If you're going to kill me. Just do it now. Do it here."

"Don't tempt me," he replied before dragging her up. When she was back on her feet, he pushed her forward.

There was silence for a time and then he spoke again, "You religious?"

"I have faith."

"You're going to need it," he said, chuckling. The rushing sound of water grew louder as they drew nearer to Grotto Falls, drowning out her pleas as she tried to reason with him.

The forest seemed to close around them, trees standing tall and imposing like sentinels of a forgotten realm. Natalie's breaths came out in ragged gasps, her mind racing for an escape plan. But every step deeper into the wilderness felt like a step further from hope. The teens didn't know she was here. No one knew she was here. At least that she knew.

She'd heard of feral humans living in the Appalachians, mountain people who lived off the land and snatched up lone hikers. For some, it was a myth, nothing but a story; for others, it held a sprinkle of truth in the form of those who chose to live off the grid, away from society.

The darkness around them was oppressive, broken only by occasional glimmers of moonlight filtering through the thick canopy of leaves. Fireflies danced in the air, their bioluminescent glow a stark contrast to the sinister purpose of Clyde.

The scent of damp earth and the rushing of water filled the air. Mosquitoes buzzed around them, drawn by the warmth of exposed skin. Natalie's clothes clung to her body with sweat and fear, her bare feet scraping against the uneven terrain.

Clyde had removed her shoes after placing her in the truck to ensure that it would be painful if she attempted to escape.

As they pressed forward, the sound of water grew louder and more distinct. The siren song of Grotto Falls drew them in with the promise of beauty and danger. Finally, the forest relented, and they emerged into a small clearing. Grotto Falls loomed ahead, its cascading waters shimmering in the pale moonlight. The falls flowed from a rocky ledge above and disappeared into the forest floor below, creating a serene yet eerie atmosphere.

Clyde's grip on Natalie's arm tightened as he led her toward the falls, his intent clear. Ricky followed, his gaze never leaving her. The dark waters of the pool beneath the falls whispered their secrets, a grim foreboding of those who had died there before and what was to come.

Natalie's heart pounded louder than ever as they reached the base of the falls. Time was almost up. "Help!" she screamed as loudly as she could, one final alarm bell ringing loudly into the world around her. Clyde wasn't deterred by it, nor did he prevent her. He joined in, screaming "Help," mocking her, and laughing.

"Scream all you want. No one will hear you out here. That's why I brought you here. When I'm done with you, you will squeal like a stuck pig."

He shoved her to the ground.

Tears flowed down her cheeks as she begged for her life. "Please. Don't do this. I've got a child just like you do. A daughter."

"And yet no one took her from you," he said, looming over her. Ricky cradled his rifle, glancing off into the darkness, almost distracted or not wishing to watch.

"I never took him from you. That was the state. I was there to ensure he was safe. I looked after Jordan as if he was my own. I don't have control over who they take and who they give us. Hell, I was in one of the homes myself," she said.

"You?" Clyde asked, his curiosity piqued.

She nodded.

"Ah. Beaten, were you? Abused? A little of both, perhaps?" he asked, grinning as if he wanted her to share her secrets. "Abuse. Wasn't it." He laughed. "Then you'll be all too familiar with what is coming next," he said, setting his gun back into his hip holster and taking out a large bowie knife.

"You want first dibs?" Clyde asked Ricky. "Or should I?"

"Be my guest," he said.

As Clyde unbuttoned his shirt, Natalie kicked him in the shins. That only garnered a laugh. "Oh, she's a feisty one. You like to play rough. News flash, so do I!" He slapped her legs out of the way and pounced on her, holding the knife's edge up to her throat. "Fight all you want. It only excites me more," he said.

Natalie spat at him and lashed out with her restrained wrists, but it was useless. He was too heavy and had the upper hand. As he lowered himself and licked up the side of her face, she turned her head away, eyeing Ricky, hoping against all hope that he would have a change of heart, that one of them at least wouldn't be an animal.

But he just stared down at her, grinning.

Just as Natalie was about to fight back with every bit of her strength, there was a snap of something, like a bullet whipping past, except it wasn't a bullet. Ricky let out a groan. He reached a hand to his throat to clasp a long projectile that had entered his windpipe. He staggered briefly, then his knees buckled and he dropped to the ground.

Clyde glanced back. "Ricky?"

Ricky looked at him before he fell face forward.

Clyde frantically looked around. He pulled away from Natalie and withdrew his gun, quickly firing rounds in every direction. "Come on, you bastard. Show yourself."

Another snap, and Clyde let out a shriek.

An arrow speared his thigh. He grasped it with one hand while shooting in the direction that it came from. As Clyde stumbled back, groaning and cursing, Natalie rolled onto her belly and scrambled to her feet. Before she could break away, Clyde was on her, grabbing her from behind.

"Oh no, you don't," he said before driving his knife into her side. She let out a gasp as he withdrew it. He had brought it up to her neck to slice her throat when there was another crack — a final blow.

He released his grip and fell backward.

Natalie dropped to her knees, pain coursing through her body. She looked back to see that an arrow had speared Clyde through the eye. On her knees, she grasped her stomach as the world around her spun.

A light appeared before her, a flashlight or something similar.

Never once did they utter a word.

Footsteps drew close, and a figure stepped into view. She couldn't make out the face of the person. They took something out of a bag and smeared it into her wound. It stung like fire. "It will stop the bleeding," the stranger said.

He dropped down, scooped Natalie up, and began to jog away from the falls. As Natalie went in and out of consciousness, she would catch glimpses of what looked like a heavily bearded man. Minutes passed. In and out of darkness she went until she felt herself being placed on gravel.

"Natalie!" a voice cried out that sounded like Dante.

"You'll be safe now," the stranger said before returning to the forest.

There was no sense of time, but when she blinked next, she was looking up at Dante and Leo. She was placed in the back of a truck. "Hurry. We need to get her to the hospital."

As she heard tires squeal over gravel, she could swear she saw a figure lurking high in a tree before everything faded to black.

33

Oregon

M inutes before the Molotov cocktail soared through the air, Bryce's heart pounded like a relentless drumbeat as he crouched in the dark living room of the small Oregon house. The night, usually a tranquil canvas of summer serenity, had descended into chaos. The homes along the street burned out of control.

Then it happened — an explosion of glass and fire.

Bryce's heart leaped into his throat as the Molotov cocktail crashed through the upper window, shattering the fragile barrier between safety and terror.

"Fire!" Colton yelled, urgency thick in his voice.

He hurried up the steps to see the flaming bottle that had landed with a sickening thud and shattered, unleashing its fiery tempest that licked greedily at the wooden floorboards.

In a frenzy of desperation, they grabbed nearby sheets

and blankets, attempting to smother the flames. The searing heat scorched their skin as they battled against the inferno, but it was a losing battle. The fire spread with relentless determination, dancing with malevolence in their path.

Then, as if fate conspired against them, another Molotov cocktail shattered a lower window, and the inferno grew with newfound vigor, filling the lower part of the house with a blaze of hellfire.

Bryce coughed hard; his lungs burned as the acrid smoke clawed into his throat. "Zoe, go down. Everyone out," he barked, his voice cutting through the chaos.

Their only choice was to flee out the back of the house.

In a chaotic scramble for safety, they raced toward the rear exit, choking on the thick smoke that had already begun to engulf the living room. Scott held open the back door as Mark was the first out, only to be cut down in a hail of gunfire.

Bryce clutched Zoe tightly to his side, her wide eyes reflecting the terror that mirrored his own. As they burst through the back door and into the moonlit yard, more gunfire erupted around them.

Bullets whizzed through the night air, the staccato percussion of violence filling their ears as Scott and Colton covered them on both sides, forcing back their attackers.

The tree line beckoned, a distant sanctuary offering the only hope of survival.

Colton led the charge, raising his weapon and firing rounds continually.

The return fire began, shots ringing out in chaotic harmony from the assailants. Flashes of muzzle fire illuminated the night, revealing the faceless attackers advancing upon them.

The grass beneath their feet seemed to shift and tremble as the battle raged on, each step taking them closer to the cover of the forest. Scott buckled, a round hitting him in the leg. Colton pulled back to help.

"GO!" He shouted.

It was like watching it all in slow motion.

As Colton attempted to ward off the attack and aid Scott, he was struck in the shoulder, spinning him.

"Keep moving, Zoe. Keep moving. I'll be right behind."

"No."

"I said go!" he shouted, returning to aid Colton.

The night was a blur with loud gunfire, bullets ricocheting off objects around them and tearing up the ground beneath. Bryce could feel the world's weight pressing down on him, the chilling reality burning into his soul.

He managed to strike two men before grabbing Colton's arm.

The trio moved fast, each one focused on the tree line.

However, it was only Colton and Bryce that would make it.

Scott was struck in the back multiple times. He offered a deathly expression that Bryce would never forget.

Inside the safety of the tree line, the deafening roar of gunfire continued even as they pressed into the thicket, clinging to a flickering hope ahead.

That hope was quickly extinguished as a stranger swung out from a tree, then another, and a third. The forest walls pressed in on them; the reality was they had been corralled from the house like lambs to the slaughter.

"Going somewhere?" one of the men said, quickly stepping in and relieving Bryce of his weapon. Colton was struck in the face with the butt of a rifle, his legs buckled, and he landed on his knees. Zoe dropped down beside him, gripping his arm.

Within seconds, they were disarmed.

"Now, which of you is Bryce?" a man said, stepping forward.

"That's me," Bryce replied.

"Um," he nodded, getting closer, sizing him up and down from his feet to his head like he was barcode. He circled him, keeping his gaze on Bryce. "Not so cocky, are we?"

Bryce said nothing. He knew better than to speak.

"What? The cat got your tongue? You sure did seem like you had a lot to say back at the house."

Bryce glanced at the other two men with him.

"Look, please, let these two go! I'll leave with you. These two aren't part of this."

"That's where you are wrong. They are every bit a part of this as you, my friend," he said, getting close to his face. "I never introduced myself. My name is Talis, by the way. And the man you killed was my brother Ryland." Before he could reply, Talis struck him in the solar plexus and gave him an uppercut with his elbow. Bryce gasped as he landed hard. Zoe went to reach for him, but Bryce put his hand up to tell her to stay back.

With Bryce down on his knees, Talis followed through with a knee to the face, knocking him sideways. He chuckled. "Well, well, not so fucking brave now, are you?" Talis crouched down beside him. "Here's what I'm going to do. I'm going to kill your friends in front of you. Well, Foster here will. As he's the guy that fucked up. The one who left my brother behind, the one I should thank for leading me to you. So maybe he isn't a fuckup," he said. "Afterward, you and I will get acquainted back at your brother's property. You remember those thick beams in the living room? I will hang you from there and take you apart, piece by piece."

As he rose, he slammed his fist into Bryce's jaw.

"All right, Foster. You're up. Put a round in these two."

Bryce tried to intervene but was kicked and punched by both Talis and the third man. Talis spat on Bryce. "And don't you even think about getting up."

He looked back at Foster. "Chop, chop, asshole. End them. Now!"

The man he called Foster took his Glock and lifted it toward Zoe. There was a look of hesitation in his eyes.

"NOW, FOSTER!" Talis shouted.

Then, in a strange twist of fate, Foster turned the gun toward the third man and shot him in the head. Talis reacted fast, shooting Foster but taking several shots to the chest. The two men fell, still alive but coughing and spluttering.

"You fucking traitor!" Talis said, reaching for his gun again.

Foster still had his in hand. He fired one round, killing Talis instantly.

A strange silence fell over the forest. Foster coughed hard, blood trickling out the corner of his mouth. He released his grip on the gun. Bryce scrambled over to him, snatching it up. Foster said something but Bryce couldn't quite make out what he said. He lived a few more minutes, choking on his blood before his eyes glazed over.

"You, okay?" Bryce asked the other two.

They gave a nod.

When the dust settled, the trio staggered away.

After walking a mile, they emerged from the forest onto a road. There, waiting in the rear of an old truck, was Jackson in the front, with Scott's wife and children.

A glance from her to them, and her chin dipped.

In one moment, relief and grief mingled for Jackson and Scott's family, who had lost everything.

As they drove away, heading for the nearest hospital to get Colton's wound treated, the full scope of what they were up against came flooding in. The situation might not improve, but people like Scott offering a hand left them with hope.

As for Talis and the others, they were just a fraction of the danger that lay before them as they would embark on a perilous journey to Tennessee.

EPILOGUE

Tennessee

Natalie's eyes fluttered open, and a harsh, white light stabbed at her vision. She squinted, struggling to focus on her surroundings. Disoriented and dizzy, she tried to piece together her situation. The room felt sterile and unfamiliar, and she was acutely aware of a throbbing pain in her abdomen.

"She's waking up," a voice whispered urgently. Natalie's ears rang, and she turned her head towards the source. It was Selena. Slowly, Natalie's senses began to return. She could hear the faint hum of medical equipment and the antiseptic scent that permeated the room. "Liam, go get Dante," Selena said.

"Where am I?" Natalie managed to croak out, her voice barely audible.

"You're at Sevierville General Hospital," Selena replied, her voice full of relief.

As Natalie's eyes adjusted further, figures began to materialize around her. Jordan stood at the foot of her bed; his eyes full of worry. Dante took a seat beside her. His face was etched with concern. Leo stood nearby, a smile lingering at the corner of his mouth. Daniel hovered at the doorway.

Natalie grimaced as she attempted to get up in bed, her body protesting the movement. "Go steady there. They treated you, but it will be sore for a while," Leo cautioned.

She glanced at Dante, who gently took her hand. "For a moment, I thought we would lose you," he admitted. "Fortunately, the stab wound had some substance in it that stemmed the bleeding."

Leo chimed in; his tone was full of knowledge. "Crushed yarrow leaves. Natives use them to create a poultice to treat cuts and bruises, and stop bleeding. Did you put that in you?" he asked.

Natalie stared back at Leo, her memory slowly piecing together the events that had transpired. She shook her head as flashes of the forest fight, the brutal attack, and the unbearable pain flooded her mind. "I don't remember much," she admitted.

Jordan stepped forward, eyes full of guilt. "My father stabbed you, didn't he?" he asked, his voice trembling.

She met his gaze with a solemn nod. "Yes."

Dante glanced at Leo, both of them sharing an unspoken understanding. "The doctor said that had the blade been half an inch to the left, it would have hit an artery. You were fortunate. Without Clyde's conversation with Jordan, we wouldn't have known where he took you." He paused. "Do you know what happened to him?"

Another rush of memories flooded her consciousness. "Someone attacked them. They were dead. You'll find them both at Grotto Falls," she revealed, her voice trembling with the weight of her revelation. "I'm sorry about your father, Jordan."

Jordan shrugged, his expression conflicted. "I'm just glad you're okay."

Dante turned to the others; his voice tinged with weariness. "Let's give her some rest. Maybe you can have the nurse swing by, Selena," he suggested. Selena nodded, and they filed out of the room one by one, leaving Natalie alone with Dante.

Dante offered her a reassuring smile. "I went back to the falls yesterday. There was no sign of animal predation. I could see blood, but Clyde and Ricky weren't there," he recounted.

Natalie shook her head, her mind grappling with the surreal events. "No, they're dead. I saw it," she affirmed.

"Are you sure?"

"Positive. I think," Natalie said.

Dante gazed out the window, where warm daylight streamed in. "What do you remember?" he inquired.

More fragmented memories flashed through her mind. "Someone else was out there — a man. I didn't see his face. I mean, I can't remember what he looked like. He carried me out," she confessed, her voice filled with uncertainty.

Dante studied her face intently, his eyes probing for answers. "When we arrived, there was no one there, Natalie. Just you," he stated.

She nodded, her thoughts swirling with confusion. "Maybe I dreamed it," she mused.

Dante remained serious. "No. Someone treated that

wound. Whoever it was, you owe your life to them," he emphasized, his voice holding a note of gratitude.

As Natalie lay there, gazing out at the town of Sevierville, her thoughts turned to her family, and a surge of worry washed over her. The world was a chaotic and uncertain place, and she had no idea about the fate of Zoe or Jackson. Her instincts told her that her daughter might still be alive; call it a mother's intuition, but she clung to that glimmer of hope.

With a heavy heart, Natalie sighed deeply. "Any word from my family?"

Dante shook his head. "Not yet. But there's still hope. Don't overthink. It would be best if you focused on getting better. Are you thirsty?"

She nodded.

"I'll go get you something," he offered, squeezing her hand gently. "I'm glad you're still alive."

After Dante left the room, Natalie glanced outside at the ruined city, wondering about the fate of her family and what lay ahead in this new world of uncertainty and danger. Hope was her only companion in the darkness, a flickering light that she would hold onto with all her strength until she was reunited with them again.

⁓

THANK YOU FOR READING
Those Who Survive
Book two will be out shortly in November 2023
Please take a second to leave a review, it's really appreciated.
Thanks kindly, Jack.

A PLEA

Thank you for reading Those Who Survive. If you enjoyed the experience this book gave you, I would really appreciate it if you would consider leaving a rating and a review. The two are vital. It's a great way to support the book. Without reviews, an author's books are virtually invisible on the retail sites. It also lets me know what you liked. It also motivates me to write more books. You can leave a review by visiting the book's page. I would greatly appreciate it. It only takes a couple of seconds.

Thank you — **Jack Hunt**

VIP READERS TEAM

Thank you for buying Those Who Survive, published by Direct Response Publishing.

Go to the link below to receive special offers, bonus content, and news about new Jack Hunt's books. Sign up for the newsletter. http://www.jackhuntbooks.com/signup

ABOUT THE AUTHOR

Jack Hunt is the International Bestselling Author of over seventy novels. Jack lives on the East coast of North America. If you haven't joined *Jack Hunt's Private Facebook Group* just do a search on facebook to find it. This gives readers a way to chat with Jack, see cover reveals, enter contests and receive giveaways, and stay updated on upcoming releases. There is also his main facebook page below if you want to browse. facebook.com/jackhuntauthor

www.jackhuntbooks.com
jhuntauthor@gmail.com

Made in the USA
Las Vegas, NV
21 October 2023

79470720R00196